"You and I aren't friends?" she said.

In the intimate closeness the serene, dark forest imparted, he lifted his head to regard her with eyes that had deepened to a navy hue. "That's a question only you can answer, Jessica. Friends trust each other. They don't suspect them of deceit and ill intent."

There was no condemnation in his tone. He'd spoken frankly, but there was understanding there, too. As if he identified with her misgivings.

"In that case, the answer is yes."

The slow arrival of gratitude, then relief and finally happiness passing over his clean-shaven features did serious damage to her defenses. Bolting to her feet, she bid him a brief good-night and reentered the house, seeking sanctuary in her room.

She couldn't allow herself to like Grant Parker. Empathy was acceptable. Concern for his health was natural. But opening herself up to a man, even for something as innocent as friendship, could very well be the first step to disaster.

Karen Kirst was born and raised in East Tennessee near the Great Smoky Mountains. A lifelong lover of books, it wasn't until after college that she had the grand idea to write one herself. Now she divides her time between being a wife, homeschooling mom and romance writer. Her favorite pastimes are reading, visiting tearooms and watching romantic comedies.

Books by Karen Kirst

Love Inspired Historical

Smoky Mountain Matches

The Reluctant Outlaw
The Bridal Swap
The Gift of Family
"Smoky Mountain Christmas"
His Mountain Miss
The Husband Hunt
Married by Christmas
From Boss to Bridegroom
The Bachelor's Homecoming
Reclaiming His Past

Visit the Author Profile page at Harlequin.com.

KAREN KIRST

Reclaiming His Past

HARLEQUIN® LOVE INSPIRED® HISTORICAL

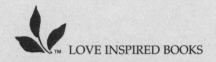 LOVE INSPIRED BOOKS

Recycling programs
for this product may
not exist in your area.

ISBN-13: 978-0-373-28346-0

Reclaiming His Past

Copyright © 2016 by Karen Vyskocil

www.Harlequin.com

Printed in U.S.A.

I will instruct thee and teach thee in the way which thou shalt go: I will guide thee with mine eye.
—*Psalms* 32:8

To Kelly Young—
who could've guessed we'd wind up in the same place? I'm so thankful for you and your family. Looking forward to many more years of friendship.

Chapter One

October 1885
Gatlinburg, Tennessee

It wasn't easy staying angry at a dead man.

Jessica O'Malley hesitated in the barn's entrance, the tang of fresh hay ripening the air. The horses whickered greetings from their stalls, beckoning her inside, probably hoping for a treat. She used to bring them carrots and apples. She used to enjoy spending time out here.

This place had become the source of her nightmares. Her gaze homed in on the spot where the man she'd loved had died defending her. The bloodstain was long gone, but the image of Lee as she'd held him during those final, soul-wrenching moments would be with her for as long as she lived.

His whispered apology, his last uttered words, came to her during those nights she couldn't sleep. At times she missed him so much it hurt to breathe. Other times she wished she could give him a piece of her mind. How could he have been so reckless, so irresponsible with their future?

If he'd been honest with her, if he'd made different

choices, she wouldn't be living this lonely, going-through-the-motions existence She wouldn't be a shadow of her former self, clueless how to reclaim the fun-loving girl she once was.

Lost in troubling memories, she was wrenched back to the present by a weak cry for help. Her empty milk pail slipping from her fingers, Jessica hurried to investigate. She and her mother lived alone on the farm. And right this minute, her mother was inside the cabin preparing breakfast. She surged around the barn's exterior corner and had to grope the weathered wall for support at the unexpected sight of a bruised and battered man near the smokehouse.

He was hatless and looked as if he'd romped in a leaf pile, and his golden-blond hair was messy. "Can you help me?"

"Who are you? What do you want?"

He dropped to his knees, one hand outstretched and the other clutching his side. Jessica belatedly noticed the blood soaking through his tattered shirt. Bile rose into her throat. Lee's gunshot wound had done the same to his clothing. There'd been so much. It had covered her hands. Her dress. Even the straw covering the barn floor had been drenched with it.

"Please...ma'am..."

The distress in his scraped-raw voice galvanized her into action. Searching the autumn-draped woods fanning out behind her farm's outbuildings, she hurried to his side and ducked beneath his arm. She barely had time to absorb the impact of his celestial blue eyes on hers. "What happened to you?"

"I...don't remember."

Struggling to help him stand, she shot him a disbelieving look. At this moment, she supposed it didn't matter how he'd come to be on her property. He required immediate medical attention. "Let's get you inside."

Several inches taller and made of solid muscle, he leaned heavily on her, his hitched breaths testament to his discomfort. His uneven gait made the distance to her two-story cabin seem impossible.

His injuries likely hadn't resulted from a wagon accident or a toss from the saddle. "Should I be worried someone will show up here to finish the job?"

The split on his full lower lip reopened when he frowned deeply. Dark blond stubble lined his hard cheeks and chin. "Can't say. My mind's gone hazy."

Can't or won't? Either he was rattled, or he was reluctant to admit the truth. Perhaps he thought she'd refuse him aid if he did.

When they reached the main door, he sagged against the notched logs, eyes closed, chest heaving. Beneath his tan, a deep purple bruise blossomed over his cheekbone. What sort of trouble had befallen him?

"Just a few more steps," she urged, compassion eclipsing suspicion. "Then you can rest."

His golden lashes fluttered, and his startling gaze locked on to hers. "Thank you."

Confusion and pain swirled in the depths, yet he'd taken the time to express gratitude. Yanking the door open, she called for her mother. He was too big and heavy for her to maneuver into the bedroom on her own, and his strength was fading fast.

"Is something the matter?" Alice advanced into the room wiping her hands on the apron stretched across her plump figure, bushy brows lifting above her spectacles. "Who's this?"

"I was about to milk Sadie when I heard him outside. Can you help me get him into Jane's room?"

Halfway to the couch, he stumbled, his hand curling into the wet, stained fabric of his shirt. A weak groan escaped him. Jessica prayed he wouldn't collapse right there on their living room floor.

"Just a little farther," she grunted.

Having spent her entire life in these mountains, her ma had dealt with more than her fair share of mishaps. Solemn yet determined, she hurried over and took his other arm. Together they got him to her sister's old room and stripped the quilt off the bed before lowering him onto it.

"Let's see your wound, young man." Alice edged his bloodied hand aside.

Jessica transferred her attention to his boots and began working them off.

"Looks like a knife's to blame." Alice's tone was grave. "It's too deep for me to stitch up. We need Doc Owens."

Grabbing a towel from the washstand, Alice leaned across and pressed it against his opposite flank.

"You go, Mama. I'll stay with him."

"I'm not sure that's the best idea."

"I am." She was far more comfortable with firearms than her ma. Thanks to her cousins' patient instruction, she'd learned to protect herself. "I can handle this."

The stranger dwarfed the bed, his body rigid atop the mattress, his head deep in the pillow and his teeth gritted. Images of Lee, wounded and dying on the barn floor, bombarded her. The boots hit the floor with a clatter.

He flinched.

"Jessica." Her ma was looking at her with a knowing, sympathetic expression that she'd grown to loathe this past year, one that made her feel as if she was five years old again. "You don't have to prove anything to me."

Sinking onto the mattress edge, she gently dislodged her ma's hand. "I'm not trying to prove anything. I'm armed. You're not. When was the last time you shot a gun, anyway?"

"Too long." With a shake of her head, Alice began untying her apron strings. Wisps of her silver-streaked brown hair had escaped her loose bun to dance about her hairline. "Are you certain you don't mind? I know how you get around this sort of thing."

"I'm certain."

"I'll hurry."

"Be careful. And don't worry about me."

"That's like telling a robin not to fly," she said wryly.

Her mother left her with the mystery man, the swish of the clock's pendulum punctuating the bed's creaking beneath their combined weight. Long lashes fanned against his cheeks. He possessed handsome, open features that made it hard to guess his age. Jessica figured him to be in his midtwenties.

His forehead screwed up. "Think I'm gonna be sick."

Seizing the patterned washbowl, she struggled to maintain pressure on his injury as he tipped over the side of the bed. Unwanted sympathy welled in her chest. He collapsed against the pillow minutes later, perspiration dotting his brow.

Blond strands stuck to his forehead, and the impulse to smooth them back surprised her.

"False alarm, I guess," he murmured.

"Hold the towel in position. I'll be right back."

Jessica darted into her room across the hall and retrieved the tin of homemade ginger candies from her bedside cabinet.

"Try one." Resuming her spot, she held one out to him. "They're good at relieving an upset stomach."

When he'd complied, he glanced out the single window situated square in the middle of the log wall. Jane's old room faced the rear of their property. There wasn't much behind the cabin besides the well and outhouse. Beyond the small clearing, a thick deciduous forest dominated their property.

"Where are we?"

"In my home."

"No, I mean what part of the country?"

"Tennessee. The eastern section. Gatlinburg, to be exact. About a day and a half's ride from Knoxville."

A worried crease pulled his eyebrows together. "I don't know why I'm here."

An air of uncertainty shrouded him. Was there a legitimate reason her earlier questions had gone unanswered?

"Have you hit your head?"

He sank his fingers into the short blond locks. He grimaced as he tentatively probed a place behind his ear. "Something did. There's a knot here."

"Can you tell me your name?"

"Of course. It's…" Uncertainty flashed in his blue, blue eyes. "It's, ah…" He blanched. "I—I don't know. I can't remember. I can't remember anything."

Jessica studied him. Either he was a seasoned con man, or the blow had scattered his memories.

Hands fisting in the mattress ticking, he fought the panic rippling through him.

His head felt as if it had been crushed beneath a loaded wagon wheel. The flesh where he'd been gutted like a fish burned hot, and the redhead's shifting weight as she stemmed the blood flow only served to inflame it further. The ache in his busted ankle was bearable by comparison.

Shoving all that aside, he tried to sort out the facts of his life. He'd woken facedown in the woods not far from this cabin, with no idea how he'd gotten there. A blank, black void prevented him from remembering. Faces scrolled through his mind, vaguely familiar and yet not. One clear memory replayed itself—a young boy calling to him, beckoning him to come and climb a tree.

"What's the last thing you remember?"

The ginger candy dissolved on his tongue. His stomach had calmed as she'd said it would.

"Waking up on your property." Hurt. Disoriented. "Before that, I recall patches of information. People whose identities and how they relate to me I can't grasp."

Disbelief shimmered in eyes the color of forest moss. She had expressive eyes, almond-shaped and rimmed with cinnamon-hued lashes and topped with bold, slashing eyebrows. High cheekbones were offset by a smattering of freckles across the bridge of her nose. Her expressive mouth twisted in open irritation.

"I don't blame you for not trusting me," he said. "I wouldn't believe me, either."

Her gaze dropped to his wound for a second before skittering to the window draped with lacy white curtains. Beyond the glass, the cloudless sky was a brilliant blue. He realized he didn't even know what month it was. Or the year.

The panic pounced, constricting his lungs until he thought he'd suffocate.

Focus on the here and now. Maintain control.

"Your name is Jessica, right?"

Seated close, her chocolate-hued skirts spread over the ticking, she had to lean across him to reach his injury. Her long hair, restrained by a shiny brown ribbon, spilled over her ivory blouse like deep red silk. "Is it just you and your ma living here?"

"Why do you ask?" She visibly bristled.

"No reason." He gestured to indicate the space decorated

in bold hues of red, white and blue. The handmade quilt folded over the footboard had repeating diamond shapes, and a flag design dominated the hooked rug beside the bed. Maps of various sizes had been pinned to the wall. A stack of books joined a dusty jewelry box atop the dresser. "I hope I haven't taken over your room."

"This used to be my sister's. She's married now."

Her reticence wasn't surprising. Why wouldn't she be concerned for her safety? She couldn't know his intentions, whether or not he meant her harm.

Unease niggled at the base of his skull. "Have you lived here your whole life?"

"Yes."

"Suppose that means I'm not a local, seeing as you don't recognize me."

"Your accent isn't Southern."

"It's not exactly Northern, either. I could've moved here at some point."

"Perhaps." She shifted again, her hand digging into his flank. He sucked in a sharp breath. "Sorry," she mumbled. "Look, I'm not going to hand you an opportunity to take advantage of us, so you might as well cease with the questions. As soon as Doc gets here, he's going to stitch you up and take you away. I'm certain the sheriff will be interested in discussing your situation."

His unease grew. What sort of man was he? The law-abiding, church-going sort? Or someone who lived according to his own code of ethics? Not knowing was tougher to handle than any physical discomfort.

"Meeting with the sheriff is a good idea," he said, exploring the knot beneath his hair again. "I apologize for making you uncomfortable. And for invading your home like this."

She said nothing, contemplating him with that cool,

assessing gaze. "Pretty words. You play a convincing victim. I'm reserving judgment until we see whether or not your likeness matches one of the town's wanted posters."

Victim? That label didn't sit well with him. He wasn't about to argue with her, though.

"You're right to be wary of me." Weariness that went far beyond his physical condition settled over him like the blackest night. He lifted his hand so that it hovered above his leaking wound. "I'll take over now."

His unenthusiastic hostess removed herself from the bed and backed toward the door, leaving the faint scent of roses in her wake. A rose with thorns, he thought, soaking in her innocent, vibrant beauty that seemed to be at odds with the prickly, glaring distrust in her eyes.

"You must be thirsty. I'll bring water."

"Could I trouble you for a mirror first?"

Inclining her head, she disappeared into the room across the way again, returning with a carved handheld mirror.

"Appreciate it."

She hovered a moment before quitting the room and giving him the privacy he craved. Heart thundering, he slowly brought the mirror to face level and peered at his reflection. No spark of recognition. No jarred memory. Nothing.

He was staring at the face of a stranger.

Chapter Two

"I've completed my examination."

Gatlinburg's only doctor—middle-aged, distinguished and a stranger to frivolity—entered the kitchen after being closeted with their visitor for more than an hour.

Jessica gave the vegetable soup a final stir, the aroma of potatoes, carrots and pungent greens causing her stomach to rumble.

"How is he?" Alice poured hot, black coffee into a blue enamel mug and carried it to him.

Depositing his scuffed medical bag on the table they used as a work space, he accepted her offering and sipped the steaming brew. "He's a fortunate young man. If the cut had been any deeper, I would've had to perform surgery. Now, if we can stave off infection, he should heal without complications."

"Poor man." Alice twisted the plain wedding band on her fourth finger. Jessica's pa had been gone for many years, but her mother liked the reminder of him. "We heard his suffering clear out here, didn't we?"

Jessica clamped her lips together. His pitiful moans still echoed through her mind.

"He refused my offer of laudanum," Doc said.

"It's quiet now." Jessica busied herself slicing up the corn bread, trying not to think of the agony he'd endured. For all she knew, he'd been the one to instigate the violent encounter. He could be a thief. He could've ambushed someone, and that person fought back.

"He eventually lost consciousness." Silver hair gleaming in the midmorning light streaming through the kitchen window, Doc cradled the mug in his bear-paw hands.

Jessica shook her head to dislodge the image of the blond stranger in Jane's old bed, as weak as a kitten and vulnerable.

"He claims to have lost his memory," she said. "Do you believe him?"

"While I haven't personally treated any patients with amnesia, I've read about numerous cases. Each one is slightly different. The young man has suffered head trauma, so it's plausible."

Her ma's age-spotted hands rested on the chair back. "Not everyone has a hidden agenda, Jessica."

Tired of the vague references to Lee and his perfidy, she sighed. "We know nothing about him." Wiping the crumbs from the knife, she addressed the doctor. "Besides, it's hardly our problem. You'll be moving him to your residence right away, I assume."

He grimaced. "My rooms are occupied with other patients, I'm afraid. If you're uncomfortable with him here, I can look for another family to take him in."

"What about his injuries?" Alice asked.

"At this point, moving him would exacerbate them."

Jessica hugged her middle to calm her churning insides. "Ma, he could be a dangerous criminal. He could have enemies searching for him."

"Or he could be an upstanding young man who met

with an unfortunate accident. Would you turn him out on the slim chance he's pretending to have amnesia?"

As much as she hated to admit it, her mother had a point. There was no way to know for sure. What if he was one of the good guys, and they turned him away? His further suffering would be her fault.

"Would one of your nephews be willing to spend a few nights here?" Doc shifted his weight. "Having another man around might ease your concerns."

"They've got their own families."

"Will might do it." Her cousin Nathan's young brother-in-law wouldn't mind. Will Tanner was always up for an adventure, but levelheaded enough that he'd be helpful if danger presented itself.

"Good idea. I'll go and speak to him after lunch." Pulling serving bowls from the hutch, Alice addressed the doctor over her shoulder. "Would you care to join us, Doc?"

"Next time, perhaps. My wife's expecting me." Draining his mug, he gathered his bag. "I'll come tomorrow and check on the patient. If you have any problems before then, you know where to find me."

"Jessica, would you mind seeing Doc out while I deliver soup to our young man?"

Our young man? She suppressed the urge to roll her eyes. Her mother's never-ending well of compassion was admirable most days. Today was different.

"I'll take it to him." This was the perfect time to deliver a warning. He'd soon discover she'd do anything to protect her family. Past mistakes had carved lessons onto her heart that she wasn't about to repeat.

"Thank you, sweetheart."

Jessica didn't miss her look of surprised approval. No doubt she thought Doc's assessment had erased her misgivings.

"What are we supposed to call him?" she asked Doc. "If he's going to remain here for any length of time, we can't keep referring to him as *the patient*."

He stroked his chin in thoughtful concentration. "I suggest you discuss the matter with him. Let him choose a name."

Ma's smile held a world of sympathy. "Hopefully he'll remember his true name before long."

Jessica wished she'd inherited a smidgen of her ma's positive outlook.

While the pair conversed on the porch, Jessica assembled his meal.

He appeared to be asleep when she entered the room. Sliding the tray onto the bedside table, she brought a chair from the dining room and sat, prepared to be patient. She noticed Doc had cleaned up his hands. Pink and raw in places, one knuckle was busted, indicating he'd used them in the scuffle. For fending off an attacker? Or for inflicting damage?

Uncertainty waged war inside her. He didn't look dangerous. Lying there in her sister's old bed, he looked forlorn. In need of a helping hand. And if they didn't help him, who would? They had ample space, food to spare, and, unlike many households in these mountains, there were no children underfoot. He'd have peace and quiet to speed his recovery.

This blond-haired, blue-eyed stranger was someone's son. Possibly someone's brother or cousin or even husband. If one of her loved ones was in the same predicament, she'd be begging God to keep him safe. To place him in the path of decent people.

While Jessica wasn't pleased with her mother's decision, offering him shelter and meeting his basic needs didn't mean she had to suspend caution. Even before her life became entangled with Lee Cavanaugh's, her outlook hadn't been all sunshine and rainbows. Now it was positively morose. She anticipated the worst. Expected people to fail her. Or deceive her.

God was no doubt displeased with this manner of thinking, but she wasn't sure how to undo what had been done.

He stirred, the quilt covering his lower body sliding low on his waist. His bloodied shirt had been disposed of, and a long-sleeved white cotton undershirt hugged his shoulders, sculpted chest and flat stomach. Thick padding covered his wound beneath the fabric.

The man would benefit from a bath and a shave. He wore his fair hair short on the sides, with slightly longer strands sweeping over his forehead. The brown cast of his skin indicated he worked outdoors.

"How long have I been out?"

His raspy inquiry snapped her out of her inspection. "Nearly an hour. I've brought you soup and some buttered bread. Do you feel up to eating?"

Hefting himself up so that the headboard supported his back, he studied the tray's contents. "I'll try the bread first, thanks."

When he'd finished, she handed him the still-warm bowl. "The soup is rather strong. If it's not to your liking, I can make a thin broth."

"No need to go to any extra trouble." His disconcerting gaze locked on her, he tested it. "It's very good."

"Did Doc give you anything for that busted lip?"

The bowl cradled against his chest, he shook his head. "It'll heal soon enough."

"Why didn't you want anything for the pain?" She gestured to the padding beneath his shirt. "Must've been horrible."

"Medicine messes with your head. I figure mine's messed up enough." Shadows passed over his face. "Plus, I'm uncomfortable with the idea of not being in control of my actions."

A stilted silence blanketed them. When he'd polished off half the contents and handed the bowl back to her, he rested his folded hands on his middle.

"I didn't expect to wake and find you watching over me."

The muted mischief in his eyes needled her. "That's not what I was doing," she huffed.

"Why don't you tell me the true reason, then? Afraid I might swipe something of your sister's?"

She arched a brow at him. "It's been decided that you will remain here until you've recuperated."

"I can tell you're pleased." Wry humor touched his mobile mouth.

He would laugh at her, would he? Her movements measured, she made a show of removing the Colt Lightning from her ankle holster. Barrel pointed to the wall, she lazily spun the full chamber. "I have no problem protecting what's mine." She smiled tightly. "A benefit from growing up with three competitive, slightly overbearing males."

Her warning didn't shock or anger him. If anything, his humor increased, joined by open admiration. "A woman who can take care of herself. I like that. So you have brothers?"

"Cousins. Their family's property adjoins ours."

"And you have one sister?"

"Four, actually. I'm the youngest."

"Are you the only one still living at home?"

The question was innocent enough, yet it unleashed a rock slide of hurt and disappointment. She was the last unwed O'Malley sister. Growing up, Jessica hadn't obsessed over boys, hadn't daydreamed about her future husband. She'd wanted a family of her own, of course. Someday. Once she'd reached marriageable age, she'd become friendly with a few interesting men. Nothing serious had developed. She'd been content with her single life until a dashing young man from Virginia moved to town. Suddenly, love and marriage became a priority. She'd wanted it all.

She replaced her weapon. "My life's details aren't important. Yours are. Doc thinks you should think up a name for yourself."

His expression altered, and she almost felt sorry she'd introduced the subject.

"Right. I suppose I do need one." His exhale was shaky. "Nothing comes to mind."

"You could choose something classic, like John or James. Or you could go with a decidedly Biblical name, like Hezekiah. Or Malachi."

The softening of his mouth gave Jessica a strange feeling…something akin to satisfaction that she'd lightened his burden.

"Any more suggestions?" he said.

She strove for something unexpected. "Wiley? Fentress?"

"This is too bizarre."

"If I were you, I'd settle on something simple. You don't want to get too attached."

"On the other hand, I might be saddled with this name for the rest of my life." He absently rubbed the knot behind his ear.

"You remind me of a boy I went to school with. His name was Grant Harper."

That startled him out of his melancholy. "I do?"

"He had the same fair coloring as you." And the same roguish streak cloaked in innocence.

"What happened to him?" His eyes narrowed.

"Nothing dramatic. His family moved away about five years ago to be closer to his grandparents."

He stared up at the rafters, quiet for long minutes. "Grant, huh?"

"What do you think? Can you live with it?"

"It'll do. Just don't expect me to answer to it right away."

"Understood." She rose to leave.

"Jessica?" His expression turned earnest. "You have nothing to fear from me. I won't harm you or your mother."

She didn't answer. Nodding, she left him, all too aware of how convincing a person could be when the stakes were high.

He stared at the doorway his intriguing hostess had vacated rather abruptly. He wondered what or who was responsible for the guardedness in her eyes. His arrival on her doorstep couldn't be the sole cause.

Nevertheless, she didn't want him here.

He'd rather be anywhere but here, at the mercy of strangers, an unwelcome guest with no past and an uncertain future. His sole possessions were the clothes on his back. He had nothing with which to repay their kindness. No matter what type of man he'd been before, it galled him now to be a recipient of charity.

So he was to be called Grant. He had no strong feelings about those particular five letters. It was nice and ordinary. A simple name, Jessica had said. But it likely wasn't the one he'd been born with.

What am I supposed to do, Lord Jesus?

His heart rate doubled. That had been a spontaneous

prayer. He must be a man of faith. Wasn't difficult to believe in a divine Creator. All a man had to do was look around and see the evidence… Someone hung the stars in the sky, molded the mountains, carved the riverbeds, imagined the vast varieties of animals into being.

He squeezed his eyes shut and offered up a plea. *Heavenly Father, I'm in desperate need of Your guidance. The doctor's not sure if I'll ever recover my memories. I'm lost. Alone.*

"Grant?"

Mrs. O'Malley approached his bedside, her eyes kind behind the spectacles.

"I hope it's all right that I call you Grant. Jessica told me you'd settled on it."

"Yes, ma'am."

There was little resemblance between her and her youngest daughter. Short and plump, the woman had liberal amounts of gray streaked through the brown hair she wore pinned into a thick bun. She was dressed conservatively in a serviceable blouse and black skirt, a ruffled apron with pockets covering the entire front. She possessed a maternal air he'd missed growing up.

Hold on a minute. How had he known that?

"Is your head paining you, son?"

He realized he'd been gripping his head. "I—I think I've remembered something."

"Oh? That's wonderful."

Alice didn't press him. "Nothing specific. It was just an impression."

"Any progress, no matter how big or small, is a positive thing." Smiling, she eased into the chair. "Doc said to tell you he'll bring a cane when he checks on you tomorrow. You're not to put weight on that ankle."

"I can't thank you enough for allowing me to stay, Mrs. O'Malley. I regret putting you out like this."

"Call me Alice, please. You're not a burden. The good Lord has blessed us, and we're eager to pass those blessings on to others. We're happy to aid you in any way we can."

Her daughter didn't share in that particular sentiment. "As soon as I'm able, I'll work off my debt." He'd show Miss Jessica O'Malley that he wasn't a lazy, no-good excuse of a man who preyed on women's generosity.

"Don't worry about that. Concentrate on getting well." Cocking her head to one side, she lifted a finger to stop her spectacles' downward slide. "How has Jessica been treating you?"

"She's been very attentive."

While she hadn't tried to hide her dislike, she'd taken pains to see to his comfort. There'd been compassion in her expression when he'd embarrassed himself by almost being sick in front of her.

Alice twisted her hands. "Jessica isn't one to hide her feelings. She's always been my most outspoken offspring. If she does come across as somewhat difficult, bear in mind that she's been through a terrible ordeal and hasn't allowed herself to heal."

He kept his silence. Inside, his thoughts whirled out of control. To what was she referring to?

"I probably shouldn't have mentioned it." Glancing toward the hallway, she sighed. "A mother never stops worrying about her children." Pushing out of the chair, she said, "I've got an errand to run. Try to get some rest."

When she'd gone, he turned his attention to the view beyond the window glass, not really seeing the trees arrayed in brilliant crimson, orange and gold framed by majestic mountain ridges. Curiosity ate at him. The alluring, feisty redhead was as much a mystery as his past. The only difference being that, with time, persistence and a little finesse, he could unravel hers.

Chapter Three

Of all the farms in these mountains, he just had to go and wind up on theirs.

Jessica didn't need another complication. She had enough to deal with without adding an aggravating male to the mix. Chopping the mound of raisins into tiny slivers, she tried to rein in her frustration.

Why did You lead him here, Lord? Why did You choose us to be his caretakers?

Of course, there wasn't an answer. There never was. She'd been asking God why for a long time. She'd come to despise the silence.

Laying down the knife, she turned to check the almonds bubbling atop the stove. The heat from the firebox wrapped around her, and she was considering opening the rear door to let in fresh air when she heard the slide of stocking feet across the floorboards.

"What are you doing out of bed?" she exclaimed.

"The walls were closing in." His lips contorted into a half grin, half grimace.

Looking scary-pale and about a second from collapsing, their patient—Grant, she must remember—reached for the closest sturdy object, which happened to be a ladder-back chair at the table. She rushed to his side. Without thinking, she wrapped an arm about his waist and took some of his weight as he slumped into the seat. Hovering there for a moment, she waited to make sure he wasn't going to lose consciousness.

"You could've ripped the stitches open." Her fingers digging into her waist, she felt the sting of temper flare in her cheeks. "And Ma said you weren't supposed to walk on that ankle."

"It's sweet how concerned you are for my well-being," he panted, an outrageous twinkle in his eye.

"You keep mistaking my intentions," she said through gritted teeth. "The fact of the matter is, the faster you heal, the sooner you leave."

"Ah. Well, I promise to be a good boy and return to my room before Miss Alice comes back."

Jessica rolled her eyes. She refused to give in to his charm.

Satisfied he wasn't going to slide to the floor, she retrieved the kettle and set about fixing him tea, uncomfortably aware of his steady regard. It had been ages since she'd spent one-on-one time with any man outside her family. Perhaps she wouldn't be so bothered by his presence if he were older and had warts on his nose.

"Smells like Christmas in here. What are you making?"

"A cake."

"What's the special occasion?"

Crossing to the hutch, she removed a delicate blue-and-white teacup and saucer. "Mrs. Ledbetter is turning fifty on Sunday. She commissioned me to make her birthday cake."

"You must be a talented baker."

She shrugged. "I know my way around a kitchen."

For years now, she and Jane had earned income by providing desserts to the Plum Café. Every day save for Sunday, they'd baked pies, cakes and assorted treats for delivery before the evening meal. When the café switched owners in August, the sisters hadn't anticipated the new one wouldn't require their services. The canceled agreement had come as a shock, and the extra money she'd grown accustomed to had all but dried up.

These personal orders helped but weren't consistent.

Grant sat with one arm tucked against his ribs, his busted hand resting protectively over his wound. "Have you ever thought about opening your own shop?"

Jessica inhaled sharply. Lee had asked that exact question right there on their front porch. At the time, she and Jane had been comfortable with their arrangement with Mrs. Greene, the former owner. The notion had struck them as far-fetched. In recent weeks, dogged by a restlessness she couldn't pin down, she'd revisited the idea.

"I mean, I haven't sampled your food," he went on, "so I couldn't say if folks would pay money for it. For all I know, this Mrs. Ledbetter hired you because she feels sorry for you."

She set the cup carelessly on the work surface, and it rattled in its saucer. "I'll have you know, folks around here clamor for my baked goods. My sister and I have a reputation as the finest bakers this side of the Tennessee River."

Soft laughter rumbled through his chest. Jessica stood immobile, affected by his grin, the flash of straight, white teeth, the way his entire face lit up like a vivid autumn day. Between those sparkling bright eyes and the boyish smile, this man was downright lethal to a woman's good sense.

"You are infuriating, you know that?"

"And you, Jessica O'Malley, are easy to rile."

Attempting to stifle her growing irritation, she proceeded to ignore him as she readied his tea. She didn't say a word when she placed the cup and honey jar in front of him.

She gasped the instant his fingers encircled her wrist and prevented her from moving away. His skin was hot, rough in places, the bones underneath strong. Working man's hands.

His face tilted up in appeal. Up close, in this sunny, cheerful kitchen, she could see the large bruise on his cheekbone, the split in the middle of his lower lip, threads of navy interwoven with cerulean blue in his irises. There was a jagged scratch on his neck she hadn't noticed before.

Despite the fact his presence was like a splinter beneath her skin, this man had endured a lot of pain. Nothing in his current situation was familiar. Her heart thawed another degree, and it frightened her.

"Apparently I'm a tease." His soft voice cloaked her. "Maybe I grew up with a passel of sisters."

"It's also possible you have a fiancée or wife somewhere out there who's willing to put up with you."

Dismay creased his brow, and he released her. "Maybe."

Feeling as if she'd kicked an injured dog, she went and removed the almonds from the stove and transferred the heavy sack of flour to the counter. How would she feel if her entire life had been wiped clean like a slate? Her loved ones, her home, forgotten?

It hurt to imagine.

Measuring out the flour, she risked a glance at Grant, who was quietly sipping his tea, lost in thought.

"Would you like for me to wash your hair? After I finish with this?"

At his startled reaction, she bit the inside of her cheek. Where had that come from? Her guilty conscience?

He lowered his cup, touched a hand to his nape. "That would be wonderful. If you're sure you don't mind."

"You wouldn't make it to the stream in your condition," she quipped, striving for an offhanded tone. "This is the next best option."

He lumbered to his feet. "And I'm sure you'd appreciate it if I didn't smell like yesterday's hog slop."

Jessica almost admitted that was not the case. She'd been in close contact with him twice now and hadn't been offended. He smelled of earth and leaves, leather and spruce. He smelled like the forest.

"That's right," she replied instead. "I'd much rather you smell like my favorite rose-scented soap."

"Roses. Now, that's masculine." His attempt at light-heartedness was unsuccessful. "Thanks for the tea." There was a stiffness to his manner that hadn't been there before. "I'll leave you to your work."

Returning her spoon to the bowl, she wiped her hands on her apron and trailed him to the dining space that housed a larger, more formal table. Between the busted ankle and tender side, his progress was incredibly slow.

He stopped her with an upheld hand. "No need to follow me. I can make it on my own steam. May take a while, but I'll get there."

She started to argue—her wish to be rid of him not the *only* reason for her concern—before thinking better of it. She may have grown up in an all-female household, but having Josh, Nathan and Caleb for neighbors and playmates had taught her much about the male ego. Grant was already beholden to them, dependent on their whims. He wouldn't appreciate any further coddling.

Returning to the kitchen, her attempts to push him out of her thoughts failed spectacularly.

He woke with aching muscles and a head full of cotton.

Contemplating the yellow-hazed dusk blanketing the mountain view, he took a full minute to remember where he was. The soft click of metal alerted him to the fact he wasn't alone. Adjusting the pillow beneath his cheek, he studied his self-appointed sentinel in the glow of lantern light, admiring the way her hair shimmered like liquid fire rippling over her shoulder.

The light smattering of freckles added an air of playfulness to her otherwise elegant features. False advertisement, in his opinion. He'd yet to glimpse any upbeat emotion in her. He wondered how she'd look without the sour attitude, found it tough to imagine her laughing, her eyes brimming with warmth and good humor.

What had stolen her joy?

A furrow pulled her fine eyebrows together, and her mouth was again pressed into a frown. Her focus was centered on the half-finished project in her lap. Various-colored yarns filled the basket at her feet.

"What are you working on?"

She lifted her molten gaze, her expression frustratingly blank. "A new rug for the rear entrance."

"You shoot, bake and create works of art out of yarn and burlap. You're a woman of many talents."

"No more than any other woman in these mountains."

"I've been out awhile, haven't I? Did you put something in my tea?"

Abandoning her task, she folded her hands together in a show of exaggerated patience. One flame-hued brow arched. "Yes. I doctored it so that you'd sleep the remainder of your recovery away. Guess I didn't put enough in there."

Grant laughed, then winced when his stitches pulled and pain radiated toward his hip.

"You were asleep when I came in to wash your hair," she said. "I didn't want to disturb you."

He noticed the quilt had been adjusted, pulled up to chest level and tucked around him. Weak and trembling from his ill-advised journey through the cabin, he hadn't bothered with it when he'd lain down earlier. She must've thought he was chilled. While the thought of Jessica watching him sleep was unnerving, being the recipient of her nurturing instinct filled him with strange fluttery sensations. Especially considering her antipathy toward him.

"Instead of waking you, I went exploring in the general area around the smokehouse. I found something."

He carefully maneuvered into a sitting position, his stomach going sideways. "What is it?"

Putting her things in the basket, she rose and, crossing to the corner, retrieved an alligator-skin travel bag.

His heart threatened to burst from his chest as she placed it on his lap. He ran his fingertips across the bumpy surface. "Doesn't look familiar."

"I almost missed it. It was half-hidden beneath a shrub, some of the contents strewn over the ground."

His fingers fumbled on the clasp. One by one, he lifted out items that proved ambiguous. Two changes of clothes, sturdy trousers with well-worn hems and solid-color shirts, didn't spark recognition. Socks. A black handkerchief that looked new. A razor and shaving soap. Basic traveling necessities that could belong to anyone.

Then he saw the Bible lying in the bottom. His gaze shot to Jessica's. Her expression was unreadable as she stood, hands folded behind her back.

He balanced the heavy tome in his hands. His heartbeat thundered in his ears. There, on the filmy, delicate first page, a name had been scrawled in blocky letters. "I can't make out the first name," he murmured. "Parker is the surname."

"Does it trigger any memories?"

"No." Defeat marred his tone. He rubbed the coffee-colored stain obscuring much of the first name. "This looks like an uppercase *G*."

"Your name could be Gabriel." Something flickered in her eyes. He sensed she wanted to trust this wasn't an act.

"Or Gilbert."

Leaning over, she studied the entry. "I can't decipher it."

"Why can't I remember my own name?" Frustration built inside him. Closing his eyes, he pinched the bridge of his nose. "We can't know for sure if this is truly mine."

He would not give in to the panic. *Keep it together. She already thinks you're suspect. Falling to pieces won't help your case.*

She unfolded a shirt and held it out in front of her. "Looks like it would fit you."

Regulating his breathing, he forced his gaze to hers. "I know you have theories about me. I'd like to hear them."

Jessica lowered the shirt, her surprise evident. "I doubt that."

"I can't say for certain, but I have a feeling I'm a practical kind of guy. No use avoiding the unpleasantness of life. Just delays the inevitable."

"All right." Sinking into the chair once more, she finger-combed her mane with long, meditative strokes. "Most obvious theory? You're an outlaw on the run from authorities or rival criminals."

"Am I a notorious outlaw or a basic, run-of-the-mill criminal?"

"You're a man who's conflicted about your misdeeds."

"That's good to know," he said wryly. "Next theory."

"You stole another man's wife."

He shook his head, such a thing unfathomable. "I stole another man's horse."

She tapped her chin. "You swindled someone in a business deal."

This game of pretend wasn't helping his dark mood. "Let's move on to the theories where I'm the good guy, shall we?"

A slim gold ring with a ruby setting flashed on her right hand. "Okay. You were traveling through the area, minding your own business, when you were ambushed by ruffians."

"Sounds plausible." And much more palatable than anything else she'd thrown at him. "There's no money in this bag or on my person. I wouldn't have traveled without funds."

She nodded. "You could've stored the money in your saddlebags, which they took along with your horse."

He rested a hand atop the Bible. "Could I be a circuit-riding preacher?"

She looked dubious. "We don't really have those in these parts. Are there notes on the pages? A preacher would probably have written down thoughts and ideas, underlined important verses."

While the pages appeared well-worn, and a couple of passages in Psalms had been underlined, he didn't see any handwriting. "I could've recorded my thoughts and sermons in a separate journal."

"The Bible could mean one of two things—either you treasure it so much you couldn't bear to travel without it, or you treasure the person who gave it to you. A parent or grandparent would be the most likely candidate."

"I uttered a prayer earlier. It wasn't something I actively thought about."

"That's good." Clasping her hands together, she said, "Jane is better at this than I am. She's more inventive."

He seized on the rare revelation of personal information. He was done discussing himself. "Does she live nearby?"

"A couple of miles away. She's married to a wonderful man, Tom Leighton. They're raising his young niece, Clara, together."

The wistfulness in her voice wasn't lost on him. Did she long for a husband and children? What were his own opinions about love and marriage?

"Do your other sisters live in Gatlinburg, as well?"

"All but one. Juliana makes her home in Cades Cove."

He pressed into the headboard, the wood digging into his shoulder blades. "Cades Cove. That name means something."

She scooted to the seat's edge. "What? Did you live there? Could you have family there?"

He had no answers for her. "Is it about two days' ride from here?"

"Yes."

"I'm not sure how I know that." He raked his hands through his hair, tugging a little at the ends. "Could you write to your sister? Ask her to check with her neighbors and the town leaders? Perhaps someone would recognize my description."

Hands twisting together, she pondered his request. "I'll write immediately after supper and post it tomorrow." Standing, she adjusted her blouse and, flipping her ponytail over her shoulder, made to leave.

"Jessica?"

"Yes?" The one word carried a world of strain. Indecision.

"What will it take for you to believe me?"

Her inner struggle was reflected on her face. "Doc believes you. My mother believes you. I value both their opinions."

"I'm more concerned with what *you* think."

"My first instinct is to believe you."

The triumph swirling inside was tempered by a heavy dose of restraint. "But?"

"My instincts have been wrong before." The raw grief he glimpsed in her jolted him. "My sister almost died because of me. I can't afford to be wrong about you."

She left him with more questions than answers, the desire to reassure her, to make things good for her again completely unexpected and decidedly irrational.

He couldn't fix his own problems. What made him think he could fix hers?

Chapter Four

"**Y**ou're so lucky." Teeth flashing in the gathering shadows, Will carried a water bucket in each hand. "Nothing exciting ever happens to me."

Walking beside him through the tranquil woods, Jessica shook her head. Because of his towering height and sturdy frame, the fifteen-year-old had the appearance of a man. And while he was mature in some ways, times like these reminded her he had plenty of growing up yet to do. Despite the absence of his parents—he'd been raised by an infirm grandfather and his older sister, Sophie—he'd turned out fine.

"Count your blessings, Will. Trust me. Excitement isn't always a positive thing."

"Easy for you to say. Your life isn't all about chores and schoolwork."

Jessica recalled the time when her biggest irritant was having to write a history report or prepare a speech to deliver in front of the other students. Such innocence seemed like a hazy dream.

They emerged from the trees close to where Grant had hours earlier. The outbuildings were mere outlines, the details obscured by encroaching darkness. The great, hulking barn was impossible to ignore. Her memory conjured up smoke belching out the wide entrance, and she could almost taste the acrid stench of burning wood and hay.

Coming even with the structure, her gaze strayed to the patchy grass and the spot where Tom had dragged Lee's lifeless body before returning inside and putting out the fire. Moisture smarted. She blinked rapidly, appalled that she still hadn't mastered the grief and regret. If only it hadn't happened here. If only she didn't have to face the lingering images each and every day.

Will reached the porch steps before noticing she hadn't followed. "You coming?"

"I'll be along in a minute."

The door slapped shut behind him. Setting her own full pail on the ground, a little of the water splashing out, she trudged through the grass and stopped directly on the spot where Lee had lain. Heart expanding near to bursting, she knelt and pressed her palm flat against the hard, warm earth. Blades of grass tickled her skin.

"Why can't I forget, Lord?"

She'd crouched over him in shock, his unmoving hand locked between hers, lost in sorrow to the point she hadn't given a thought to Jane's gunshot wound. Tom had had to walk over to her in order to get her attention and convince her to assist her sister.

At the repetitive drum of an approaching rider, she shot to her feet. Jessica squinted at the lane, less than thrilled when she recognized the mount and its owner, Sheriff Shane Timmons. His low instructions carried in the still air, his horse slowing and eventually coming to a halt yards from where she waited.

Shane touched his brim. "Evenin', Jessica."

She clasped her hands at her waist. "Hello, Sheriff."

He dismounted and crossed to her in three easy strides. She held his sharp azure gaze with difficulty. He treated her with nothing but kindness and respect, and yet she couldn't help thinking he saw her as weak and naive. After all, what intelligent female involved herself with a criminal?

"I hear you got yourself a visitor."

"That's right."

Swiping off his hat, he tunneled his fingers through his light hair. Perusing her face, he opened his mouth to speak, but she held him off.

"I'll take you to him."

His concern plain, he acted the gentleman and didn't remark on her avoidance. Dipping his head, he extended his arm to indicate she precede him. Her progress across the yard was accomplished quickly. She would take him to Grant and escape into her room. Or rather upstairs to Nicole's old room, now dedicated as a storage area for their sewing supplies.

Her mother and Will greeted Shane with friendly enthusiasm, a far cry from her own stilted welcome. Unlike her, they didn't have cause to be uncomfortable in his presence.

"He's taken over Jane's old room," she said over her shoulder, ushering him past the grouping of sofas and chairs and into the hall. Stopping just past the entrance, she waved him in. "I'll leave you to it."

He paused. "I'd like you to stay for the interview."

Peeking inside, she saw Grant propped against the pillows, assessing them with undisguised wariness. "I don't see how I can be of assistance."

Patience smoothed Shane's rugged features. "You were the one who found him. And you'll know if there are changes in his story."

"Fine." She sighed.

Inside, she introduced the two men. The room's size

struck her as inadequate all of a sudden. Too confining for the competent, bent-on-justice sheriff and Grant, who, despite his weakened state, exuded quiet strength.

Shane stood at the foot of the bed, one suntanned hand gripping his Stetson and the other resting atop his Smith and Wesson. Jessica sat in the only chair, wishing she could start the day over, wishing it was an ordinary, boring day like all the rest.

"Doc tells me you've lost your memory."

Grant grimaced, the hand closest to her curling into the bedding as he nodded. His turmoil troubled her, evoked sympathy she'd rather not deal with. She stared at his busted knuckles and experienced the strange urge to link hands with him, a small gesture to soothe his anxiety.

How do you know he deserves your sympathy? There could be innocent people out there...victims of his cruelty.

She forced her attention to the rectangular rug covering this section of floorboards and studied the fading flag's stars and stripes. Deep in her heart, a voice protested that Grant wasn't a cruel man. A thief or swindler, perhaps, but not cruel.

She listened as he recounted his brief knowledge of the day's events. Shane's lingering silence brought her head up. Both men were regarding her with unsettling intensity.

"Care to add anything, Jessica?" Shane said.

Grant's mouth was set in a grim line, his neck and shoulder muscles stiff with tension. A thin vein was visible at his temple.

"No. Nothing."

The sheriff riffled through the Bible she'd found, squinting at the pages. "Can you think of anyone else this might belong to?"

"We haven't had company in months." She pointed to the bag tucked against the wall. "The bag looks relatively free of debris and dirt. I figure it hasn't been out there long."

He slid the book onto the dresser behind him. "What are you expecting to be called?"

"I've decided to go by Grant for now."

"You could adopt the surname Parker, if you're of a mind to. Good chance this stuff is yours."

"Grant Parker. Doesn't sound horrible."

Shane tapped his weapon handle. "I'll search my wanted posters tonight. Tomorrow, I'll post letters to the lawmen in nearby towns."

"I understand."

"The O'Malleys are good friends of mine. Don't make them regret giving you shelter, or you'll have to answer to me." The warning in his tone mirrored his expression.

"You have nothing to worry about on that front." Grant's chin jutted. "I wouldn't do anything to harm Mrs. O'Malley or her daughter. Besides," he drawled with a sideways glance at her, "I'm convinced Miss O'Malley is capable of fending for herself."

Shane made a noncommittal noise and moved toward the hallway. "Walk me out, Jessica?"

With one final look at their patient, she followed the other man out and onto the porch. Night had fallen and so had the temperatures. The air was cool and crisp, with the faint twang of moist earth and chrysanthemums. Rubbing her arms, she leaned against the railing, thankful for the cover of darkness. Like Grant, she'd been the focus of Shane's professional interest once upon a time, and it hadn't been a pleasant experience.

He put his hat on. "I can send my deputy over to keep an eye on things tonight if you need."

She fixed her attention on the sliver of moon in the velvet expanse. "We'll be fine."

"I can't guarantee he's harmless."

"He's hardly in the shape to ambush us." She surprised herself by defending him. "I'm armed and so is Will."

At his huff, Jessica crossed her arms. "Will may be young and obnoxious, but he's a right good shot. I know you've heard of his rifle skills."

"That is a full-grown man in there, not a skittish deer."

Light spilled from the windows. In the space between them hung the unspoken remembrance of her stupidity and willfulness. Last year, when Jane had first spoken of her suspicions that Lee was involved in the illegal production and sale of moonshine, Jessica had rejected them outright. She had been in love with the man. She thought she would've known if he was involved in unlawful activity. She'd been blind. And so, so wrong.

He studied her a beat longer. "Your cousins aren't going to be happy about this."

Josh, Nathan and Caleb would indeed be furious. "As it wasn't my decision to keep him, they'll have to take their complaints to my mother."

"Be on your guard. And come to me at the first hint of trouble."

Unlike last time, his expression intimated.

"Good night, Sheriff."

Spinning on her heel, she crossed to the door. Her hand was on the latch when he called after her.

"I'll come back tonight if I find anything matching his description."

With a nod, she retreated inside, anticipating a long, uneasy night.

The bottle of laudanum called to him.

Grant shifted again, unable to find relief. He could take the doctor's prescribed amount. Wouldn't mean he was weak. The dose would allow him to sleep and find temporary release from the incessant hammering inside his skull, the radiating pain in his side and the dull throb in his ankle. Not only that, it would make the questions stop.

What was he doing in these mountains? Where had he come from? What had been his destination? Was he a danger to the occupants of this cabin?

On the other side of the window, pricks of light pierced the black sky. He could easily identify the patterns they made. Who had taught him the constellations?

His gaze shifted to the rafters overhead. Too low, he thought. The walls too close.

He yearned for open spaces and fresh air. The fact that he couldn't get outside without assistance was depressing.

Muffled snores filtered in from the living room, where the O'Malleys' young relation slept on the sofa. Will Tanner didn't strike him as a worthy protector. Jessica had introduced her cousin's brother-in-law when he'd first arrived with Alice, and the young man had studied him with barely concealed awe. As if Grant was an infamous outlaw like Jesse James or in league with Sam Archer and his gang. Problem was, he couldn't rule that out. No theory—no matter how unpleasant or disturbing—could be dismissed.

Grant massaged his temples in a vain attempt to drive away the headache.

The ornate clock he'd glimpsed on their mantel chimed the hour. One o'clock in the morning. The hours until dawn stretched out before him. Morning wasn't going to be much better. Nothing would be better until his mind decided to function again.

Grant suppressed a groan of frustration. Here he was, a grown man, feeling sorry for himself. He had his life, didn't he? He hadn't died out there in the forest. Alone. Nameless.

He fluffed the pillow again, stilling when he heard a soft cry. Jessica's door wasn't visible from his vantage point, but he'd seen her rush past this room soon after the sheriff left, and she hadn't emerged since.

Pushing aside the covers, he moved like an old man, fighting exhaustion as he hobbled to his door. He hesitated. Gripping the frame, he steadied himself. His frown deepened. She was definitely crying. Her anguish leached through the walls, drawing him closer, concern blocking out self-preservation. If they caught him wandering about in the middle of the night, they'd assume the worst. Sheriff Timmons would have him locked in a cell before dawn.

He moved as quietly as he could. The ropes of her bed creaked, and her weeping became muted. He lifted his hand to knock. Instead, he laid it flat against the wooden surface and debated what to do. She didn't know him. Certainly didn't trust him. What made him think she'd willingly share her private pain?

He dropped his head. She wouldn't. Not with a suspicious stranger with a questionable past.

Chapter Five

"Grant."

Lids shut against the subdued light, a quilt cocooning his sore body, he struggled to recognize the melodious voice. His life was decidedly female-free.

"Your food is gonna get cold if you don't wake up."

A woman had prepared him breakfast? Couldn't be.

When a slender hand wrapped around his wrist and tugged, his eyes shot open. A familiar redhead stood staring down at him, impatience lining her perpetual frown. Yesterday's events flooded his mind.

"Jessica." His voice was rusty from sleep, yet his relief was audible.

A small part of him had worried he'd forget what few memories he'd retained.

He eyed the tray on the bedside table, the scents of peppery sausage, eggs and sweet molasses wafting toward him. The stack of fluffy flapjacks glistened with melted butter. Steam rose from the blue enamel mug.

"If you'll sit up, you can have your breakfast in bed. Ma and I have a full day of chores." Flipping her ponytail behind her shoulder, she picked up the tray. "I don't have time to chaperone you."

"That's a shame." Grant pushed himself up so that he rested against the headboard. "I was hoping you'd stay and hold my hand. Perhaps read me a storybook. I think one about a prince and a vexing princess would suit me."

Jessica set the tray on his lap with enough force to make the dishes rattle. The coffee came dangerously close to sloshing over the rim.

"I'll be back in fifteen minutes to retrieve it."

In the seconds before she straightened, her face hovered about six inches from his, and he noticed that her eyes were puffy, the surrounding skin ravaged by grief. His late-night trek to her room fresh in his mind, he wondered how long she had lain there and suffered alone. How come he wished he was in the position to offer her comfort?

Before he could form a coherent sentence, she swept out of the room, her nut-brown dress swishing and boots clacking against the boards. The main door slammed. He heard movement coming from the kitchen area. Probably Alice cleaning up the breakfast mess.

Grant picked up a fork and scooped a mound of scrambled eggs. The delicious taste registered, and he felt certain he wasn't accustomed to being waited on. He didn't have proof. It was strictly a gut feeling.

Jessica returned as promised a quarter of an hour later, as fresh and vibrant as an autumn flower, her cheeks flushed from exertion.

Examining his almost-empty plate, she stopped short. "You need more time?"

"No. As delicious as it was, my appetite hasn't returned to normal."

Nodding, she avoided eye contact and reached for the tray. "No worries. Our hogs will enjoy the leftovers."

"Would you mind sending Will in?"

Cinnamon-hued brows rumpling, she balanced her

burden against her hip. "He left before breakfast. He has responsibilities at home. What did you want with him?"

Grant attempted to frame his needs in a delicate manner. "I need to go outside, yet I was ordered not to put weight on my ankle, and Doc hasn't delivered my cane."

In addition to the pressing urge to answer the call of nature, he was desperate for fresh air and a view other than these four walls.

An exaggerated sigh escaped her lips. Depositing the dirty dishes on the bedside table, she retrieved his boots and crouched beside the bed.

"What are you doing?"

"Helping you."

Pushing the covers aside, he carefully swung his feet to the floor, his wound protesting. He cradled his middle.

She noticed, of course, but merely waved for him to lift his good foot.

"I can put my own boots on," he muttered through his embarrassment.

"Not with that stab wound, you can't."

Her fingers were gentle atop his sock as she guided his dusty boot on. He stared at the crown of her head. Restrained by a slightly askew ribbon, her hair was clean and shiny, like a luminous red flame.

"Thank you."

"For what?"

"The food." He waved a hand to where she knelt on the rug. "This."

"It's my goal to see you recovered and on your way as quickly as possible."

On his way to where? "I may not be going far. How's the Gatlinburg jail for creature comforts?"

Holding his other boot between her hands, her dark green gaze flashed to his. "Shane said if he didn't come back last night, we'd know he didn't find anything. I should've mentioned it sooner."

If his heart had been encased with rocks, this news released a couple of them. "So now I wait for reports from the surrounding towns."

"I suppose so." Lips thinning, she contemplated his swollen ankle and set the boot aside. "Let me see if we have something to wrap this foot."

He waited in that corner room, trying to distract himself from his predicament and failing. Trying to remember *anything* beyond waking up in the forest and failing.

Jessica reappeared just as his anxiety reached its peak, threatening to make his chest implode.

"I was unsuccessful. I'm afraid you'll have to go out sans shoe."

"It's fine." Tugging down his pant legs, he pushed to his feet and began to hobble toward the door.

She stepped directly into his path, hands on her hips. "Trying to do it on your own will only hinder your healing."

"Your concern is touching, Miss O'Malley." He smirked, and his torn lip smarted.

Her ire sparked. "Will you accept my help or not, Mr. Parker?"

"I don't have a chance against your stubbornness, do I?"

Rolling her eyes, she moved close to his side and anchored her arm around his waist. Grant curved his arm about her shoulders, her softness and warmth a shock to his equanimity. Their progression proved awkward. Her head knocked into his chin several times. He was trying not to lean on her too much, which served to pull at his stitches. It was a relief to reach the yard.

The main cabin, barn and outbuildings inhabited a small clearing in what amounted to a massive mountainous forest. The tips of the mountains, arrayed in vibrant autumn attire, were visible above the treetops. To their left, a rutted dirt lane merged with a wider one in the distance. A sizable vegetable garden boasted fat orange pumpkins and yellow squash, broccoli and cabbages. Chickens strutted near their coop. A rural paradise.

Removing his arm, he said, "Can I ask you something?"

Jessica retreated a safe distance away. "You can ask. I may not answer."

"Were you and Sheriff Timmons a couple?"

She gave a huff of disbelieving laughter. "What? No! He's at least a decade older than me. He's not the type of man I'd be interested in. What gave you that idea?"

"I got the impression you weren't comfortable having him around. I thought maybe you and he…"

Her jaw snapped shut, and the shadows returned. "That's not the case."

"What's wrong with the sheriff, then?"

"We are not discussing my preferences."

He didn't heed the warning in her expression. Scraping his fingers along the itchy stubble lining his cheek, he admitted, "I heard you crying last night."

Consternation flushed her cheeks a bright apple red. Shame and raw anguish passed over her features.

"Your mother mentioned—"

Jessica gasped. Splotches of hot color crept up her neck. "She talked to you about me? What did she say?"

Wrong move. Wrong words. Should've kept his big mouth shut.

He held his palms up. "Nothing specific. She said you'd experienced some difficulties. That's all."

Her thick auburn lashes swept down, shutting him out. "That was not her place." Mortification laced her tone. "What could she have been thinking? You're a *stranger*."

"True. And I have no past experiences to draw on that would help you whatsoever. I shouldn't have brought it up."

"Stranger or not, amnesia or not, you can't help me. No one can. I got myself into a mess, all right? The ramifications are mine to deal with alone."

"You sure it has to be that way?"

"I appreciate your concern, Grant. I do. But you're not gonna be here long enough to matter."

Jessica watched him limp across the yard and disappear around the corner of the cabin. No wonder he'd flat out dismissed her offer of assistance. She'd been rude.

Humiliation had spurred the hasty words. That and outrage. Knowing her mother and Grant had discussed her spectacular mistakes made her burn with embarrassment. That she hadn't divulged specifics didn't matter. Grant hadn't earned their trust. He was a stranger in their home.

A handsome stranger whose presence made her evaluate her current circumstances and the sad fact that she was alone. Helping him outside in what had amounted to an awkward side embrace, she'd been overwhelmed by his latent strength, the power coiled in those honed muscles. His heat and earthy scent had taunted her, reminding her of what she might never have—someone special who meant more to her than everyone else on earth, someone worthy of her trust and admiration.

The longing for love and romance scared her. Under absolutely no circumstances could she be attracted to this man. He was the worst possible person to reawaken long-buried dreams. If she ever decided to reenter the world of courting and suitors, she would take the safe route. A pity the reverend was triple her age and happily married.

Several riders entered the lane behind her. Swinging around, she registered her cousins' approach with mixed feelings. Josh, Nathan and Caleb were more like brothers than cousins. Having grown up on neighboring farms, they'd shared meals and holidays, gotten into mischief together, stuck up for one another. And while she loved them dearly, she didn't appreciate it when they stuck their collective noses into her business.

Josh was the first to dismount and approach. The oldest brother, he wore his wheat-colored hair short. A trim mustache and goatee framed his mouth. The quiet, intelligent type, he looked to be on a slow simmer.

"We heard about your visitor," he said, grip on his waistband tightening.

Nathan joined him, his silver eyes stormy beneath his hat's brim. "What were you thinking, Jess? Will came home this morning spinning wild tales. Are they true?"

Raven-haired Caleb stalked over, the angry scar around his eye more pinched than usual. He didn't have to say a word. All it took was one imperious glare for her to guess his thoughts.

Jessica squared off against the trio. "First of all, he isn't *my* visitor. So all this protective outrage is wasted on me." She made a circling motion in the air. "Grant is Ma's project. Take your complaints up with her. Second, he's suffering from several wounds, not to mention memory loss, so leave him alone."

Caleb's mouth twisted into a cynical slash. "You believe his story?"

"I haven't made my mind up yet."

Grant's sincerity seemed awfully authentic, and she found herself leaning toward belief. But resistance lingered. Look at how Lee had convinced her he was a run-of-the-mill farmer, when right under her nose he'd been cooking up moonshine to distribute across the state and beyond.

Their expressions turned frosty. Looking over her shoulder, she saw Grant register their animosity and come to a halt. Caleb made to move past her. Slapping her hand again his chest, she inserted steel into her voice. "He's injured."

"So?"

"So take it easy."

"Relax, cuz. I'm just gonna talk to the man."

Trailing behind them, praying for a peaceful outcome, she studied Grant's busted-up face. Wariness was notable in his stiff shoulders and stance, but the determined set of his jaw said he wasn't going to back down. The cabin wall behind him providing support, he didn't waver beneath Caleb and Josh's onslaught of questions. The righteous defiance in his clear gaze shifted her perception of him, eradicating many of her doubts. There wasn't a hint of discomfort in him. No telltale signs he was protecting a lie.

If she *were* to accept his account of events, it wouldn't be a case of her judgment opposing everyone else's, as in Lee's case. Her own mother and the respected town doctor trusted Grant.

Not speaking, Nathan listened, content to let his brothers do the interrogating.

The longer it went on, the more Grant's physical weakness began to show.

Pushing past Nathan, she walked between the brothers to stand beside Grant. He glanced at her in surprise.

"Who's interested in blackberry cobbler? And coffee? I'm sure Ma's wondering what's keeping us."

Caleb and Josh exchanged matching looks of displeasure. Too bad. She wasn't about to stand by while they ambushed him.

Nathan lifted his hat and fluffed his dark hair. "I've just had breakfast, but I won't pass up your cobbler."

"Then it's settled." Linking arms with Caleb, she urged him in the direction of the porch steps. "So how are Rebecca and the kids?"

"In between feeding and changing the baby, Becca's teaching Noah how to paint faces on pumpkins and gourds."

She smiled at the image his words spawned. Caleb's wife was a gifted painter. In fact, one of Becca's paintings hung on the wall across from Jessica's bed. Young Noah was a sweetheart, and he loved being a big brother to three-month-old Isaac.

He angled his face so that his mouth met her ear. "Tread carefully with this one, cuz. While I suspect he's telling the truth, there's no way of knowing his history and whether or not it's a violent one."

Her smile vanished. Of course he was alluding to her past. Her discernment would forever forward be called into question. Teeth clenched, she merely nodded, quickly disengaging her arm once they entered the house.

He was right. Grant Parker was a puzzle. One no one might ever be able to solve.

Chapter Six

For a while there, Grant thought he might get stabbed a second time. Or shot. Or, at the very least, punched.

Jessica's relatives were not pleased she and her mother had taken him in. The scarred one especially looked as if roughing Grant up a bit would make him feel better. Alice O'Malley's presence dictated they be polite. Still, the unspoken strain in the crowded living room was palpable.

Although he tried not to appear fixated on his perplexing young hostess, his gaze insisted on sliding in her direction against his will. Seated on a low cushioned stool beside the unlit fireplace, Jessica held a delicate china teacup in her hands, the saucer on the stool beside her. She'd served up the cobbler for everyone except herself and him. His excuse? He'd probably cast up his accounts if he attempted to eat anything more. As for hers, he wondered if she was too nervous to eat, concerned about maintaining her waistline or the kind of person who enjoyed the act of cooking more than actually sampling the fare. He found himself wondering a lot of things. Such as why she'd come to his rescue outside when he'd obviously messed up by mentioning her private grief.

The brief excursion outside his bedroom had winded

him. While he longed to recline in his borrowed bed, doing so would impart the notion he was either weak or hiding something. Instead, he'd sunk into the closest wingback chair, the soft, worn cushions like a gentle hug. Focusing on the conversation flowing around him took his mind off his body's state of perpetual soreness.

There was talk of extended family members, both young and old, as well as the state of Josh's furniture business in town. Sophie, who they'd explained was Will's sister, was expecting twins. From the way Nathan's expression lit up, Grant surmised the proud father-to-be wasn't daunted by the prospect of caring for two infants at once.

Ensconced in the chair nearest his, Alice beamed. "Grant, Sophie practically raised Will, what with her pa off roaming the country and her ma dead. Her grandfather helped as much as he could. I miss that gentle soul."

On the other side of the coffee table, the three O'Malley brothers sat side by side on the sofa. Their collective focus shifted to him.

He gripped the mug's handle tighter. "Congratulations."

Nathan considered him. "Thank you."

Caleb leaned over and set his empty bowl on the walnut table with a clatter. "What about you, Parker? You remember having any children?"

Jessica gasped. The silence that followed could've suffocated him. Or was that the panic that refused to leave him entirely, crouching in the shadows and waiting for a chance to pounce?

To cover his anxiety, he lifted his mug and sipped the aromatic brew.

"Caleb, I don't believe that's appropriate." Dabbing her mouth with a napkin, Alice frowned at her nephew.

"I'm simply curious."

"No, you're trying to evoke a reaction," Jessica retorted, her eyes full of fire. "It's rude." Shooting to her feet, she started collecting the discarded dishes. "Now that you've all met Grant, it's time for you to go. Ma and I have ten bushels of apples to turn into apple butter by day's end."

To his surprise, Alice didn't refute her daughter. "Yes, we do have a busy day ahead of us."

Grant nestled the mug against his thigh. "I don't mind answering the question."

Everyone in the room stared at him.

"I don't know if I have children. Or a wife. For all I know, I could have a family out there waiting for me to come home." The words sounded like a foreign language to his ears. He rubbed his thumb over his left ring finger. It was bare. There wasn't an indentation or sun line indicating he'd ever worn a ring. He couldn't fathom having a wife, let alone children. "I may not have my memories, but I have a sound mind and enough good sense to know that these ladies are well-loved in this community and by your family. I wouldn't dare repay their generosity with ill-treatment."

Josh slapped on his hat and stood. "Let's hope you're telling the truth, because we won't tolerate anything less than gentlemanly behavior. Not only do we know every square mile of these mountains, we've had plenty of practice hunting down criminals. It'd be in your best interest not to cross us."

His brothers stood as well, their expressions no less cautionary.

"Understood."

Alice ushered them to the door like a mother hen with her chicks. The affection the older widow harbored for them was written in her lined countenance. Made him lonely for something he wasn't sure he'd ever had.

Drawing on all his strength, Grant leveraged himself out of the comfy chair and relieved Jessica of the bowls. She didn't protest. In the warm, sunlit kitchen, she emptied the mugs' leftover contents into a scrap pail one by one. He leaned his hip against the wooden counter. The tangy scent of ripe apples teased his nose. Baskets brimming with the bright red and green fruit lined three walls.

"I'm sorry about that."

"They're your family," he said. "They care about you."

"I care about them, too," she said drily. "Doesn't mean they aren't annoying sometimes."

"Be thankful you have someone to annoy you."

Her luminous gaze sought his as she lowered the last cup into the dry sink. "You may not have been married, but you do have a mother and father. Possibly even siblings."

He studied the cheery yellow curtains, the pie safe shelves crowded with baked goods, the burlap rug at the door boasting a rooster pattern. He hadn't been hatched in a coop. He'd been born to parents and raised in a home. What sort of parents he'd had and what sort of home life he'd experienced were questions he could add to the growing list of unknowns.

"The family tree page in the Bible was left blank. I could be an orphan."

She toyed with one of her ear bobs. "Or…your folks couldn't read or write."

Impatience dogged him. Edging around her, he went to the basket beneath the window and, choosing an apple, brought it to his nose and inhaled deeply. He wasn't sure which foods he favored and which he avoided.

"What variety are these?"

"Macintosh."

"How does one go about making apple butter?"

Jessica explained the process. Once all the apples were

quartered, they'd start three fires out in the yard. One to boil down cider, another to heat the quartered apples and a third to turn cider into a sugar-like substance. Once that first batch of cider was half its original amount, they'd add the apples and sugar, along with cinnamon and nutmeg. This process would take the entire day.

He glanced at the dirty dishes piled in the dry sink, the bowl of bread dough rising on the stove. His presence was adding to their already considerable load of chores.

"I'll help you."

"You look as if one flick of my finger could knock you over." Her expression was dubious. "You should be in bed resting."

Pointing to the table, he said, "I can sit there and peel apples while I rest."

"You'll regret pushing yourself too hard."

Her concern appeared to center around his health this time and not on how his arrival had disrupted her life.

"Before I leave, I'm going to find a way to repay my debt. I don't have any money." The tips of his ears burned. "What I can offer you is physical labor. I can do chores. Tend the animals. Fix whatever needs fixing around the farm."

A wave of light-headedness washed over him, and his hand shot to the window ledge. Jessica's washcloth slipped to the floor unheeded. Striding over, she dipped beneath his arm and sidled close against his side.

"Let's get you to your room before you fall flat on your face." Her palm was warm on his lower back.

"I'll go crazy staring at those four walls." He switched course and headed for the table. "I just need to sit down for a few minutes."

She accommodated him without a word. When he was seated, she perched on the table corner and crossed her arms. "I can't help but wonder what sort of skills you have."

Taken aback, he raised his brows in question.

One delicate shoulder lifted. "You offered to tend the animals, but how do we know you have experience with them? You might've grown up in a crowded city."

Grant searched hard for a silver lining. "I might've been a newspaperman. Or a wealthy shipping magnate."

The tiniest of smiles played about her mouth. "You were so wealthy you resided in a seaside mansion with dozens of servants and indoor plumbing."

"I like the sound of that." Stroking his light beard, he said, "On the other hand, I could've been a poor but happy traveling circus performer."

Her eyes widened. Her lips curved into a full-on smile that dazzled him. When a husky chuckle bubbled up her throat, Grant couldn't help but share in her amusement.

"Perhaps you'd like to juggle a few of those apples to test that theory."

Smiling, he shook his head. "Maybe when I'm in top form."

They continued the silly game for several minutes, each of them proposing more and more outlandish professions. By the time Alice joined them, Jessica had been transformed. Her eyes sparkled with good humor. Her teeth flashed white with each spurt of laughter. The glimpse of tiny dimples charmed him.

Splaying a hand against her middle, she panted, "My stomach hurts from laughing."

Her mother stopped beside the pie safe looking both pleased and confounded. "It's good to hear you laugh again, dear."

Pushing off the table, Jessica moved to retrieve the towel from the floor. "Yes, well, Grant has quite the imagination. He's convinced he was either a stage actor or a patent medicine salesman."

Alice's jowls quivered with laughter. "There are endless possibilities, to be sure. Now, young man, it's time to change out that bandage. I'm sure you'd appreciate a shave, as well."

"Yes, ma'am."

As he shuffled into the living room, leaving Jessica to her work, Grant wished the lighthearted moments didn't have to end.

Jessica heard movement in Grant's room and sat up. She'd come to bed over an hour ago, weary to the bone yet unable to sleep. Her shoulders and the muscles of her upper back ached from the constant stirring required to ensure the apple butter didn't scorch. Her hair and skin smelled like a mixture of cloves and cinnamon.

His door latch clicked. Seconds later, the floor creaked. What was he up to?

Wide-awake, she pushed the thick quilt off her legs and, after lighting the lamp on her bedside table, shrugged on the housecoat that covered her from chin to toes and went in search of him. No light came from the kitchen. Will's obnoxious snoring sliced through the darkness. Jessica jiggled his feet hanging off the end cushion, and he shifted onto his side, thankfully cutting off the noise.

The scrape of wood across floorboards drew her to the nearest window. She could make out Grant's shadowy form in the rocking chair. Taking care to be quiet, she slipped outside.

His head snapped up. The lamp's muted glow fell on his face, highlighting his freshly shaven jaw and glinting in his clean locks.

He's handsome. So what? Gatlinburg has dozens of attractive men.

"Did I wake you?" His husky voice cut through the frogs' song echoing through the woods. Soon it would become too cold for the creatures.

"I'd have to be asleep for you to do that." Choosing the rocker on the other side of the door, she set the lamp near her feet and folded her hands in her lap. "Have you ever pushed through exhaustion until you're not sleepy anymore?"

"I'm not sure." Wearing a rueful grin, he pushed the chair into motion with his foot. "I have an excuse to be awake. I had a long nap after lunch. You, on the other hand, didn't stop moving the entire day. I expected you to be snoring right about now."

"Will was doing enough of that for the both of us."

His laugh was soft, affectionate. "I heard."

Jessica reached for her ponytail out of habit, only to remember she'd left her hair unbound. Grant caught the movement. His gaze sharpened. In the dimness, she couldn't decipher his expression. Uncharacteristic self-consciousness seized her.

"You have beautiful hair." His voice deepened. "Like a flame. Or a sunset." Scraping a hand over his face, he grimaced. "That sounded better in my head."

She couldn't help smiling. Funny, she'd done more of that in the past twelve hours than in the past twelve months. "I believe we can rule out poet."

"I believe so." Turning his attention to the sky visible beyond the overhang, he said, "Did you know the constellations are different in summer and winter?"

"I didn't. Where did you learn that?"

"In a book maybe. Sailors need to be familiar with the stars' patterns, right?" His mood seemed to shift. "Enough guessing for one day. Tell me about Gatlinburg. Tell me about yourself. Your family."

Jessica complied. While living in a small town had its disadvantages—there was no hiding one's mistakes, no secrets—she loved the mountains, the lush forests and sparkling streams, the diverse wildlife. She described the heart of town and the businesses established there, two of which were owned by her family members. Her sister Nicole had married the mercantile owner. And Josh and Kate operated a combination furniture store and photography studio. Grant asked questions from time to time. He possessed a keen intelligence, and she tempered her admiration with the reminder that not all criminals were dumb. Some were geniuses. Some were adept at deceiving those closest to them...

Stop it. You can't live the rest of your life thinking the worst of people.

A small shadow emerged from the barn and trotted across the yard. As the black cat neared, the lamplight glinted off its golden eyes. Cinders hopped onto the porch and, bypassing Jessica, went over and sniffed Grant's socks and pant legs.

"Who's this?" He stretched out his fingers.

"Her name's Cinders. Careful, she's not all that friendly."

Belying her words, the black feline butted her head into Grant's palm, eager for affection. Then she promptly leaped onto his lap.

"You were saying?" Grinning, he slid her a sideways glance.

Jessica watched Cinders lap up his attention. "I've never seen her do that."

"So you named her that because of her coloring?"

"Jane named her. Our older sister Megan used to entertain us with stories. For me, the scarier the better. Jane's the opposite—she hates to be frightened. One night, after a particularly harrowing tale, this kitten hopped out of the shadows and pounced on poor Jane. Her fur was streaked with ashes. I'm not sure how she got so filthy."

Grant sneezed. "You don't know where she came from?"

"We searched the woods for her mother and came up empty. Cinders didn't make it easy for us to care for her, but we managed. I get the impression she regards us as necessary but annoying."

His tanned, capable-looking hands gently stroked her sleek fur. He sneezed again. Dipping his head, he murmured, "You and I have something in common, don't we, Cinders?"

Another sneeze overtook him, and he winced. Either his head or his side was paining him. Maybe both. Her mother had applied fresh ointment and gauze that morning and told her it looked the same as yesterday. Taking in his profile, Jessica worried over the possibility of infection.

Only because he'd be forced to stay here longer, she reassured herself. Her focus must be on her own life, her own problems. Not someone passing through their lives. They would do their Christian duty and send him off with warm wishes.

Jessica frowned. "Grant, I think you may have a sensitivity to cats."

"I can put up with itchy eyes and a runny nose for my newfound friend. After all, she's the first one I've made here in Tennessee."

"You and I aren't friends?" she said partly in jest, the tiniest bit hurt that he'd discounted her.

In the intimate closeness the serene, dark forest imparted, he lifted his head to regard her with eyes that had deepened to a navy hue. "That's a question only you can answer, Jessica. Friends trust each other. They don't suspect them of deceit and ill intent."

There was no condemnation in his tone. He'd spoken frankly, but there was understanding there, too. As if he identified with her misgivings.

"In that case, the answer is yes."

The slow arrival of gratitude, then relief and finally happiness passing over his clean-shaven features did serious damage to her defenses. Bolting to her feet, she bid him a brief good-night and reentered the house, seeking sanctuary in her room.

She couldn't allow herself to like Grant Parker. Empathy was acceptable. Concern for his health was natural. But opening herself up to a man, even for something as innocent as friendship, could very well be the first step to disaster.

Chapter Seven

The closer Jessica got to town, the easier it was to breathe.

Rising before dawn, she'd completed her chores, fixed breakfast and dressed for church all before her mother emerged from her bedroom. Alice had been surprised, to say the least, but willing to keep their patient company. Jessica had woken Will and asked him to see to Grant's needs before he left.

She hadn't wanted to face Grant across the breakfast table and witness the questions in his eyes. The brief moment of camaraderie between them last night had unsettled her, as had the unexpected longing to remain there on that porch with him, exploring the connection she felt, learning as much about him as possible. It wasn't wise, getting attached to an outsider, and she was determined to be wise.

A brisk breeze tunneled through the forested lane, rustling the multicolored leaves that hadn't yet fallen. Crossing the wooden bridge suspended above the wide but shallow river, she eyed the church's steeple rising toward the cloud-dotted sky and framed by Mount Le Conte's gentle slopes. The shops on either side of Main Street blocked her view of the white clapboard building, but she knew the churchyard would be bustling with parishioners.

Attending services used to be a pleasant, peaceful endeavor, a time to sing hymns and reflect on God's glory, to delve into God's Word and be encouraged by fellow believers. That had changed after she became involved with Lee. Caught up in a whirlwind romance, she had allowed her relationship with her Creator to become less of a priority. Her prayer time and daily Scripture reading had suffered. Lee had become her main focus and now she couldn't seem to move past the shame and self-recrimination to find God's peace.

After the tragedy, folks formed opinions about her involvement with Lee and his associate, John Farnsworth, who was sitting in a jail somewhere in Virginia. Those with sympathetic attitudes saw her as a gullible young woman who'd been blinded by love. Others weren't so kind. They thought she'd been privy to Lee's activities all along and had chosen to keep quiet. Either way, the fact that every single person in Gatlinburg was aware of her most private failure made life uncomfortable.

Spotting Jane and her family beneath the tallest, oldest oak on the church's property, she veered toward their wagon. Six-year-old Clara ran to greet her with a hug. "Auntie Jessica!"

Caressing Clara's bouncy brown curls, Jessica smiled at the little girl who'd charmed her way into her affections. With her dark hair and sparkling bright green eyes, she looked enough like her uncle Tom that she might be mistaken for his biological daughter. Since both her parents were deceased, Tom had taken her in and treated her as his own.

"Is that a new dress?"

Clara's smile widened as she performed a pirouette.

A buttery-yellow color, the dress was trimmed in white ribbon, and a wide sash encircled her waist. "Auntie Nicole made it for me."

Jessica's older sister Nicole was an excellent seamstress. She filled orders from her shop in the rear of the mercantile she owned with her husband, Quinn. "It's lovely."

Taking Jessica's hand, Clara tugged her over to where Tom was assisting a very pregnant Jane from the wagon. Seeing her identical twin sister in that state was strange. This was Jane's first child, so her peculiar reaction was to be expected, Jessica supposed. Plus, it gave her a clear picture as to how she herself would look if a man as trustworthy and steadfast as Tom Leighton ever entered her life and decided he wanted marriage and a family with her.

"Jess."

Jane's face, a mirror image of her own, crumpled with worry as she came near. Wearing one of the handful of dresses she'd let out to accommodate her growing form, she'd arranged her red hair in a sophisticated twist and accessorized with two ornate pins. Folks were able to distinguish between them because of their hairstyles. Jane favored more formal upward styles, while Jessica preferred to simply restrain the mass with a ribbon.

"I was in the mercantile yesterday afternoon when I heard the news. I wanted to come at once, but Tom urged me to wait until today. How are you coping?"

"It's odd having a stranger in the house, of course, but it's a temporary situation. Ma's there to change the bandages, and Will provides added security at night."

Not that they needed protection from Grant, she silently conceded.

Tom joined his wife, his arm coming protectively about her shoulders. "See? What did I tell you? Your sister is made of sturdier stuff than you think." He winked at Jessica.

Angling her face up to his, Jane shot him a smile that made Jessica feel as if she were intruding on a private moment. "I'd like a few minutes with her, if you don't mind."

"We'll be inside." Tom dropped a kiss on her forehead before holding out his hand to Clara. "Come along, my little bird."

The child obeyed, but not without numerous glances over her shoulder as they crossed the spacious expanse to the church steps.

Jessica pointed to Jane's round tummy. "How's the wee babe?"

"Active." Her countenance went dreamy until her gaze cleared. "Don't try to distract me. I want to know every single detail about this man. How old is he? Is he kind?" Her nose scrunched. "Or grouchy? Oh…is he covered in filth? Of all the homesteads in these mountains, why did he have to pick yours?"

"Grant didn't exactly pick us."

"He knows his name? I thought he had amnesia."

"We chose it for him. Couldn't exactly address him as 'Hey, you.'"

Jane absently rubbed her tummy, her manner assessing. "There's something in your voice…your expression…" Her hands stilled. "He's young, isn't he? And handsome. *Jessica*—"

"There's no need to worry, Jane." She held up her palms, bitterness rising up. "I learned my lesson well. I'm not about to repeat my mistakes. No unsuitable men for me. Actually, there aren't any men, suitable or otherwise."

"What happened with Lee is over and done with. It shouldn't stop you from seeking love and happiness. I want you to have what I have, just with the right man."

A pair of young men dressed in their finest clothing strolled past. "Hey Jess."

"Hello, Pete."

"Lookin' mighty fine today." Lowell turned and walked backward, wiggling his brows suggestively. The light in his eyes was harmless, however. "Sit with me?"

"Not this time." She rustled up a smile to soften the refusal.

"I'm not giving up hope."

Pete elbowed him. With a tip of his hat, Lowell spun forward and loped toward the church.

Jane's expression was shrewd. Before she could voice her obvious opinion, Jessica said, "I'm not interested, and you know it. Besides, he's only teasing."

"I disagree." Sadness surfaced. "At some point, you have to forgive yourself and move on. We all make choices we wish we could undo."

Memories overtook her. Jane had been the one to first suspect Lee was involved in suspicious activity. After witnessing him selling moonshine to several locals, she'd pretended to be Jessica in order to investigate and had discovered an abundance of evidence on his property. Jessica had not only been livid over the pretense, she'd stubbornly refused to believe the man she adored could be a criminal. Her stubbornness had nearly cost them both their lives. Lee hadn't been so fortunate.

As if interpreting her thoughts, Jane linked their arms and began walking. The service would begin in minutes. "Lee made his own choices, just as we did. His death is *not* your fault."

"You've said that before."

"I'll keep on saying it until you accept it."

Jessica inhaled the brisk air, her attention on the fenced-in cemetery adjacent to the building. They'd held a funeral for Lee in the days following the fire. But Lee's family had wanted him buried in their home state of Virginia, so they'd arranged for his body to be transported there. It hurt not to have a grave to visit or decorate with flowers.

They stopped at the base of the steep steps. On either side of the double doors sat containers of yellow, orange and purple mums, their bright hues cheerful against the stark white structure.

Jane turned to her. "Promise me you'll be careful."

"Grant isn't dangerous."

"I'm talking about guarding your heart."

Jessica frowned. "I never said he posed a threat to my emotional well-being."

"You didn't have to."

Seated across from Jessica in the O'Malleys' confined dining space, Grant watched her mix bite-size pieces of ham with collard greens, pinto beans and corn bread and sprinkle the pile with Tabasco hot sauce. Scooping up a large portion, she guided the fork to her mouth, pausing when she caught him staring. "What?"

"That's...disgusting."

"Not to me." Shrugging, she went back to ignoring him, something she'd been doing since her return from church.

He turned to Alice, seated in between them at the table's end. "Has she always done that?"

A fond smile creased the older woman's features as she smoothed the napkin in her lap. "Her pa liked his food spicy. Before Tabasco was available, he grew hot peppers and concocted his own sauce. When Jessica was about six or seven, she wanted to try it and he allowed her to.

We could tell that it was too much for her, but she dug in without complaint."

Grant shook his head, pointing with his fork. "Do you sprinkle hot sauce on your baked goods, as well?"

Her nose wrinkled in disgust. "Of course not."

"What do you prefer? Spicy or sweet?"

She sipped her coffee. "Spicy."

"Interesting, coming from a baker."

Grant tucked into his food, eating one selection at a time. No mixing for him. The lady's tastes mimicked her personality. While he didn't know her well, he'd already glimpsed both spicy and sweet aspects of her nature. Last night, he thought they'd made a connection. Her initial wariness gone, she'd treated him as someone worthy of her trust. When she'd finally admitted that she believed his account of events, he'd been relieved. But then she'd clammed up and retreated inside, and he'd woken this morning to find her already gone. He couldn't shake the feeling she'd done that deliberately to avoid him.

She'd arrived home right before lunch and given him the briefest of greetings before disappearing into the kitchen to help Alice.

What does her opinion matter, anyway? You're not staying.

His throat tightened. Without his memories, there was no way to understand his potential, no way to know what kind of life he was meant to lead. He had no money, no physical possessions and no reputation to recommend him. Anyone who hired him would be taking a risk.

Lost in thought, he didn't pay heed to the women's conversation. A slice of apple pie appeared at his elbow minutes later and, startled out of his reverie, he looked up into Jessica's inquiring gaze. She'd noticed his distraction, had she?

"When did you have time to make this?" he said.

"There's always time for baking."

"Baking helps her sort through her problems," Alice inserted.

"Ma."

"It's not a national secret, my dear."

Circling the table, Jessica resumed her seat, taking her time arranging her skirts. Had she always been this private? Or was it that she didn't want *him* knowing her personal quirks?

Apparently satisfied the fabric was folded and draped to her liking, she lifted her head, her eyes meeting his. Grant's heart jolted anew at her loveliness. She was dressed more formally today in an exquisite lavender outfit. The scooped neckline was demure, the form-fitting bodice overlaid with lace. A cameo brooch attached to a ribbon choker drew his gaze to the swan-like grace of her neck. Delicate pearl ear bobs winked at her ears. A bold choice considering her deep red hair, her outfit's lavender hue gave the appearance of fragility, like a rare wild flower vulnerable to the elements. The fire in her green eyes belied that notion. Life events may have weakened her confidence, but Jessica was a fighter.

He deliberately turned his attention to the dessert. She may be pure pleasure to look upon and great fun to tease, but he wasn't free to pursue any woman. He had to accept that he might never be in that position...not without knowing whether or not he had someone special in his life. Or if he had a bounty on his head.

The pie's lattice crust was light and flaky, the thin apple slices coated with cinnamon, nutmeg and just the right amount of sugar. He couldn't prevent a groan of appreciation.

"Now I understand why Mrs. Ledbetter hired you to

do her birthday cake. You weren't kidding—you *are* the finest baker this side of the Tennessee River."

Alice's bushy brows shot toward her hairline, and Jessica squirmed in her seat. "I said that in the heat of the moment. It was an exaggeration."

"I don't think so. You have true talent."

"You're not the only one who shares that opinion," Alice said. "Up until a few months ago, she and Jane supplied desserts to the Plum Café in town. Every day they'd bake cakes and pies. All sorts of goodies. When Mrs. Greene sold to the new owner, we never suspected he'd terminate their agreement."

"Either the man's taste buds are messed up, or he's a fool."

"Plenty of people have complained, but he won't listen. Apparently he's accustomed to having everything done in-house."

"A businessman who turns a deaf ear to his customers' wishes won't be in business for very long," he said.

"It's Gatlinburg's only café. He doesn't have to worry about competition." Jessica's tone was weighted with disappointment.

"How frequent are orders like Mrs. Ledbetter's?"

"It varies. Sometimes I'll have several in a single week, other times I'll go for long stretches without any." Her chin lifted, determination smoldering in her gaze. "However, with the holidays right around the corner, I'm sure things will pick up."

"I'm certain they will, dear." Alice patted her hand. Pushing away from the table, she removed her dishes and went to the kitchen.

Grant wondered how the reduction in income had impacted the women's lives. Their farm appeared to be in proper working condition, as did their home, which was tidy and comfortable. Some of the furnishings were well-worn. And a couple of the dishes could stand to be replaced. Certainly feeding a grown man like him on a regular basis might strain their resources.

"You never answered my question."

"Which one?" she said.

"Why don't you open your own shop?"

"It would be a huge undertaking. I've seen how much effort Josh and Kate put into their business. I have responsibilities here. I can't leave Ma to deal with everything."

"You might consider hiring someone to help Alice during the busier seasons. I'm guessing Will would appreciate the extra money and wouldn't require a high wage."

"There's another option." She traced her cup's rim in methodical circles. "My sister and brother-in-law have offered to give me counter space in the mercantile. I could display my goods there."

"Sounds like an ideal situation. What's holding you back?"

An air of grief veiled her features. "It's difficult to explain."

Her lips pressed into a thin line. She wasn't going to open up to him, and it bothered him. Someone or something had hurt this woman, and she wasn't about to reveal her inner scars to him. Didn't stop him from wanting to try to ease her distress, though.

A heavy rap on the front door intruded on the moment. There was no mistaking Jessica's relief. Dropping her napkin on the chair, she hurried to answer the summons. From his vantage point, he could see the doc's bulky form and cropped silver hair.

Hope sprouted in his chest. Maybe he'd found some useful news in his medical journals. Snatching up the cane, he went into the living room.

"How are you faring, Mr. Parker?"

"My headache's gone."

"Good." Transferring his bag to his right hand, he gestured toward the bedrooms. "Let's go evaluate your other ills."

Jessica hung his black bowler on a peg by the door. "I'll get you some coffee, Doc. Would you like a slice of apple pie to go with it?"

Grant smiled. "I suggest you say yes."

The severity of Doc's face eased, and a twinkle entered his eyes. "I'd like that, Jessica. Thank you."

In the bedroom, Doc probed his swollen, discolored ankle. "You should have full range of motion in a week. Two at the most." He proceeded to apply fresh bandages to his side. A distressed sound escaped before Grant could stop it. "You'll have soreness in this area for a while. The skin around the stitches is red, but I don't see any signs of infection." Wrapping up his old bandage for disposal, he indicated Grant should button up his shirt. "You're a fortunate man, Mr. Parker."

In some ways, perhaps. But he was far from restored to his former self. "None of my memories have returned. Is there anything I can do to speed the process?"

"I reread the articles on your condition." He frowned. "Unfortunately, there's nothing you can do to regain your lost memories. It's a game of wait and see."

Not what he'd been hoping to hear. Not even close. He fisted his hands. "I can't accept that."

Sighing, he laid a hand on Grant's shoulder. "My advice is to take life one day at a time. Don't pressure yourself to remember. Don't make rash decisions. You're with a good family. They'll give you the time you need to heal and decide where to go from here."

Grant sank onto the bed, weariness invading his soul.

Doc Owens let himself out, closing the door behind him. Low conversation hummed through the walls. He supposed he was giving the women an update on his condition.

What am I supposed to do, God? I'm lost without my past. Aimless. A ship sailing on the wide-open sea with no compass, no origin and no destination.

Lying flat on his back on the lumpy mattress, he closed his eyes, his future as murky as his past.

Chapter Eight

"Jessica, you're not leaving early, are you?"

In the arched entry to the well-appointed parlor, she reluctantly turned to address Jane's best friend, Caroline Turner. The Turners' home was one of the largest in Gatlinburg. Many community meetings were held here because of that fact, along with Louise Turner's desire to be viewed as a proper and welcoming hostess.

Caroline didn't share her mother's aspiration to be the most beloved town member. They were frequently at odds. Add to that a complex relationship with her father, and the pretty blonde found it a challenge to be content.

Through the windows flanking the fireplace, orange blended with encroaching deep blue sky. "I have chores yet to do."

Nothing that couldn't wait until the morning, of course, but she'd grown tired of the sly stares. Jessica had purposefully arrived five minutes after the meeting started. The annual harvest fair was only weeks away and, as she was in charge of coordinating the food booths, she'd had no choice but to attend. With the unending questions in the other women's eyes, she'd decided to skip the refreshments in favor of escape.

Your rush to get home doesn't happen to have anything to do with a certain endearing stranger, does it?

Rejecting that thought outright, she slipped her reticule over her wrist and wished the door was a few steps closer. Caroline looked intent on having her curiosity satisfied.

"Can't you stay long enough to have some carrot cake and lemonade? You slipped out of church yesterday before anyone could corner you. I'm sure I'm not the only one who's dying to hear about your guest."

She half turned to indicate the young women seated on the plush blue sofa and overstuffed striped chairs. They were staring at her like a pack of hungry dogs waiting for bits of choice meat.

"Is it true he's a member of the notorious Jenkins gang?" Pauline Cross piped up, her eyes as big as saucers.

"I heard he nearly died in your arms, and you saved him just in time." Laura Latham pressed her hand over her heart. "How romantic."

Caroline's expression urged her to confess all. "As you can see, there are multiple rumors being bandied about town. Now's your chance to tell us the true account."

Grant's arrival on her doorstep had naturally reawakened folks' speculation about her. Once again, her actions would be discussed at length and judged. Irritation fired through her. She'd never expected to be in this position again.

"There's not much to tell," she hedged.

Wilda Haynes put her palms together in a pleading gesture. "You're the only one of us who's ever had anything exciting happen to them. Don't keep us guessing!"

Exciting? That wasn't a word she'd use. *Irksome. Confounding.* Those better described how she viewed Grant's intrusion into her life.

Jessica related the basic facts, glossing over his injuries

out of respect for his privacy. Their questions ranged from the outrageous to the intrusive. Finally, she'd had enough.

"I have to go."

Caroline escorted her to the door. "I know you didn't enjoy that, but being secretive would've fueled the flames of their imaginations. The talk should start to die down now."

Jessica didn't bother to hide her discontent. "Let's hope you're right, because I don't plan on repeating any of that."

The strange drive to protect Grant had taken her unawares. If it turned out he possessed a notorious past, the damage to her already shaky reputation would be immeasurable.

Bidding her hostess goodbye, she descended the polished wood steps and wound her way down the path to the lane. The Turners lived on the opposite side of town and, eyeing the darkening sky, she wished she'd brought her horse.

Grant dominated her thoughts during the long walk home. After Doc's visit yesterday, he'd remained in his room the entire afternoon. He'd declined supper. At her mother's request, Jessica had gone in later and offered to play a game of chess or checkers with him. His mood hadn't been difficult to read. He'd been somber, the vibrancy in his blue eyes dulled. He'd thanked her for the offer and claimed exhaustion, but she hadn't bought the excuse.

Somewhere in the dense woods flanking the lane, an owl hooted. The rustle of birds and small animals moving about in the darkness didn't scare her. She'd grown up here and was used to the wildlife. But what about Grant? Not knowing the details of his life—from the mundane to the momentous—must be eating away at him. That he'd been able to tease and smile at all was a testament to his fortitude.

Passing the snake-and-rail fence that marked the edge of their property, she wrapped her thin shawl more snugly about her shoulders. The lack of the sun's heat lent a nip to the air that chilled her skin. The strumming of a guitar reached her. Startled, she lengthened her stride. Her ma didn't play. Neither did Will.

The porch came into view. Grant sat in one of the rocking chairs, his new friend Cinders curled up at his feet and a guitar in his hands. His head was bent to study the strings. A lantern had been placed on the roughly crafted table. Caught in its circle, his fair hair shone like the sun's rays. Stubble darkened his jaw. A twig snapped beneath her boot, and he looked up. There was a sadness about him that touched a corresponding chord deep inside her. He knew trouble intimately, the same as she. Her trouble was behind her, the scars deeply embedded. Grant's was present, affecting him right this minute, and she wondered how he'd come out of it. If he'd fare better than her. She hoped so.

"Hi." The haunting tune faded.

She ascended the steps. "I didn't know you played."

"Nor did I. Your ma noticed my interest and suggested I try it, so I did. She told me it belonged to your pa. I hope you don't mind my testing it out."

"Not at all."

"Alice is inside. Will had to run home for something. Should be back anytime."

"Okay."

She made to move past, determined not to care or involve herself in his business in any way, until he caught her hand. Heat from his skin instantly enveloped hers.

"Sit with me for a little while."

Jessica almost got lost in his fathomless eyes. In his grasp, her hand felt small and protected. It was such a wonderful sensation, this contact with a virile, intriguing male. That was why she had to disengage.

Pulling free, she tried to think of a good excuse not to stay.

"Please."

The humble plea reminded her of their first encounter. It did strange things to her resolve. Maybe because she wasn't used to hearing the men in her life say it. *Or maybe you can't handle the loneliness wreathing his features.*

"Okay," she said again, promising herself she wouldn't linger long. Taking the other rocker, she slipped off her reticule and laid it on her lap.

"How was your meeting?"

"Same as usual." *You were the main topic.*

"What's the usual?"

"Hmm, let's see." With her boot, she set the rocker in motion. "The committee leader, Louise Turner, gives everyone time to fawn over her latest acquisition—tonight it was an anniversary gift—a new ruby brooch given to her by Mr. Turner. Once that's accomplished, she expounds on our upcoming event. That would be Gatlinburg's annual harvest fair."

Humor bracketed his mouth. "What does one do at a harvest fair?"

"There are pie-eating contests. Music and dancing. Skillet tosses and sack races. And then there's the judging… who has the prettiest quilt, the tastiest pumpkin bread, the most flavorful blackberry preserves. It can be quite intense, let me tell you. These mountain women take their crafts seriously."

A chuckle rumbled through his chest. "I'm sure it's entertaining. Just as I'm sure they are all jealous of you."

"Me? Why?"

"No one else's desserts could possibly compare to yours."

He caught her wince and wagged his finger at her. "I'm right," he crowed. "How many years in a row did you win the blue ribbon before they asked you—politely, I'm sure—to refrain from entering?"

She rested her head against the chair, not surprised that he'd guessed the truth. For someone with no knowledge of his own identity, Grant was exceedingly perceptive.

"Five. And Jane and I entered together."

Whistling, he thrummed a couple of notes. "Five. Impressive."

They fell silent. Was he thinking the same thing she was? That he might not be here come fair time?

"I didn't recognize the song you were playing before. What is it?"

"Something I made up." He shrugged. "Or maybe I heard it as a child."

"Can you play anything else?"

Wrapping his long fingers about the guitar's neck, he started and stopped a couple of times before selecting a melody that was both sad and moving. He then transitioned into a lively tune she recognized. Listening to him play, she found herself humming along and mentally joining her fiddle to his guitar. She used to play most every day. Chasing chords, exploring new sounds and practicing old favorites gave her satisfaction and contentment. She'd stopped after the fire.

She didn't realize until this moment how much she missed making music.

"That was beautiful, Grant."

"Thanks." Leaving the instrument in the chair, he drifted

over to a porch post—still favoring his hurt ankle—to stare up at the night sky. "I have no idea who taught me."

His voice was ragged. Dejected. Joining him, she let the opposite post support her weight. "The accident was just a few days ago. Be patient with yourself."

"That's what Doc said."

"He may not have a winning personality," she said drily, "but he knows what he's doing."

"I skimmed through my Bible today. I can quote Scripture. Not only from Psalms and Proverbs, but from the New Testament, as well."

"You could've learned them as a child."

"Or I could have attended seminary."

"You're worried you aren't a good person, aren't you? That's why you're clinging to this theory." Reaching out, she touched the back of his hand. "These are farmer's hands. Or a dock worker's."

"That doesn't prove I'm not a preacher."

"Doesn't prove you're not a gunslinger, either."

"Why do you insist on believing the worst about me? What is it that you see in me, Jessica?" The anguish roaring to life in his beautiful eyes stole the breath from her lungs.

"I—I'm sorry. You're right." Her face felt on fire. "I apologize."

She fled.

"Wait. Jessica—"

Inside the cabin, she sagged against the door, regret washing over her. Her suspicious nature had hurt him. She'd known it was destructive, but she'd assumed she was the only one affected by its bitter poison.

Her mother looked up from the sewing project on her lap. "There you are. Isn't it something about Grant's playing ability? You and he should play together."

Her fiddle lay in its case, unused for months. Making music had been beyond her capabilities.

Her legs were heavy as she forced them across the room. "When is he leaving?"

Alice's hands stilled, the needle and thread hovering midair. "What's wrong? Did he say something to upset you?"

"No, I—I just think that the longer he stays, the easier it will be for him to depend on our hospitality." She forced the untruth through stiff lips.

"Oh, I don't see that as a possibility. Grant isn't one to take advantage."

"How can you know that for certain? He's been here a handful of days."

Lowering the material, she sighed. "What is this really about, Jessica?"

"Nothing. Never mind. I'll be in my room if you need me."

Her countenance a reflection of concern, Alice slowly nodded. Her mother wasn't one to push, something Jessica greatly appreciated in moments like this.

In the kitchen the next morning, Grant found Will at the table devouring a large portion of biscuits and gravy and fried eggs. His mouth full, he lifted a hand in greeting.

Alice turned from the stove, her spatula suspended above the pan. "Good morning, Grant. How did you sleep?"

He couldn't tell her the truth, that thoughts of her daughter had kept him up half the night. "Fine. And you?"

"Like a baby." Pouring him a cup of steaming hot coffee, she set it on the long counter between them and nodded to the table. "Have a seat. I'll have your breakfast ready in a jiffy."

Grant did as she suggested. Taking the seat opposite Will, he wondered where Jessica was and if she planned to avoid him today. He hadn't meant to upset her. His frustration had boiled over, and he'd lashed out at her. *Great way to repay her hospitality, Parker.*

"You have school today?" he said, wrapping his hands about the mug.

Will chugged half the contents of his glass, then used his sleeve to wipe the excess milk from his mouth. "Yep. Wish I could skip."

Alice slid a plate in front of Grant. She shot Will a don't-you-dare glance. "Nathan and Sophie would have your hide. You know how important it is to finish your learning."

"I guess." The look on his face said he didn't agree.

The aroma of salty bacon hit Grant's nose, and his stomach rumbled in response. The biscuits were light and fluffy, the white gravy dotted with sausage bursting with savory goodness.

"If I don't start doing physical labor soon, I'm gonna need larger trousers," he said.

She chuckled and returned to the stove. "Better hurry, Will. You don't want to be late."

Grunting, Will finished off his drink and carried his dishes to the dry sink. "See you tonight."

He was rushing out of the kitchen when Jessica appeared. "Oh, hey, Jess."

"Morning." She sidestepped out of his way, her gaze locked on Grant's. The main door slammed behind the boy.

Grant tried to think of something to say to break the tension suddenly permeating the room and came up blank. She looked as fresh as a daisy in her sunny yellow blouse and dark brown skirt. Her hair wasn't in its usual ponytail. Shining red locks spilled over her shoulders. Only the top strands had been pulled back and restrained with a crooked ribbon. The casual style made her look younger and softer. More like a woman and less like a warrior. His mouth went dry.

Whatever she saw in his gaze caused her to break eye contact, and she hurried to pour herself some tea.

"Good morning, my dear," Alice greeted. "Do you have any orders to work on today?"

"No. Why? Do you need my help with something?"

"I was hoping we'd get those bushels of green beans preserved."

"I'll get started on it right after breakfast."

"Thanks, dear. Here you go."

Grant had kept his attention on his plate during their exchange. In his peripheral vision, he saw Jessica's slow approach. He couldn't have her feeling uncomfortable in her own home.

He gave her a welcoming smile, one he hoped communicated that last night didn't have to ruin today. "Does your harvest fair host a competition for autumn queen?"

"What?" She sank into the chair Will had vacated, her brows pulling together. "Oh, um, no. Why?"

"Because you'd win the crown today. I like your hair like that."

Her full petal-pink lips parted as becoming color tinged her cheeks. "That's sweet of you to say."

The urge to cradle her hand seized him. Aware of their audience, he cleared his throat. "I'll help with chores today," he told Alice. "I'm assuming you have to break the beans first."

"That's right. But Doc said you should focus on getting your strength back."

"If I sit still any longer, I'll lose what's left of my mind. It's not strenuous work, anyway."

"If you're sure. You and Jessica can break them while I get the jars washed and ready."

What felt like a tiny lightning bolt of pain arced through his skull. He flinched, and then it was gone. Neither woman noticed.

"Are you sure you wouldn't rather read a book or practice the guitar?" Jessica suggested, her reluctance to spend time with him plain.

She didn't want him around. She'd made that clear from the moment he collapsed in her yard. He tried to mask how much it bothered him.

"I'm well enough to help you. I won't be around for long. Take the assistance while you have it."

Blowing lightly on the tawny liquid in her china cup, she lowered her gaze.

A second spasm streaked through his head. His fork clinked against the plate. Pain exploded behind his temple. He rammed his chair back, leaned over and gripped his head with both hands.

Chapter Nine

"Grant!"

Barely aware of Jessica kneeling beside him, he squeezed his eyes tight and willed the pain to stop. An image flashed in his mind. Not a face, but an object.

"Grant, what's wrong?" Her fingers trembled where they cupped his knee. "What can I do to help you?"

"My head." He concentrated on his breathing. "Hurts."

Alice's soft tread neared. "Should we fetch Doc?"

"No." Somehow, his hand found Jessica's, and their fingers wound together. He drew strength from the contact. "It'll pass."

Gradually, the intensity lessened until he could straighten and meet their anxious gazes. "I remembered something," he wheezed.

Jessica sat back on her heels. "What?"

"A star. Made of silver, I think. It was blurry."

As if just noticing their linked hands, she disengaged and stood. "A star? What does that mean?"

Alice scratched her head. "A piece of the puzzle, that's what it is."

"It might not mean anything." Grant closed his eyes and tried to recall more details. Nothing. Nothing but emptiness. A sense of helplessness swamped him, followed swiftly by a tidal wave of fury. He wanted to plant his fist in something. Shake the walls. *Why did You allow this to happen, God? I thought You were supposed to care about me.*

He shot to his feet so fast the women took a step back. His wound protested the sudden, careless movement.

"I need air."

No one spoke as he hobbled through the dining area and into the living room. By the time he reached the door, Jessica had caught up to him.

"I'm going with you."

"Jessica—"

"I can show you the spot where I discovered your travel bag." Her chin jutted. "You might see something I overlooked."

Grant wanted to ask why she was insisting but figured he wouldn't like the answer. "Lead the way."

Jessica stuck close to Grant's side as they meandered through the woods. He was using the cane to navigate the uneven terrain. While his countenance no longer bore the vestiges of pain, he was too pale for her peace of mind. Seeing him like that had been difficult. Not just the physical anguish he was dealing with, but the mental turmoil, as well.

He didn't seem inclined to conversation, and she didn't press him. The forest provided ample distraction. Grant was like a scientist on a mission, absorbing every detail, stopping intermittently to study a plant, test a tree's bark or touch an insect's body. He was familiar with the constellations. Perhaps he was a professor at one of those expensive universities back East.

They reached the stream crisscrossing their property.

About four feet wide at this spot, mossy rocks of all sizes littered the streambed and banks on either side. The trees grew close together here, and the forest floor was hardly visible through the layer of fallen leaves. Their orange hue contrasted nicely with those bushes and saplings that were still green.

"This is spectacular." Leaning on his cane, he did a slow circle and surveyed their surroundings with appreciation.

"Spring and summer are wonderful," she said. "The forest is a canvas of lush greens and browns. Autumn is the best season, in my opinion. It brings these mountains to life."

"I can see why anyone would want to live here. It's peaceful. You have abundant wildlife to sustain your family. Rich soil for growing things."

"My only complaint is that everyone knows your business. You are already the talk of the town, and you've only met a handful of its residents."

His brows lifted. "You're serious?"

"I am."

Taking a seat on one of the larger boulders, he wrapped both hands around the cane. He looked troubled. "I've been thinking. What if I was ambushed, and the person responsible wanted to make sure he finished the job? What if he returns? You could very well be in danger."

Jessica began to pace. She should've thought of that possibility.

"I couldn't live with myself if I brought that sort of trouble to your door."

"We'll be prepared," she said. "I carry a gun on me everywhere I go."

"Is that typical around here?"

Deliberately ignoring his assessing gaze, she crouched at the water's edge and watched the pinkie-sized minnows darting beneath the surface. She shouldn't have let that tidbit about Jane and her brush with death slip the other day. His curiosity had been piqued. "Depends on the woman, I suppose. I happen to think it best to be prepared."

"Have you ever been in a situation where you've been forced to use it?"

She bent closer to the water so that her hair hid her profile. The questions needled her, prodded her fortified defenses. After Lee's death, she'd given an account to the sheriff and that was it. Her family and friends had respected her privacy and given her the space to work through her grief. Folks talked about what happened, but never to her face.

"No, I haven't."

While she'd brandished her weapon in a bid to free Jane from John Farnsworth, she hadn't had a chance to use it. Lee's coldhearted boss had had a knife to Jane's throat and would've hurt her if Jessica hadn't forfeited her gun. She'd never felt such a formidable mix of helplessness, dread and rage. The helplessness had been the worst.

Rising to her full height, she considered him. "You should have a means to protect yourself. You weren't wearing a gun belt or holster when I found you, but that could've been stolen along with your other possessions." Pulling out her gun, she handed it to him. "This one's a four-chamber. I've got a six-shooter at home you'd probably like better. Want to get some practice in before we break beans?"

A slow, mischievous grin curved his lips. "Let's see... shooting practice or preserving vegetables? Which should I pick? It's a surprisingly tough decision. I like guns. I also like to eat."

Jessica's mouth went dry. Injured and out of his element, Grant was handsome and endearing, his charm a powerful draw. She hated to think how she would've fared against him in his normal life.

"You're incorrigible."

"I'll take that over infuriating any day." He winked.

She threw up her hands. "Wait here while I get you a gun and ammunition."

At home, her ma didn't take pains to mask her pleasure, smiling and nodding at Jessica's practical explanation.

"What are you so excited about? It's shooting practice. That's all."

"It's good for you to concentrate on someone else's needs for a change. To focus outward, instead of inward."

Speechless, Jessica took a longer time to return through the woods than she'd taken to reach home. Her mother's observation reverberated through her mind. The implication had been clear—she was selfish. Too absorbed in her own problems to notice or care about others'.

She couldn't argue or defend herself. Her mother was right. Since the moment she and Jane were taken captive and her life was lifted from the pages of a gothic novel, she'd wrestled with destructive emotions. Memories tormented her. Remorse consumed any and all crumbs of peace she managed to seize. The ardent wish to change the past, the choices she made, was a constant, living thing inside her. The futility of such a wish didn't prevent it from existing.

Selfish. Self-absorbed. Those were ugly flaws. What troubled her was the fact it had taken a stranger in need to bring her attention to them.

Her family and friends must really love her to put up with such behavior for so long. While she couldn't rid herself of the guilt and grief, she could make sure it didn't overflow to those around her. She couldn't go on like this. Not if she didn't want to wind up a bitter, lonely old woman.

Grant was exactly where she'd left him, still on the boulder, managing to appear deep in thought yet aware of his surroundings. The cane was propped beside him, her gun resting on his thigh and the barrel pointed away from them. He was wearing one of the two outfits in his travel bag—slate-gray trousers that hugged his muscular legs and a sea-blue shirt that molded to his shoulders. He'd rolled the long sleeves up, revealing tanned, toned forearms and thick wrists. Sunlight speared through a break in the trees and lit on his short blond hair. Several locks fell across his forehead. That, combined with the hint of shadow along his jawline, gave her the impression of a rakish pirate.

Oh, come on, Jessica. Leave the frivolous imaginings to Jane.

At her approach, he came and relieved her of the ammunitions pouch. They switched weapons and, setting the pouch at his feet, he examined the Smith and Wesson Schofield revolver. He let out a low whistle. "Nice. I used to have one like this, except the barrel was longer."

Popping open the chamber, he didn't seem to realize the significance of his words.

"You did?"

His gaze lifted and locked with hers. "Yeah...I did." A muscle ticked in his jaw.

To distract him, she lifted the tin can she'd brought. "I say we put this here." She strode to the boulder he'd vacated and set it on top. "I'll even let you go first."

The worry smoothed from his face, and he smiled. "Oh, no, a gentleman always allows the lady to go first."

She kicked up a shoulder. "Whatever you say."

They readied their weapons and moved a sufficient distance away from the target. She had no trouble hitting it.

Friendly competition between the males and females in her family was commonplace. Grant's unchecked admiration sent warmth fizzing through her. Unlike some men of her acquaintance, he wasn't intimidated by a woman's competence.

Then he stepped up to shoot, and it was her turn to be impressed. Moving farther away from the can didn't hinder his ability.

"You're amazing," she gushed, inwardly cringing. She sounded like an infatuated schoolgirl.

He shrugged off her praise as he gathered their things. "I can say the same about you."

"You're a better shot than I am. You're better than any of my cousins."

He grabbed up his cane, and they started for home. "I know what you're thinking."

There was a heaviness to his bearing that hadn't been there before.

"That's not arrogant at all," she quipped. "Tell me, what's on my mind?"

He turned his head toward hers, his eyes deep, endless pools of blue. "You're thinking only a bank robber would possess such skills."

"Wrong." She met his gaze head-on. "I was thinking only a lawman would."

He came to a halt, knuckles loosening on the cane's knob-like handle. "Honestly?"

"There are two sides to every coin, after all."

"Without solid proof of who and what I was, I have to strive to stay positive. Hope for the best outcome."

Jessica could empathize with his situation. Without hope, how was he to move forward with confidence? How would she find the strength to begin anew? She couldn't shatter his tenuous foundation, despite the lingering voice inside her head telling her that whatever he'd been involved in couldn't have been good.

He should be exhausted. The day had been a full one. Between the three of them, they'd washed, snapped and canned three bushels of green beans. He'd been grateful for something to do to keep his mind occupied. His proficiency with the gun troubled him more than he'd let on. Safe to say he wasn't an ordinary postmaster or storekeeper. The image of the silver star remained embedded in his mind as well, and he yearned for answers.

Alice and Jessica had proved excellent company. For all her prickly ways, the feisty redhead was a dutiful daughter who clearly loved and respected her mother. The haunted light in her eyes awakened Grant's protective instincts, and he wished there was some way he could chase away her sadness. Those rare moments when her guard lowered and she gave in to humor, she became a different person, her bright smile and husky laughter infectious.

Whatever secrets she was harboring, they were chipping away at her contentment. He'd wanted to press her at the stream, to demand answers, but it wasn't his place. He had no stake in her life. He was just a traveler passing through.

Grant didn't need his memories to know he didn't like inaction, detested feeling powerless.

He walked over to where Alice and Jessica were washing the supper dishes. "Thanks for another excellent meal, ladies. While you're finishing up here, I'll do the milking. Just tell me which pails you prefer me to use."

"Aren't you tired?" Alice said.

He couldn't explain the restlessness plaguing him. His injuries pained him, but he wasn't ready to rest. "I'm too young to be going to bed at seven o'clock."

Alice's smile was indulgent. "Jess, would you mind taking him out to the barn and showing him the tool room? You can introduce him to Sadie while you're at it."

Nodding resignedly, Jessica finished drying the plate in her hand before removing her apron. The yellow ribbon in her hair drooped and looked close to falling out. Her skin was damp, and there were shadows under her eyes. She looked as if she could use a hug.

"I'm sure I can find what I need," he said. "You don't have to come."

"It's all right."

At the door, he took her knitted ivory shawl from the peg and offered it to her.

Murmuring her thanks, she wrapped it about her shoulders. Her long hair became trapped beneath the tightly woven yarn, and he considered freeing it. He would have if he didn't think she'd slap him.

He opened the door for her and, remembering his cane, followed her to the barn. She hesitated at the entrance.

"Is there a problem?" he said.

"N-no. No problem."

Firming her shoulders, she lifted the lamp she'd brought and hung it on a nail on the nearest wall. A small room housed tools, hoes, rakes and other gardening implements, ropes and pails. She chose one of the pails.

"How many milk cows do you have?"

"Just one." Walking briskly past a rabbit hutch and stalls that housed their horses, she stopped at the last one on the right. "She's a good producer. And even-tempered. If you're gentle, she won't kick you." Turning around, she jumped at his close proximity. "D-do you need pointers before I go?"

Her gaze was fixed on his chest. This close, he could see the rapid pulse at her throat.

What was troubling her? Grant eyed the drooping ribbon and couldn't resist. "Hold still." Propping the cane against the wooden slats, he reached out.

"What are you doing?" Her eyes went round.

"You're about to lose your hair ribbon." Working quickly, he tightened the loops, keenly aware of her rose-kissed skin, her soft breathing, the silkiness of her hair beneath his fingers. His own pulse sped up. "There. It's not perfect but should hold."

Lowering his arms, he gave her space. She swallowed convulsively.

Sensing much more than his nearness was bothering her, he tried to silence the voice inside his head begging him to test the sweetness of her mouth. *Just once*, it insisted.

"Are you okay, Jessica?"

"I'm fine." Spinning, she pushed into the stall. Going over to the Jersey cow, she scratched between its ears. "Sadie, this is Grant."

He snagged the squat stool and carried it over. "Hello, Sadie." He sat and patted her side. "I may not recall exactly how to do this, but I'm sure we'll get on just fine."

A plaintive meow came from just inside the stall door. He and Jessica turned to see Cinders rubbing against the frame, her nose sniffing the air.

"Hey there," he greeted softly. "Don't worry. You're still my main pal."

Jessica kept her attention on the straw-strewn floor. After a rocky start, he got the hang of milking and settled in to do the job. He ignored the soreness in his side. It wasn't excruciating like before. Soon, he'd be completely healed and able to put more energy into their farm.

She roamed the stall like a caged animal. When he'd finished, her expression was one of relief. Out in the aisle, he asked about the rabbits and she listed off the names.

Looking around, he noticed that much of the interior structure was newer than the roof and walls. When he commented on it, her face lost all color.

"There was a fire."

Worried she might faint, he grasped her elbow to steady her. "What happened? Was anyone hurt?"

"It doesn't matter."

"It does matter." He ran his fingers down the length of her arm until he found her hand. He stroked her knuckles with his thumb. "You've been antsy ever since we came in here. You're upset. Talk to me."

"I don't think so."

He gently squeezed her hand. "So it's okay for you to know the details of my life, meager though they might be, but I can't ask about yours?"

Her jaw was set, her eyes twin pools of misery. "I don't discuss the fire with anyone," she whispered.

"You saved my life, Jessica. Offering a listening ear is the least I can do. Besides, I'm not staying. Whatever you tell me will go with me when I leave."

Pulling free, she wrapped her arms about her middle. For a minute, he thought she wasn't going to relent. Then she spoke. "Lee Cavanaugh started the fire. He and I..." Her eyes drifted shut. A sigh passed between her lips. "We were close."

She loved him. Loves him still, by the looks of it. The realization rocked Grant. Why, he wasn't certain. Jessica was a lovely, intriguing young woman. Any man would be dumb and blind not to see her worth.

"Why would he do such a thing?"

"Because an evil man ordered him to. Farnsworth had a gun. Lee didn't have a choice but to do as he commanded."

"Wait." He held up a hand, horror shuddering through him. "This man was holding a gun on you both?"

"And Jane. She was with us."

Now her comment from the other night made sense. She'd said her sister almost died because of her actions.

"Were you hurt?" He fought the urge to touch her again.

"I suffered bruises, that's all. Farnsworth ordered Lee to douse the place with kerosene, so he did. Jane and I were tied up. We couldn't do anything but watch in terror." Walking around him, she moved to a spot in the middle of the floor, reliving the scene. Her back was to him, her head bent. "In a bid to save our lives, Lee swung the can at Farnsworth. He missed. Farnsworth shot him in the stomach. He died right here in my arms."

His heart breaking for her, Grant moved beside her and laid a hand on her shoulder. "I'm sorry, Jess. I hate that you had to live through that."

She lifted her face to his, and the anguish he saw there socked him in the gut. "But I did live. Lee didn't."

Cupping her cheek, he murmured, "You can't blame yourself for his death. You didn't pull the trigger."

"You don't know the whole story."

"Tell me."

"I—" Her lips parted seconds before her invisible barriers shot into place. "I can't. I've said enough on the subject."

Covering his hand with hers, she slowly pushed him away. Regret speared into him. "At least tell me how you and Jane escaped."

"Farnsworth turned his gun on me. Jane leaped in front of me at the last second, taking the bullet that was meant for me. She blacked out, and I thought I'd lost her. Her wound wasn't life-threatening, thank the Lord, and she regained consciousness. Tom arrived and captured Farnsworth. He helped us get Lee's body out. The animals, too.

My cousins and uncle got here in time to help him save the barn."

The burden she carried finally became clear. Guilt was paralyzing her, the same way his past threatened to do to him. She'd convinced herself that Lee's death and her sister's injury were her fault. How could he make her see the error of such thinking?

He was mulling over the issue when a throat cleared behind them. "Evenin', folks."

Jessica put distance between her and Grant. "Shane. What are you doing here?"

"Sheriff." Grant nodded. Something told him this wasn't a social call.

The sheriff leveled a look at him. "We need to talk."

Chapter Ten

"Have you discovered something?" Sweat trickled beneath Grant's collar. He shifted his weight, trying to tame the panic beast clawing for release.

Right this second, he was glad Jessica had given them privacy. He tried to decipher the sheriff's expression as he removed his Stetson and ambled over, using a nearby stall to prop up his weight.

"I haven't heard from anyone yet. Should get a response from the nearest offices this week." His hard gaze swept the barn's interior before pinning Grant to the spot. "I stopped by to check on things here."

In other words, he wanted to ensure Grant was toeing the line. Treating the O'Malleys with respect. Some of the tension left him.

"Everything's fine. I'm helping out where I can."

Shane's gaze narrowed. "You and Jessica were having an intense conversation."

While the lawman had every right to dig up Grant's past, what happened in the here and now was off-limits. "Maybe."

"What about?"

"That's between the lady and me." He retrieved his cane.

Pushing off the stall, Shane followed. "That girl has been through enough without you compounding the problem. If you hurt her, you'll regret it."

Grant ground his teeth. "You're threatening me?"

"I'm speaking not as a lawman, but as her friend."

"Rest assured, Sheriff. I wouldn't intentionally hurt Jessica. I'd like to be her friend."

He scoffed. "You really think that's wise, considering?"

Anger at the other man and the situation pounded at his temples.

Will's lanky form blocked the entrance. He must've just arrived. "Hey, Sheriff. Grant. Miss Alice wants to see you both inside."

When he'd gone, Shane speared him with a hooded gaze. "Think about what I said." Then he spun and stalked out.

Grant lagged behind, his mind full for someone who couldn't recall 99 percent of his life.

He was finishing up the milking the following morning when Jessica entered the barn. Lowering the slat on the stall door, he looked up in surprise. He'd left her in the kitchen making gravy. "Was I taking too long?"

"Oh." She fingered the gold chain around her neck. "I didn't expect to see you."

Carrying the brimming pail, he headed her direction. "What do you mean? I told you I'd be out here." His words trailed off as he tracked the downward motion of her hand, which landed on her very swollen stomach. "Uh…"

Confusion scrambled his thoughts. It was rude to stare, but he couldn't take his eyes off her changed form. "Is this some kind of joke?"

She could've put a pillow beneath her dress, he supposed, not convinced. That didn't look like a pillow.

Her eyes twinkled. A tinkling laugh escaped. "I see Jessica didn't tell you she has an identical twin sister."

"Twin?" He almost dropped the milk. This woman looked exactly like Jessica. A mirror image. If it weren't for her obvious pregnancy, he wasn't sure he'd be able to tell them apart.

She extended her hand. "I'm Jane. You must be Mr. Parker."

He mutely shook it.

Her smile was kind. "I apologize for giving you a shock."

"It is a bit much to absorb before I've had my breakfast," he said ruefully. He belatedly noticed the wedding band on her finger. Her hair was pulled off her neck in a complicated twist, a more formal style than Jessica favored.

He followed Jane outside. For someone close to having a baby, she moved with easy grace. How strange it would be to have a copy of himself in the world. He'd heard the bond between twins was a unique one. If they were as close as he imagined, no wonder Jessica had taken Jane's injury to heart.

Entering the cabin, Jane announced her presence. Grant came in behind her and stood off to the side. Alice emerged from the kitchen first, wiping her hands on her apron before hugging her daughter. When Jessica entered the living room and he watched them embrace, he couldn't help but be fascinated.

They broke apart, and Jane chided Jessica for keeping him in the dark. "I frightened the poor man."

Jessica took one look at his face and burst out laughing.

"You think it's funny, do you?" he said with mock injury. "For a minute there, I suspected you'd slipped laudanum in my water."

"You look like you've never seen a pregnant woman before." Her brilliant smile did funny things to his heart.

He arched a brow. "Or twins."

Alice shook her head. "I suppose we did leave out that important tidbit."

"Are there any other surprises I should know about? More sets of twins? Triplets?"

"No more surprises."

Jessica linked arms with her sister and nudged her toward the kitchen. "What brings you by so early?"

"I wanted to ask if you're going chestnut picking this weekend. I really want to go, but Tom thinks it's too close to my delivery. He's being very cautious."

"He's right to be." Alice lowered a stack of dishes from the wall shelf. "This is your first child. Neither of you know what to expect."

He hefted the pail onto the counter, uncomfortable with where the conversation was headed.

"In all the recent excitement, I forgot about the trip." Jessica's gaze touched on his for a brief moment. "What do you think, Ma? Should we stay home this year?"

"We have more canning to get done." Alice wore a doubtful expression. "But the chestnuts bring in decent revenue."

Leaning against the counter, Grant folded his arms and regarded the trio. "What's this about?"

"Every year around this time, families in our community go camping in the higher elevations. That's where the chestnut trees grow," Jane explained. "We spend a couple of days gathering chestnuts to sell in Maryville. They are shipped to big cities like New York and Boston, where street vendors sell them freshly roasted."

"We keep some for ourselves, as well," Jessica said. "The nuts make a fine stuffing for our holiday turkey."

Alice paused in laying out the silverware. "Jessica, why don't you go? Take Grant along with you. I'll stay and get the canning done."

Jessica's jaw went slack. "Grant and me? Alone? Ma, you know that's not possible."

"You'll hardly be alone. Your cousins and their wives will be there."

Rubbing slow circles on her stomach, Jane regarded him with unmistakable pensiveness. Jessica waved a hand of dismissal. "He's not fully recuperated from his injuries."

"How long is the trip?" he asked.

"About four hours."

"You travel by wagon?"

"Yes, but it's rough terrain. If an axle broke or a wheel needed to be repaired, you wouldn't be able to do it without risking reopening your wound."

"Could we take Will along?" he said.

"I suppose."

"The trail will be used by other families," Alice pointed out. "There will be people around to lend assistance if you run into trouble."

Jane sank into one of the chairs and snagged a biscuit from the platter in the middle. "Why are you interested in going, Mr. Parker?"

"Please, call me Grant."

Jessica set a mug of coffee at his usual setting. Murmuring his thanks, he took his seat. "I figure the more people I'm around, the better chance someone might recognize me. Will there be people from other communities?"

"Some." Jane split open her biscuit, slathered butter on each side and drizzled it with honey.

Carrying a bowl of boiled eggs, Jessica took her spot beside him. "I understand your reasoning, Grant, but I think it's risky. What if someone does recognize you and that person is the one who attacked you?"

Her question indicated she cared about his safety and that she believed in his innocence. "I'll be prepared. I'll take the gun you loaned me."

She smoothed a napkin over her lap. "I don't know."

"Jessica, I have to try to find answers, no matter the outcome."

Jane's assessing gaze bounced between them. He supposed that after the fire and the events leading up to it—not all of which he was privy to—she would naturally be protective of her twin.

Alice urged them to start filling their plates. "I agree with Grant. Besides, there will be plenty of folks around. Caleb will be on alert for danger."

The twins exchanged a look that Grant couldn't quite interpret.

Under the table, he nudged Jessica's shoe. "I have you to protect me, don't I?"

"You're a better shot than me," she retorted, mashing up her egg with more force than necessary.

"Then what's there to worry about?"

She sagged against the chair back. "You're as stubborn as a mule, you know that?"

Alice's bubble of laughter rose to the ceiling.

Jessica's chin jutted. "What?"

Jane lifted her napkin to hide a smile.

Grant shrugged. "Apparently I'm not the only one in this room who could be compared to an animal."

She rolled her eyes. "Fine. Have it your way. Let's go camping."

The excitement her words evoked had everything to do with being in a new environment and possibly finding clues to his identity, he reassured himself. It had nothing to do with spending time with the beautiful redhead.

Chapter Eleven

"You didn't mention how agreeable he is." Jane was seated on the wagon's high seat, her bonnet casting her features in shadow. "Or how pleasing to look at."

Jessica blocked the sun with her hand. She wouldn't deny that Grant was both those things and more. "I've told you before, there's nothing to worry about. He's only going to be here for a short time."

"Sincerity practically oozes off him," Jane continued, tugging on her wrist-length gloves. "No one's that good an actor. Doesn't he strike you as a humble sort? But he also has an inner strength. You can see it in his eyes."

Jane had always been the more imaginative twin. And that remark about Grant's humility was a subtle comparison to Lee, who'd possessed a charismatic personality. Her twin hadn't ever truly warmed to him.

"He has reason to be humble, Jane. He has nothing. No money, no home, no past. He's completely dependent on us for everything." She frowned, knowing he wasn't going to like what she had planned for later.

"Listen, sis, I want you to keep your wits about you."

Throwing up her hands, she huffed, "I'm not going to

keep repeating myself. You're not telling me anything I don't already know."

Her lips compressed. "He seems like a nice man. I don't want to see either of you get hurt."

"Why does everyone assume I'm going to fall in love with Grant Parker?" her voice rose.

Behind her, boots scuffing across the porch made her stiffen. Judging by Jane's embarrassed grimace, Grant had overheard every word.

Humiliation washed over her. Squeezing her eyes shut, Jessica wished for a hole to swallow her up.

"Yes, well," Jane said with false brightness, "have a safe trip. Nice to meet you, Grant."

"Likewise."

The curiosity in his voice promised this was going to be an excruciating conversation. If only she could avoid him the rest of the week.

"We'll talk in a couple of days," Jane said to her with unspoken apology.

"Don't have the baby while I'm gone."

Jessica stood back as her sister maneuvered the wagon around and rolled down the wooded lane. She waited until it had disappeared from sight before very slowly turning to face him.

Arms folded, he watched her with expectation.

"You heard what I said."

His mouth curved into an infuriating grin. "Would've been hard not to."

"You enjoy seeing me squirm, don't you?"

Dropping his arms to his sides, he walked closer. "Yes, I do."

"That's not very gentlemanly," she said hotly.

"We don't know if I am one," he retorted. "Stop stalling,

and tell me why your family thinks you're in danger of falling in love with me."

"Ugh." Covering her eyes, she massaged her throbbing temples. "It has nothing to do with you."

"Huh?"

Jessica forced herself to meet his gaze. "The man I told you about before—Lee Cavanaugh—my family didn't approve of our connection. I ignored their warnings. Bad things happened. Because of that, they've all seen fit to warn me away from another potential mistake."

"Ah."

Smile fading, his attention strayed to a point beyond her shoulder. Her carelessness had wounded him.

"Grant, I'm sorry." She laid her hand on his upper arm, the bunched muscle firm beneath his cotton shirt. "It wasn't my intention to imply... I didn't mean..."

"No need to apologize. I'm not exactly a prize catch for you or anyone else." Clearing his throat, he edged out of her hold and gave her a tight smile. "They're right to warn you away."

"This is a preposterous conversation," she said at last. "We hardly know each other. You're leaving, and I'm—" She broke off when his intense blue stare pinned her. "Not."

"Right." Gaze hooded, he nodded. "Preposterous."

"Seeing as how you're already upset with me, I may as well tell you that we're going shopping."

His head jerked back. "Shopping."

"You can't gather chestnuts without gloves. You'll also need a hat and another set of clothes."

He planted his hands on his hips. "You're forgetting I don't have a way to pay for those items."

"Consider them payment for the chores you've been doing."

His eyes darkened to navy blue, and she hated that she'd made him feel inadequate. Again. But he couldn't go on the trip unprepared.

"The small tasks I've done aren't enough to repay the food and shelter you've provided, much less provisions."

He started to return to the house. She waylaid him, her palm splayed against his chest. The thick muscles twitched. Awareness fired through her, setting her nerve endings aflame. She may not be in danger of falling for him, but her reaction to his nearness was proof enough that she was vulnerable.

Removing her hand as casually as possible, she said, "I realize this isn't easy for you. But unless you can produce a hat and gloves before Friday, you aren't going."

He had the temerity to glare at her.

She glared right back. "I suggest you set aside your pride, Mr. Parker, and accept my help."

"Pride?" he scoffed. "Not sure I know what that is anymore."

"Grant—"

"Fine. You win," he grated. "When?"

"Ten minutes."

"I'll be ready."

Watching him hobble-stomp inside, the cane whacking the floor, she released a pent-up breath. Whirling about, she strode for the barn to ready their horses. He met her exactly eight minutes later in the yard, his hair freshly combed and his expression implacable.

She handed him the reins to Galahad. "I thought riding would be easier on your ankle."

He inspected the sorrel, smoothing a hand along his neck and patting his flank. "I've been getting acquainted with him in the barn. Appears to have a fine temperament."

"He's a big baby, but a reliable mount."

Before she could move around to her horse, Grant's strong fingers captured her wrist and tugged her closer to his lean form. Pinpricks danced up her arm. She had to tilt her chin up to meet his gaze, a move that brought his generous lips into a kissable zone.

"I apologize for being testy," he muttered. "It's difficult to accept handouts."

"Would it make it any easier if I were a man?"

His blond brows lifted. "No."

"I don't know why you wound up on our property. We aren't wealthy, but purchasing necessities for you isn't going to bankrupt us. And who knows? By helping you get back on your feet, we may be helping someone else down the line. Someone who'll need *your* help."

"Beautiful *and* insightful," he teased, features softening. "I can't argue with your reasoning." Giving her hand a firm squeeze, he released her and, tying his cane to the saddle, hauled himself up. His grimace was fleeting as he righted himself. "I'm fortunate to have friends like you and Alice. No matter where I end up, I won't ever forget what you've done for me."

He should work to keep his physical distance. Not search for opportunities to be near her.

During the ride into town, he focused on the surrounding forest's untamed beauty, allowing himself infrequent glances at his companion. At ease in the saddle, Jessica had seemed preoccupied, an almost imperceptible worry pinching her forehead. Grant couldn't be blamed for thinking he was the cause. He was yet another complication in her life.

That her family was concerned about her emotional state compounded the problem. The O'Malleys were tolerating his presence—for the time being. If they knew his secret thoughts, that to him she was the perfect balance of sweet and sassy, a complicated challenge he'd readily take on if given the chance, if they found out he'd been tempted to kiss her, they'd run him out of town. Sheriff Shane Timmons wouldn't do a thing to stop them, either. He'd applaud their wisdom.

No one could learn of his regard.

While it had stung to hear her say a relationship with him would be a mistake, he couldn't argue with the truth.

The rushing of water over rocks drew him back to the present. Up ahead, the profusion of towering trees gave way to open sky. When they reached the wide wooden bridge suspended above the river, he pulled up on the reins to take it all in. Steep banks contained what he gauged to be thigh-deep water. Rocks lined the edges. In the middle section, where the river flowed unchecked, hues of orange, red and gold shimmered on the green surface, rippling reflections of the trees. He dismounted, irked that his muscles were stiff after such a brief ride. Being weak was for the elderly and infirm. He was not shaping up to be a long-suffering patient.

Bracing his forearms on the bridge's railing, his gaze trailed a pair of brown-tufted ducks floating along with the current. Jessica joined him, keeping several feet between them.

He gestured to the wood-framed buildings on the far side of the bridge. "So this is Gatlinburg."

"Yes."

Nestled in a valley, the quaint town was encircled by mountains, their rounded peaks framed against blue sky. The river curved to their left. From their vantage point, he could see the lane behind the businesses on this side of Main Street. She gestured to a wagon parked at the base of a set of steep stairs.

"That's the mercantile and dress shop my sister Nicole and Quinn own. People make deliveries at all hours of the day." Leading her horse across the bridge, she beckoned. "Come on. I'll give you the tour."

They hitched their horses to the post outside the first shop they came to. "Jane's husband, Tom, used to own the barbershop." She pointed to the wide window. "He sold it several years ago."

"And now he does what?"

"He's a farmer like most everyone else."

The main thoroughfare was a dry, dusty road wide enough to accommodate three wagons side by side. A couple of stray dogs trotted across at the far end. Townspeople traversed the boardwalks on either side or congregated in small groups. To his right, she pointed out Josh and Kate's establishment, as well as the Plum Café and the post office. The jail was farther down. On the left side of the street, the mercantile dominated much of the street front. He spied the livery beside it.

A stately white church with stained-glass windows was situated at the far end facing them, the lush, sweeping yard interspersed with trees and flanked on one side by a gated cemetery. With the mountains rising up behind it, it looked like a masterpiece painting.

"See that lane leading into the trees beyond the church? Nicole and her family live about a mile down. My other sister Megan lives that way with her husband and children." She indicated the road winding beside the river.

Grant noticed the wide-eyed stares and whispers the same time as Jessica. Some were more tactful in their curiosity than others. "We've been spotted."

"So it seems." Her demeanor shifted, her expression shuttering.

On impulse, he seized her hand and placed it in the crook of his arm, tucking her close to his side.

"What are you doing?" she demanded, eyes large in her face.

"They want something to talk about." He jerked his thumb to the gawkers across the street. "Why not give it to them?"

Slowly, her surprise transformed into something akin to impishness. "You're right." Before he could guess her intent, she went up on tiptoe and pressed her lips to his cheek. He froze. Lightning-swift heat arrowed from her lips to the soles of his feet. He felt anchored to the earth not by gravity, but by her.

Jessica's smile fascinated him. He knew, in that moment, that he was seeing the woman she used to be before the fire, before the man she loved died in her presence, before misplaced guilt and regret imprisoned her true self.

The ground rumbled beneath his boots. It took him a few seconds to realize it wasn't due to her kiss but a passing wagon.

"Now they truly have something to talk about." Tossing her head, she tugged him toward the mercantile. He would've let her lead him anywhere.

The bell above the entrance jangled when they entered. An interesting combination of smells washed over him— leather, sour pickles, the twang of dried fruit, fragrant, flowery soaps. Fat barrels lined the outer walls. Floor-to-ceiling shelving along the interior wall and behind the sales counter held everything from colorful stacks of fabric bolts to china sets to metal birdcages. Customers perusing the aisles and those waiting at the long counter to purchase their goods turned as one to see who'd come in. Grant held his breath, waiting for someone to recognize him. Maybe scream in fright and call for the law. Nothing happened.

Fingers tightening on his sleeve, Jessica moved toward the counter with confidence.

The distinguished, raven-haired man weighing a sack of sugar looked up and smiled. "Jess. How are you today?" He flicked an inquisitive glance at Grant.

"Hi, Quinn. We've come in to purchase a hat and some other things." She made the introductions. Interest gleamed in the businessman's shrewd gaze. As his hands were full, he nodded in welcome.

Jessica introduced him to her sister Nicole, who didn't resemble the twins in the slightest. Due to her impeccable clothing and regal carriage, she oozed sophistication. Where the twins were warmth and exuberance, she was cool and reserved. They were flames to her ice. Inky-black ringlets were piled atop her head, in contrast to milk-white skin and eyes an unusual shade of violet.

Grant wondered if she perhaps had a different father or was adopted. Whatever the case, she was courteous and knowledgeable and made the purchasing process bearable, considering he was spending Jessica's money. Leaving the sisters to converse while wrapping up his choices, he wandered over to the notice board. There were advertisements for garden equipment and livestock. A single job announcement caught his attention.

He couldn't survive without resources of his own. And he absolutely refused to go into further debt to the O'Malleys.

"Are you ready?" Jessica appeared at his side. He relieved her of the parcels, tucking them under one arm while opening the door for her.

"I have one stop to make before we return home," he told her out on the boardwalk. "It shouldn't take long."

"Would you like for me to come with you?" A breeze

teased free a long strand, and it snagged on her lips. He tried not to stare as she tugged it free.

"This is something I have to do on my own."

He'd expected her to question him. Instead, she pointed to a long bench in front of the mercantile's window. "I'll wait here." As he deposited the parcels beside her on the seat, she unwrapped the largest one and held it aloft. "Sun's bright today. You'll need this."

Witnessing her expectant pleasure, he couldn't refuse. Dropping the fawn-colored Stetson into place, he ran his fingers along the stiff brim and gave her an exaggerated wink. "What do you think? Is it my color?"

"It's perfect." She rewarded him with a sunny smile, one he could quickly become used to.

Heading for the livery, he rehearsed what he might say to convince the owner to give him a job. He strode into the weathered structure, pausing to get his bearings in the dim interior. The place smelled of stale hay and sweaty animals. All but two of the enclosures were occupied. On the far wall hung tools and tack. A wagon sat empty in the opposite entrance.

"Can I help you?" A stout, grizzled man emerged from the corner stall wiping his hands on the dirt-streaked smock covering his clothes.

"Are you Milton Warring?"

"That's the name."

Grant removed his hat and tapped it against his thigh. "I'm here about the employment notice you placed in the mercantile."

Warring's narrowed focus lowered, and Grant immediately stilled his hand. Letting a potential employer see his nervousness wasn't a good idea. Weakness, either, which was why he'd left the cane with Jessica.

"I'm Grant Parker. I'm staying with the O'Malleys, and I need a paying position to cover room and board."

Scraping his bristly jaw, Warring frowned. "Heard about you. They say you have…oh, what's it called?"

"Amnesia."

"That's it. Amnesia. So you don't remember anything about yourself?"

"No, sir."

"Not your ma or pa? Your home?"

"No. Nothing." He got a sinking sensation in his gut.

"That's a shame. I can't help you." Shaking his head in dismissal, he turned and would've gone back to work if Grant hadn't surged forward, hand outstretched.

"Wait. My lack of memory won't impact my ability to be a loyal employee. I'm a hard worker." He worked to keep his expression neutral, to hide the desperation boiling beneath the surface.

"You expect me to entrust my livelihood into the hands of a stranger?" He motioned to their surroundings. "You'll have to look elsewhere."

"Just give me a week. I'll work without pay. If you decide to keep me on, you'll owe me for the work I completed. If you decide not to, I'll walk away with nothing."

Grant clenched his jaw, waiting for the man's decision and despising his life in that moment.

"You'll have to look elsewhere."

His chest tight, he replaced the hat he couldn't pay for and nodded tersely. "Good day, Mr. Warring."

They both knew his chances of finding work were slim. He left the man staring after him, his pride in pieces on the floor.

Chapter Twelve

"Your friend's finished with his errand, Jessica." Pete looped his thumbs in his waistband and rocked back on his heels. "Sure don't look happy."

Lowell whistled softly. "Looks like he swallowed a pickled peach. Maybe he doesn't like you talking to us."

From her spot on the bench, Jessica angled to the left, instantly aware something was wrong. Grant stalked toward them, hands fisted at his sides, anger billowing off him in waves. A muscle worked in his tight jaw. The new hat cast his eyes in shadow, but they burned into her and the pair of men who'd stopped to chat.

Bolting to her feet, she gathered the purchases. "I have to go."

"Ditch the leech and come have pie with me," Lowell cajoled, gesturing over his shoulder to the café. "Won't be as good as yours, of course, but a guy has to take what he can get."

The paper wrapping crinkled beneath her hands. "I'm not in the mood for pie. And even if I were, I wouldn't share it with a man who resorted to calling others names in order to make himself look better by comparison."

Pete chuckled. Glaring, Lowell elbowed him. He lowered his voice. "I'm just saying what everyone else is thinking. He's a leech, Jessica, sucking you and your ma dry. Has he paid you anything for your hospitality?"

Grant neared, and Jessica was desperate to shut Lowell up. Erasing the distance between them, she warned, "Not another word, Lowell, or you'll be eating pie all by your lonesome for the rest of your life. I'll make sure of it."

Surprise flitted through his dark eyes. He put his palms up. "No call to be ornery. It was an observation. Touchy, aren't we?"

Pete stroked his chin. "I think the lady is infatuated with Gatlinburg's latest visitor."

"Sorry to keep you waiting." Grant's eyes glittered as he took in her proximity to Lowell.

"No need to apologize. These gentlemen were on their way to the café for dessert."

Jessica made a brief introduction. Lowell's smirk smacked of challenge, his brown eyes falsely innocent. "Would you two care to join us?" he said.

Grant's frown grew more pronounced. Before he could respond, she linked their arms. "We can't. I have rhubarb pie waiting on us at home. Good day, fellows."

When they reached the horses, she put their belongings in her saddlebags. Grant unwound the reins from the post and stared moodily down the street at Pete's and Lowell's retreating figures.

"They must've changed their mind about the café."

Schooling her features, she shrugged and, mounting her horse, changed the subject. He was sensitive enough about his situation without being privy to what folks were saying. "Did you get your errand taken care of?"

"It wasn't the outcome I'd hoped for." Hauling himself into the saddle, he turned Galahad toward the bridge. One thing about the new hat, it hid his eyes from view, making it difficult to determine his mood.

They rode side by side into the shaded lane, the hum of the rushing river gradually fading and replaced with birds' calls echoing through the understory. Minutes passed, and yet his profile continued to appear carved from granite.

"You seem upset."

"Talking about it won't change anything."

The self-derision in his tone caught her off guard. He was normally so upbeat that she wasn't sure how to deal with the cracks in his optimism.

"I recall saying something similar. And guess what you said?"

He turned his head to stare hard at her. Having the fullness of his intense perusal zeroed in on her made her antsy and wistful.

"Whatever you tell me will go with me when I leave," he supplied.

She made a zipping motion over her mouth. "Which means that whatever *you* tell *me* will stay."

Expression stormy, he shifted in the saddle. "I tried to get a job at the livery. The owner's hiring, but he's not inclined to take a chance on me."

"Oh." Unexpected hurt and defensiveness flooded her, and she pictured marching into the livery and giving Mr. Warring an earful. "I'm sorry, Grant."

One shoulder lifted in a careless gesture. "Told you it wouldn't change the outcome."

She nudged Caramel closer to Galahad. "You'll find something." She injected confidence in her manner. "I'm sure of it."

"Thanks for the vote of confidence."

"What are friends for?"

"For boosting one's ego, it seems." He thumbed the

brim up, giving her an unobstructed view of his eyes. "Do you plan on writing me after I leave?"

"As I won't know where you wind up, you'll have to write me first and find out." With a wink, she urged her horse into a trot, the exhilaration filling her stunted by one fact—she was beginning to think his leaving would be a bad thing. A feeling that could easily lead to trouble if she let it.

The wagon bed was packed with stacks of empty flour sacks and baskets, a pair of canvas tents, crates of food and enough personal items to last them three days. They planned to return Sunday night, but it was good to be prepared for delays. Grant studied the clouds above. Fat and fluffy, they looked harmless.

"I believe we have everything."

Jessica descended the porch steps and was in the process of tying the bold pink ribbons of her straw hat beneath her chin. Her white blouse was printed with miniature pink flowers, her skirt a refreshing spring green.

"I thought redheads didn't wear pink."

Grant couldn't resist teasing her. He'd felt sorry for himself the previous two days, stewing over the lost opportunity, until he'd decided it wasn't attractive or manly to sulk. He had his health, and he had the O'Malleys. God had provided for him. *Lord, I know You see my need for a job. I also know that with You, all things are possible.*

Planting her hands on her hips, she arched one sleek brow. "I don't care if it clashes with my freckles. I like pink."

Grinning, he moved close and gave her ponytail a playful tug. "You'd look beautiful in any color and you know it."

Not speaking, she blinked up at him, the teasing mood

gone in a flash. Interest was reflected in the green pools. Interest in *him*. He couldn't have imagined that first day that she would ever look upon him with anything other than disdain. But along with the longing in her eyes, he saw a heavy dose of restraint.

She's right to be cautious. Your past is one big question mark, as are your integrity and character. Somewhere out there might be a woman who's already laid claim to your heart. Maybe even your name.

Unable to stomach that last thought, Grant shoved it aside. He wondered about the man she'd loved and lost. What sort of relationship had they shared?

"Did he treat you well?" he blurted without thinking.

"Did who…" Her brows crashed together as understanding dawned. "That's a difficult question to answer."

"I don't think it is. Either he did or he didn't. You said your family didn't approve. Why not?"

"It's complicated." Picking up her skirts, she swept around to the far side. "We should go. Will's waiting on us."

Grant battled frustration. What was so horrible that she refused to tell him? The scant knowledge he had about her wasn't enough to satisfy the growing need to know more.

He thinks I'm beautiful.

Jessica left Grant, Will and Caleb to assemble the tents while she refilled their canteens. The clearing bustled with activity. All around her, people set up their campsites in clusters of families and friends. The air was cooler here in this higher elevation, the autumn foliage more pronounced. Afternoon light set the yellow, scarlet and orange leaves ablaze. Some of the chestnut trees were hundreds of years old, their sheer size impressive. Through the openings in the trees, she could see for miles, the mountain ridges marching into the distant horizon.

"Hello." A young woman about her age nodded and smiled in greeting as she passed.

Jessica smiled and continued picking her way across the chestnut-strewn, hilly terrain, her thoughts straying into places they had no right to go.

He thinks I'm beautiful.

Lee had been lavish with his compliments. So much so that she hadn't taken them to heart. Grant's praise was altogether different. His sincere admiration had rattled her.

Admit it, even without his memories, Grant Parker is a better man than Lee ever dreamed of being.

Instantly guilt flooded her. It wasn't right to compare her deceased beau to a living, breathing virile man. Still, she couldn't help noting the differences. When she thought of Grant, the description *steadfast* came to mind. Strength of purpose. Serious, yet able to appreciate the humor in life. Grant was light and laughter.

Lee had been dark and compelling, a swirling eddy that beckoned her closer to discover what was beneath. Compared to the local men, he'd seemed exciting and adventurous. Even a little mysterious. From the moment they collided outside the café and globs of buttermilk pie rained down on him, the handsome, brash newcomer had pursued her with flattering single-mindedness. He'd dazzled her with stories of life in Virginia as a wealthy businessman's son. He'd wooed her with romantic picnics. Delighted her with thoughtful gestures...flowers, badly written poetry, candy, inexpensive trinkets. Spending time with Lee made Jessica's small-town life less dull, less mundane. He was her perfect match.

Or so she'd believed.

He'd presented himself as a God-fearing man in pursuit of a simpler life. It wasn't until those weeks prior to his death that she'd realized she hadn't *truly* known him.

A single question nagged her. How could she have loved a man who'd deceived her so convincingly?

She knelt at the stream's edge, cold water trickling over her hand as she dunked the first canteen beneath the surface. Preventing this flourishing friendship with Grant from becoming meaningful was crucial. There were so many reasons why caring for him could prove disastrous it made her head swim.

The next man she allowed into her heart must lead a life that was above reproach. His reputation had to be untarnished. He'd be safe. Uncomplicated. Boring men didn't turn out to be criminals. They didn't lead double lives.

A dismayed cry snapped her out of her reverie.

"My dolly!" Farther down the bank, a girl who reminded Jessica of her niece, Clara, was tugging frantically on her older sister's sleeve and pointing to the object bobbing in the current.

Capping the canteen and placing it in the grass with the others, she hurried to join the girls. "Can I be of assistance?"

They lifted matching brown eyes to hers. The older one nodded. "Yes, please. My sister's doll fell in."

The stream wasn't wide, nor was it particularly fast. With no time to remove her boots or stockings, however, she wound up with soggy feet and dripping pantaloons. Handing the toy to its owner, Jessica smiled despite her uncomfortable state. "There you go."

"You saved Winnifred." The little girl sighed. Unmindful of her dress, she hugged the drenched doll to her chest.

"Thank you, ma'am." Her sister wore a look of relief. "Winnifred is her only doll. She would've been devastated to lose it."

"Happy to help. My name's Jessica. What's yours?"

"I'm Eve." She tilted her head to the side. "This is Lydia."

Lydia blinked shyly up at her.

"Nice to meet you both." Jessica bent to wring the excess water from her hem.

"We have to go."

"See you around, girls." She watched the pair hurry off, Eve lecturing Lydia as they went.

Laughing to herself, she didn't at first notice the woman rushing toward her.

"Jessica!" the woman squealed. "I'm so happy you're here!"

She caught the impression of red hair and a familiar smile before being crushed in a tight hug. Arms pinned to her sides, she inhaled a fragrance she'd recognize anywhere. Lavender.

"Juliana?" Her voice came out muffled, wonder filling her. What was her oldest sister doing here?

Gripping Jessica's shoulders, Juliana leaned far enough away to scan her face with unchecked joy. "Evan and I were searching for a good spot to camp when we saw Caleb. I couldn't believe my eyes. And then he told us you were here. I abandoned them without a word, I'm afraid." She laughed, hugging her again.

"Why didn't you write and tell us you were coming? Ma will be inconsolable for a week once I tell her."

It had been seven months since they'd last traveled to Cades Cove. Because of the farm's many responsibilities, they visited once or twice a year. Juliana and Evan hadn't been able to come to Gatlinburg as often as they liked, either.

"This trip wasn't planned. At the last minute, Lucas and his wife volunteered to care for the children."

"That was thoughtful of Evan's cousin. I'm sure you two appreciate the opportunity to be alone, but I would've liked to have seen James and Sammy."

Her nephews were growing so fast. James was four years old, Sammy two. Both boys resembled their raven-haired, blue-eyed father.

"You look well," Jessica observed.

Marriage and motherhood agreed with Juliana. An inch or two taller than Jessica, she wore her hair in a neat twist and preferred to wear comfortable, unfussy dresses.

Linking arms, Jessica led her to where she'd abandoned her things. Contentment she hadn't known for months stole over her. Growing up, Jessica could always count on Juliana's practical advice.

"I've missed you."

At the rare admission, Juliana's expression became concerned. "I received your letter about Mr. Parker. Did you get my reply?"

Crouching to refill the remaining canteens, she shook her head, her hair swinging forward.

"We asked around. Evan spoke with the sheriff and reverend. No one has heard of him."

Grant would be disappointed. "It was worth a try."

Moving to stand upstream, Juliana studied her closely. "Caleb introduced us to him. He's a polite man. Ma must think highly of him to condone this trip."

"You know how she feels about those less fortunate."

As thrilled as Jessica was to see her big sister, if Juliana warned her off Grant, she was likely to upend the contents of the canteen over her head.

"It says something about your opinion that you'd agree."

Twisting on the lid, she couldn't rein in her testiness. "What are you getting at, Jules?"

"Nothing. Just that it's wonderful of you to help someone in his position."

"Wonderful?"

Moving to take the filled containers, Juliana shot her a quizzical gaze. "What were you expecting me to say?"

"Oh, the same as almost everyone else in this family. That I should be careful not to fall for his charms. They act like I'm the biggest featherhead in east Tennessee. Like I don't have a single functioning brain cell. I'm not the only O'Malley to make a grave error in judgment."

Clueing in on her disgust, Juliana nodded her understanding. They strolled toward the clearing in the woods where most of the campers had chosen to spend the weekend.

"Do you know how many letters I've received these past months?" Juliana said. "Not only from Ma and Jane, but Megan, Aunt Mary, even Nicole, and you know how fond she is of writing." She turned her green eyes on Jessica. "They've had to stand by and watch you suffer because you insisted on shouldering your grief alone. They feel helpless. Can you blame them for wanting to see you happy again?"

Jessica wasn't sure she deserved to be happy. "No, of course not."

They reached their site and found Will assembling firewood and Caleb assisting Evan to erect a tent. All around them, the bustle of activity echoed through the forest. Children chased each other through the grass, weaving in and out of the chaos. Mothers called out warnings to be careful. Someone nearby played a jaunty harmonica tune.

Grant emerged from his tent balancing a crate against his uninjured side. He was wearing a borrowed gun belt about his waist, and the six-shooter she'd loaned him nestled in a holster on his left hip. Seeing Juliana and Jessica together, he stopped short. Shook his head and smiled. "No one could deny your heritage. What I don't get is where Nicole fits in."

Juliana laughed. "He hasn't met Megan yet, has he?"

"No." With her blond hair and blue eyes, Megan took after their mother's people. "Nicole is the spitting image of our paternal grandmother."

"That explains things. I guess." His gaze bounced between them. "Where do the red hair and freckles come from, then?"

"Both our father and grandfather were full-blood Irish," Jessica answered, adding the canteens to the supply pile.

"While our ma's side is English," Juliana supplied.

"Nature's funny like that." Grant's focus turned inward even as he scoured the expansive clearing, as if waiting for someone to pop over, shake his hand and supply all the answers he was seeking. The discussion about their heritage had to have sparked questions about his own.

"Jess, I'm going to start unpacking the supper supplies. We've got loads to share. You know what Evan's appetite is like."

"I heard that," he called.

Jessica smiled, meeting her brother-in-law's wink and wave as he fit the canvas over the poles. Evan hadn't changed in the years since he'd married her sister. As handsome and intense as ever, with his jet-black hair and blue eyes, he loved Juliana to distraction.

"We'll pool our resources," Jessica said.

"Good idea."

She turned to Grant, dreading telling him that Juliana and Evan hadn't discovered anything useful. He was counting on someone here recognizing him. What happened if someone did and the answers they supplied weren't what any of them wanted?

Chapter Thirteen

Jessica was basking in the fire's warmth, listening as Juliana and Evan caught everyone up on recent events in Cades Cove, when Grant sank onto the log beside her. His closeness warmed her more effectively than the nearby flames. The sun had set a while ago, but the mountainside was lit up with all the campfires.

He pointed to her bowl of pinto beans, into which she'd crumbled corn bread and topped it with sauerkraut. "You going to eat that?"

"I was planning to. Why?"

"Doesn't look all that appetizing."

She jabbed her fork in the air. "You worry about your own food, mister."

"If you insist." He shrugged. "I just thought you might like to add some zest to it."

Angling her knees toward his, she held the warm bowl aloft. "I forgot my Tabasco sauce, and Juliana doesn't use it."

"*You* may have forgotten it." The firelight flickered in his eyes. His hair flopped onto his forehead in that rakish way she found appealing. "I didn't."

He reached behind the log and produced the skinny bottle, giving it a little shake right in front of her nose.

"You brought it?" His thoughtfulness touched her.

When she reached out, Grant hid it behind his back, his playful mood palpable. "I sense that I have a bit of bargaining power right now."

"Grant Parker, you give me that bottle this instant."

Stroking the short, pale bristles covering his chin, he mused, "What should I ask for, I wonder."

"No bottle, no cookies." She smirked.

He considered her with his head tilted to one side. "What kind of cookies?"

"Oatmeal raisin. Bigger than your fist."

"I forfeit." He held out the Tabasco, and she grabbed it happily, dousing her meal while he made a grunt of mock disgust.

Picking his own bowl off the ground, he dug in with gusto. It had been a long, grueling day of travel and work to get their site set up. He was no doubt famished, not to mention exhausted. She worried he'd demand too much of himself.

He bumped her shoulder with his. "Your sister is nice."

Jessica shot him a sideways glance. "Are you insinuating I'm not?"

"*Nice* isn't a word I'd apply to you, no."

She socked him in the arm. A chuckle rumbling through his chest, he rubbed the spot. "Ouch, lady. See what I mean?"

The conversation across from them had ceased. Jessica blushed when she realized the others were observing them with keen interest. Juliana and Evan, their chairs pulled close together, were flanked by Will and Caleb.

"Grant's right." Will spoke with a full mouth. "You don't have the reputation as the nice O'Malley sister."

Jessica's jaw sagged. "Are you serious? After all the cake and pie I've plied you with?"

He laughed, and Caleb joined in. A shame his wife, Rebecca, couldn't come. Baby Noah had a cough, and they didn't think it wise for him to travel.

Juliana stuck up for her. Sort of. "Jessica can be accommodating when she puts a mind to."

"I'm beginning to feel offended."

Grant remained silent beside her, absorbing every word, looking entertained.

Caleb leaned forward and rested his elbows on his knees. "Juliana, tell Parker about Jessica and old man Brantley."

Juliana obliged, recounting how, as a determined nine-year-old, Jessica had insisted on visiting Zeb Brantley every day for a month. Believing his grumpy attitude stemmed from loneliness, she'd taken her fiddle and played for him.

"Alice mentioned you haven't played in a long time," Grant said, perplexed. "Why did you stop?"

"I don't know. Too busy, I guess."

He studied her, clearly not buying her excuse. She slid her glance away.

"At that point in time, she'd only just started to learn to play." Juliana smiled, green eyes twinkling. "She wasn't what you'd call talented."

Caleb guffawed. "It sounded like a cat screeching for its mate."

Will winced. "Poor Zeb."

"So I'm guessing his mood didn't improve?" Grant's gaze locked with hers. Humor mingled with admiration.

Her stomach did a little flip. "After a month, he finally asked me to leave the fiddle at home and read to him instead."

"She visited him once or twice a week for over a year," Juliana said, the fondness in her tone unmistakable.

"And then he died." A lump formed in her throat. It had been ages since she'd thought of the gentle man who'd been like a substitute grandfather.

"Do you remember that bird she saved?" Caleb broke the silence. "Its wing was broken, right?"

Juliana launched into another story of Jessica's antics. Grant lapped it all up. By the time they'd finished supper, she was sick to death of hearing about herself.

"Stop." She dumped out her cold coffee. "I think you've entertained Grant with enough stories to last a lifetime."

"I'm not bored," he protested.

"I am."

"Then let's play some music."

"What are you talking about?"

"While packing the guitar, I grabbed your fiddle on a whim. I knew we'd have some free time on our hands, and what goes better with a warm fire on a cool night than music?"

"That was presumptuous of you."

"Yes, it was," he agreed without apology. "But I don't remember playing with anyone else, and I'd like to see how well it works."

"Come on, cuz," Caleb drawled, depositing his empty plate in the grass beneath his chair. "Just a few songs."

The others waited for her decision. Her twin maintained that Jessica had been blessed with courage and boldness. Jane had aspired to those attributes, and that was why she'd decided to investigate Lee herself. Since his death, Jessica hadn't felt brave. She'd retreated inside her dreadful isolation. She'd allowed her circumstances to steal joy from her life. Steal her love of music and the comfort she derived from it.

"I'm rusty," she warned.

A slow, triumphant grin curved his mouth. "I have no memories of playing before waking up on your property, so we're even."

Striding to his tent, he retrieved their instruments, a new energy humming in him. Matching anticipation leaped to life inside Jessica, and her fingers itched to hold her bow again. To draw it across the strings and wait for the resulting notes to blend in a familiar tune.

Grant handed her the case with a flourish. Settling beside her, he took out her pa's guitar and situated it on his lap. From Juliana's expression, Jessica knew her sister had recognized it.

Perceptive as always, Grant paused and directed his comment to Juliana. "If this is awkward for you, I won't play."

At Evan's questioning glance, Juliana explained. To Grant, she said, "I'm glad it's being put to use. Pa would be, too."

Evan urged her close to his side and pressed a kiss against her temple. Smiling, Juliana snuggled in close and splayed her hand on his chest, the wedding band on her left hand winking. Caleb sat sprawled in his chair, legs stretched in front of him and crossed at the ankles. Will pulled a blade of grass through his teeth, knees bouncing.

Nodding reverently, Grant strummed a few notes while Jessica readied her instrument. She held the fiddle across her lap like a guitar and carefully plucked each string. Hearing that they were in tune, she picked up the rosin cake and rubbed it over the bow hair so that it would better grip the strings.

"What do you want to try first?" he asked.

"Do you know any hymns?"

"How about 'Amazing Grace'?"

It took them a few minutes to find their stride. He was patient, strumming softly, allowing her to reacquaint herself with her fiddle and the movements. The familiar notes came flooding back, as did the rush of contentment, and she found herself smiling like a fool. They concentrated on hymns at first, switching to folk songs later. Grant played in a way that allowed her to shine, showcasing her instrument's capabilities. For their last song, she chose one that would put the emphasis on his abilities. There were several spots where she'd lift her bow from the strings and pluck them softly as he continued to play. As they played together, an unexplainable emotional connection wove through the music and joined them in complete harmony.

When they'd finished, and not only their group but the surrounding campers were clapping and whistling, Grant's eyes shone with pleasure. Jessica laughed a little, her own spirits zinging with delight.

"What a treat," Juliana exclaimed. "I hope you'll play again before we leave."

Grant looked to Jessica, a hint of vulnerability in him. "I'd like that."

Jessica nodded, her heart dangerously soft and impressionable. "Me, too." When Juliana started stacking the soiled dishes, Jessica put out a hand. "I'll take care of those."

"We can do it together."

"No. You and Evan are rarely alone. Take advantage of your time together. Go take a stroll."

Disquiet flared briefly in Juliana's eyes before Evan caught her hand and brought it to his lips. "Jess is right. You deserve a break." Motioning to the tree line, he said, "Let's walk."

Her manner only slightly subdued, Juliana agreed. Jessica watched the pair weave their way through the throng, confusion surging. It appeared something was bothering her sister. But what?

Grant returned from his tent then, scattering her thoughts. "I'll take the basin."

She resisted. "It's heavy."

"That's why I'm going to carry it."

"And what about your wound?" She pitched her voice low, positive he didn't want his physical condition discussed in front of the others.

His stare was unwavering. "It's fine."

All too familiar with his obstinate nature, she allowed him to take it, gathering wash towels, soap and a lantern. They weren't the first ones at the stream. The points of light up and down the hillside were an enchanting sight, as was the trickling water glittering like golden fireworks.

They found a semiprivate spot and got to work

"You're one fortunate lady, you know that?" He swiped a towel over the dish she'd scrubbed clean. "You've got roots. Stories to remind you of how you became the person you are today."

Jessica hadn't taken stock of God's blessings in her life. She'd been too busy concentrating on the negatives. Once again, Grant's presence had pointed to a deficiency in her life. *I'm sorry, God. Help me appreciate all the ways You provide and care for me.*

The soap slippery in her hand, she paused to study Grant's profile. *And please, Father, help him. Guide him to the answers he deserves.*

Shortly before dawn, Jessica was startled awake. She stared at the canvas ceiling and blinked the bleariness from her vision. Objects in her tent gradually took shape in the lingering gloom. She lay still, the air cool on her face, her ears straining for clues. But there was nothing beyond the usual hushed forest sounds.

Crawling from beneath her covers, she lifted the flaps and peered out. If there was a bear out there scavenging for food, she needed to know about it. Being surprised in her bed by a wild animal wasn't how she meant to pass the weekend. In the midst of their tent circle, the fire's disintegrating logs glowed orange. High above the tree canopy, countless stars winked in the inky expanse.

A guttural cry shredded the hush blanketing the campers. Jessica's head whipped to the right. That had come from Grant's tent, situated several feet from hers. Will's was on her left side. Caleb's beside his. Evan and Juliana were sleeping opposite, yards away from the fire.

It came again, followed this time by an emphatic, slightly frantic "*No.*" There was no discernible movement inside. *He's dreaming.*

Pulling her housecoat lapels together at the throat, she didn't stop to put on boots before hurrying over. The dew-moistened grass soaked through her stockings. Crouching at the opening, she hesitated, darting a quick glance around. The assumptions folks would make about this had her heart knocking furiously against her rib cage.

She couldn't go inside. What would Grant think if he woke to find her in his tent, hovering over him in the dead of night? Her mouth went dry. Lifting the flaps, she squinted into the darkness, feeling as if she were invading his privacy. He tossed and turned on the pallet. More indecipherable words slipped out. Snagging his ankle, she jostled it.

"Grant," she hissed. "Wake up."

He didn't respond. Balancing her weight on one hand, she leaned farther in and shook harder. "Grant!"

"Huh—" He bolted to sitting, his forehead ramming into hers.

"Ouch!" Pain registered as hands clamped onto her shoulders.

"Jessica?" His voice was like a gunshot in the dark stillness. She covered his mouth.

"Shh!" she whisper-shouted. "You don't want to wake the entire camp, do you?"

He went very still. She became aware of several things at once. His undershirt-clad chest rising and falling. The weight and warmth of his hands. His spruce and leather scent permeating the space. And his face, wreathed in shadows, was but a breath away. Against her palm, his lips were incredibly soft.

Slowly, reluctantly, she let it fall to her lap.

"Why are you here?" His sleep-ravaged voice sounded almost angry.

"You were dreaming. Not the good kind."

"What?"

Suddenly, being this close to him wasn't such a good idea. "I'll explain out there."

Scrambling backward, she stood and hugged her house-coat more tightly about her.

He emerged a minute later and loomed close. "What's going on?"

"I was dead asleep when I awoke to the sound of you talking in your sleep, so I came to check on you."

Rubbing a weary hand over his face, he sighed. "You should've let me sleep. It would've passed."

Face-to-face with him in the predawn hours, she felt a trifle silly. Perhaps he was right.

"What were you dreaming about?"

"The same dream I've had for three nights straight."

"Did you remember something?"

"I didn't want to tell you. I've no clue who the man is or what it means."

"What man?" She stepped forward, accidentally landing on his foot. Also shoeless. "Sorry."

"In my dream, I'm struggling with a man. He lunges at me, and I grab him. We go down and then I wake up. I don't recognize him, but I do know he's angry with me."

"Grant, this is good news. I think I have paper among my things. We have to record the details and take them to Shane. We can sketch his likeness and compare them to the jail's wanted posters."

He clutched her arm before she could retreat. "That can wait until after breakfast."

"But it's fresh in your mind. You might forget something important."

"Go to bed before someone discovers us and assumes the worst. I can't marry you, Jessica. Not even to save your reputation."

Shock rendered her mute. Then irrational hurt filtered in. Ripping free of his hold, she jutted her chin. "Who said I'd marry you, anyway?"

"Jessica—" Exasperation riddled his tone.

"Good night, Grant." Escaping to her tent, she slumped onto her pallet and buried her flaming face in the pillow. "Next time I'll let you suffer through your nightmares alone."

She was the most infuriating woman on the planet.

Scooping a handful of chestnuts from the ground, he dropped them into his sack and tried not to eavesdrop on her and Juliana's conversation. Their group had moved higher up the mountainside after a cold breakfast of ham and biscuits. She'd rebuffed his efforts to speak in private. His comment had upset her, and she refused to let him explain.

Their predawn interaction dominated his thoughts. His defenses practically nonexistent, he'd come close to kissing her. Dangerously close, in fact. He'd yearned to pull her into his arms. Only by God's grace had he found the strength to refrain.

If one of her family members had seen them, or one of the campers…they would've misinterpreted the innocent exchange.

A hand clamped onto his shoulder. "Something on your mind, Parker?"

Caleb's gaze traveled a deliberate path to Jessica, indicating he'd picked up on her icy attitude.

"Plenty."

Not that he was about to share any of it with her cousin. Like the sheriff, Caleb didn't approve of his associating with her. Stooping lower to the ground, he pried a stubborn nut from its prickly burr.

Caleb joined him beneath the branches and got to work. "My youngest cousin can test a man's patience. Jane's a sweetheart. Jessica, on the other hand, possesses the will and stubbornness of an ox. Always has, always will."

His casual assessment evoked a swift, defensive reaction in Grant. Swiping his sleeve across his sweaty brow, he turned to study her, the smile she gifted her sister tinged in sadness. He wished he could take away the hurt, but how?

"Nothing wrong with a spirited woman." He speared Caleb with his gaze. "Personally I wouldn't want one who catered to my every whim. Maybe you're too close to see that Jessica can be sweet the same as her twin."

The other man's knowing smirk made Grant feel as if he'd been snared in a trap.

"Is that so?" Caleb drawled, brows lifting.

"No need to lecture me," he retorted. "I've already gotten an earful from your good friend the sheriff."

His dark eyes continued to study him. Grant held his gaze. At last, Caleb shrugged. "We don't want to see her get hurt again."

"She's mentioned her former beau a time or two. How bad was he?"

Anger shimmered around Caleb and, with that wicked scar, he looked deadly. "The worst kind of manipulator. She's convinced he loved her, but his actions proved otherwise."

Both men stopped what they were doing when a pair of young girls approached the women. The smaller one with brown curls and a shy smile handed Jessica a piece of paper. Grant's lungs seized as Jessica's face brightened with pleasure. She was breathtaking. And very, very sweet.

Bending to hug the girl, Jessica's eyes met his and darkened to twin pools of forest green. For an instant before she schooled her features, she looked young and vulnerable. He shared in Caleb's anger, wishing this Lee person was around so that he could show him what he thought about his treatment of her.

"What happened between them? What exactly did Lee do to her?"

"She'd be livid if I told you. If you haven't noticed, my cousin is the private sort. She'll tell you when she's ready."

He wasn't certain she'd ever be ready, that she'd ever trust him enough to bare her heart. The knowledge cut deep. He was getting in way over his head. Jessica would never be his to love or protect, comfort or cherish.

If he was smart, he'd pack his bags and move on before it was too late.

Chapter Fourteen

"I've cornered you at last. Unless you plan on running again."

Her hands submerged in the water, Jessica ignored Grant's dig. No use denying she'd been avoiding him the entire day. While ridiculous, the humiliation she felt burned beneath her skin, as did the infuriating wish that he'd take her in his arms and profess his ardent admiration. Had she learned *nothing* from Lee?

Snatching up a towel, he sank onto the bank and began drying the clean dishes. Waning sunlight washed the mountain in a pinkish-yellow haze. A few yards away, a squirrel scampered between the trees.

"I don't know about you, but I could sleep for a week."

Against her better judgment, she spared him a glance. He looked as ruggedly appealing as ever, his skin slightly red from hours in the sun. "How's your wound?"

"A little sore, is all." His eyes were like a bright summer sky, trailing blissful heat across her face.

Nodding, she scrubbed the skillet's surface. Weariness dogged her movements. Hopefully she'd sleep too soundly to hear anything that night, be it wild beast or man. There'd be no repeat of last night's foolishness.

A cloud of gnats whirled on the opposite bank. She observed their progress into the forest.

"After this, what do you say we pull out that paper of yours and record what I remember about the man in my dream?"

"You don't need me for that. I'll give you the writing supplies once I'm done here."

Grant's fingers tangled in her hair, and she gasped, jerking her gaze to his. "You, ah, had something in your hair." He pulled out a misshapen leaf and held it up for her inspection.

She continued to stare at him, and he dropped his hand to his lap. "You didn't let me finish earlier."

"No need." She strove for a casual air, hoping he wouldn't see the hectic pulse at her throat. He didn't want to marry her. So what?

"Yes, there is." He sighed. "If you hadn't dived into your tent, I would've said that I can't marry anyone because I don't know if I'm already married. It has nothing to do with you personally."

Oh. Annoyed at the relief rushing through her, she flipped her ponytail behind her shoulder. "Like I said, your marital status makes no difference to me."

One blond brow quirked, his expression challenging. He opened his mouth to speak and was prevented by the arrival of Eve and Lydia. Eve hefted a container full of dirty pots and utensils. "Do you mind if we wash here, Miss Jessica?"

"Not at all."

Setting it on the ground with a thump, Eve handed a towel to Lydia. Seeing their interest in Grant, Jessica introduced them. Both girls blushed at his charming greeting.

"Did you like my drawing, Miss Jessica?" Lydia asked.

"Very much. You're a talented artist. Thank you, again."

"What did you do to deserve such a gift?" Grant asked her, stacking a clean mug atop the rest.

"She saved my dolly from drowning," Lydia piped up, her eyes big and adoring.

"I see." Grant's smile was centered on Jessica, and her insides went all mushy, despite her earlier irritation with him. "Well, that's a *nice* thing to do."

Unable to form a coherent response, she concentrated on finishing her task and fleeing his confounding presence. When the basin became full, he went to retrieve another. Content to listen to the girls chatter about their older siblings and home in the outskirts of Cades Cove, she was washing her last plate when Lydia cried out.

Jessica's head shot up in time to see the knife fall into the water. Lydia stared in openmouthed horror at her flattened hand. Eve grabbed her wrist and paled.

"Miss Jessica! She's cut herself. It's bad!"

Feeling as if she were moving through a gallon of sticky syrup, she reached Lydia and, taking her small hand, inspected the injury. Blood spurted from the gash. The girl's crying rang in her ears. Suddenly, she was back in the barn, the stench of kerosene strangling her and the blood pooling on Lee's stomach. Fear rendered her limbs useless. He was going to die, and there was nothing she could do to prevent it.

"Miss Jessica—" someone was tugging on her sleeve "—you have to do something."

And then Grant was there, nudging her out of the way, ripping a towel into strips. She watched, numb to the core, as he soothed the child and quickly bound her hand.

"Can you get her to your parents?" he asked Eve.

"Yes, sir." Pointing to a nearby site where a man and woman conversed by a fire, she said, "That's them."

"Your ma can see to her wound. I'll come by and check on her in a bit."

"Thank you, sir." With a furtive glance at Jessica, Eve curved a supportive arm around her sister and led her away.

Jessica didn't realize she was crying until Grant came and wiped the moisture away with his fingertips. Lacing his fingers through her cold ones, he nodded upstream. "Come with me."

Blindly she went with him, fresh guilt compacting upon old guilt. Following the water's meandering path, he led her farther into the dense forest, and when she stumbled for the second time, he released her hand, wrapped his arm about her waist and guided her to where there were no people.

Stopping in a copse of fir trees, he pressed a handkerchief in her hand.

"I couldn't help her. I wanted to, but I…" More tears slipped down her cheeks, and her hands shook as she attempted to sop up the mess.

Grant stayed close, caressing her arm, his eyes brimming with understanding. "I know."

Shame barreled through her at the remembrance of Eve's parting glance. "She needed me, and I couldn't help her."

"Like you couldn't help him."

Jessica sniffed, too distressed to argue.

"Tell me about Lee. Tell me everything."

Her head bowed, she stared at their dusty boots and the leaf-littered ground. "No."

The truth would change his view of her, and she craved his good opinion.

He gently tipped up her chin, giving her no choice but to meet his gaze head-on. "You've held it in for far too long, my sweet."

"I made a horrible mistake," she whispered.

"I don't matter, remember? So you can unburden yourself and not worry about the future."

The tenderness in his manner brought on a fresh wave of sorrow, and she wanted to tell him he was wrong, that he most certainly *did* matter. That despite her best efforts, her heart had decided he was important.

He pulled her into his embrace, his arms linking low on her back. She cried into the curve of his neck and shoulder, the steady thump of his heartbeat reassuring beneath her cheek. He held her until there were no more tears left to be spilled, and his shirt was damp.

She stirred. Loath to leave the haven of his arms, but aware she couldn't remain there forever, she made to move away. Grant's hold tightened. He pressed a kiss to her temple, his breath stirring her hair, before releasing her.

He didn't let her retreat, however. He joined their hands, his expression telling her he'd wait here until Christmas if need be.

So she told him how Lee had convinced everyone that he'd come to Gatlinburg in search of a simple country life. There'd been no reason not to believe him. She told him about Jane's suspicions, how she'd witnessed him selling homemade moonshine to locals.

"I refused to believe her, so she pretended to be me and wangled an invitation to his home." After all the crying, her eyes were puffy and her throat full of needles.

His jaw dropped. "Jane tricked him into thinking she was you?"

"Doesn't strike you as the type to do something that bold, does she?"

His incredulous gaze roamed her face. "I'm guessing you didn't take the news well."

"I was incensed. Hurt, too. I felt betrayed. So much

so that I didn't care that she'd found evidence of a major moonshine production."

His frown turned thoughtful. "Revenue collectors turned their attention to this area in recent years. They were determined to enforce the excise tax."

"Yes. How did you…"

"Not sure." Pulling away, he tunneled his fingers through his hair. "Did Lee catch on?"

"Yes. He told her that his business associates were dangerous, and that she should keep quiet. He promised he'd get out as soon as he made enough money to set us up for a good life."

He should've known she didn't care about excess material wealth.

"She didn't heed his warning, did she?"

"No. Tom discovered her pretense, as well. They went to Shane with their information."

"That's why he makes you uncomfortable. He knows the whole story."

Pacing away, she lifted her face to the weakening rays of the sun slanting through the trees. The colorful patchwork of leaves filled her vision. She wondered what it would be like way up there, far above the cares of the earth.

"How did you wind up in your barn?"

"Jane came to Lee's place looking for me. She stumbled upon him and his boss, John Farnsworth. And then I swooped in, waving my weapon around, positive I could save her."

Grant gently turned her to face him, the fierceness wreathing his features at odds with his touch. "What you did was extremely brave and noble."

"She never would've been at his mercy if I'd listened to her. I was stubborn and stupid and—"

"Stop," he commanded. "You were in love with the

man. Of course you weren't going to believe him of wrongdoing. Not without seeing the proof with your own eyes."

"I still don't understand how I missed the signs he was hiding something. I feel like the biggest idiot on earth."

"That's what con artists do. They prey on people's belief in basic human decency." The matter-of-factness in his tone took them both by surprise. Stroking his light beard, he shook away his confusion. "So you confronted them on Lee's property. Why were you on yours?"

"Farnsworth planned to cover up our deaths by burning our barn to the ground." A shudder racked her frame. "I'll never forget that man's face. There was no compassion in him, only evil."

"Is he dead?"

"He's spending the rest of his life in prison."

Cupping her cheek, Grant murmured, "Thank you."

"For what?"

"For trusting me. It's a strange thing not to be trusted. Or needed."

Jessica's heart fluttered in her chest. Heady emotion crashed through her, bittersweet and poignant and wistful. For the first time since Lee's death, she experienced hope.

Above their heads, a pair of robins burst from the branches. With a rueful smile, Grant put distance between them. "You ready to return to camp?"

She balled the soaked handkerchief in her fist. "I'd like to see Lydia and apologize."

"You have nothing to apologize for. But we can stop and see her." He started walking, and she fell into step beside him. She felt his perusal. "Did talking about it help?"

"A little."

"You still hold yourself responsible, though."

Jessica didn't respond.

"He deceived you, Jessica. By keeping his criminal

activities secret, he put you in danger. You couldn't control his actions. In the end, he decided to fight back. To try to save you and your sister. And Jane made her decision. She chose to protect you."

"I can't stop thinking if I had gone to Shane in the beginning, we never would've ended up in that barn."

"You can't know for sure what the outcome might've been. And what about Lee's culpability? He's the one who was breaking the law." Banked anger glittered in his gaze. "Have you ever considered your grief might be marring your perception of things? If he hadn't died, if Lee was sitting in prison right now, would you feel differently?"

Grant continued walking, unaware that she'd stopped cold. He finally stopped and turned.

"I've been so angry at him. Angry at a dead man. What kind of person does that make me?"

"A sane one. He's not around for you to focus your anger on, so you turned it on yourself."

His argument resonated with truth, a powerful truth that made sense of everything she'd experienced. "How did you get to be so wise?"

"I offered an objective perspective, that's all."

She shook her head in disbelief. "You were able to do what no one else has in all these months."

"What's that?"

"Make me see reason."

He had another nightmare that night.

Not about the stranger. This time he dreamed Jessica was trapped in a raging inferno. He woke gasping for breath, his skin drenched and heart pounding.

She wasn't the only one angry at a dead man.

Grant found it impossible to rationalize how any sane person could treat her with such disrespect. To deceive her, put her very life in danger… That Lee had sacrificed himself trying to save her was his only redeeming quality.

Shoving off the blanket, he emerged into the quiet night and inhaled the crisp, fragrant air. Face lifted to the heavens, he turned in a complete circle, studying the stars. He could breathe easier outside. He was more comfortable in open spaces than confined by tent or cabin walls. Had he led a nomadic life?

His gaze fell on Jessica's tent, and he half wished she'd come out, despite the risk. He would've liked to talk with her. Find some excuse, like a crooked ribbon or stray leaf, to touch her hair. Tease laughter into her wide green eyes and color in her cheeks. He still could hardly believe she'd opened up to him about her past. Holding her, comforting her, he'd felt more at home in his own body since he'd woken with no idea who or what he was

Upon their return, their first stop had been at Lydia's campsite. Although subdued, she'd warmed to Jessica's apology and hug, taking pride in showing them her bandaged hand. Her parents had been effusive in their gratitude. Jessica's family members hadn't been pleased at their extended absence. One look at her grief-ravaged face, and they'd turned accusing eyes on him. But then she'd smiled, taken out her fiddle and asked him if he'd like to play with her. Bemused, Juliana and the others had gathered around and listened as his guitar and her fiddle joined together in song.

They'd played for hours. Other campers brought chairs and blankets and settled in to listen, which had made him self-conscious. As if sensing his unease, Jessica had caught his eye and smiled her encouragement. The pure pleasure in her face made his worries disappear and his heart expand with happiness.

The guilt and sorrow so prevalent in her had receded.

He couldn't take credit for the change. He'd only said what others had likely tried to say countless times before. She just hadn't been ready to hear and accept the truth until now. In this instance, the fact he was an outsider had actually been a good thing.

Grant prayed she'd be able to move forward with her life, pursue dreams that were important to her. Leaving her wasn't going to be easy, he realized. He'd miss her.

He liked her and her family. Liked her charming mountain town.

Perhaps she'd agree to exchange letters.

His spirit heavy at the prospect of never seeing any of them again, he returned to his tent and, lighting a lamp, dug in his travel bag for his Bible. His fingers encountered an unusual bump in the lining. Removing the items one by one and placing them on his pallet, he squinted into the bag. There weren't any rips in the seams. Running his hand flat against the bottom, he frowned. Something was in there.

Pulse skipping, he located his pocketknife and worked open the seam along the long side. He peeled the lining away. The air inside the tent seemed to constrict, cutting off the oxygen. His throat closed.

Black velvet pouches. Four of them.

Dread spread like black ink from his chest into every part of his body.

Fingers trembling, he dumped the contents of the first pouch onto his bedding. Gold and precious gems winked up at him. Necklaces. Ruby rings. Diamond bracelets. Emptying the rest, he lifted the most ornate piece and held it on his palm. The brooch's pearls glowed in the circle of light, the diamonds scattered rainbow-hued prisms. These pieces couldn't be fake.

Closing his fist around it, he didn't register the sharp edges cutting into his skin.

He slumped over, his forehead resting against the bed, and fought the resurging panic. Sweat beaded on his brow, and his heart pumped so hard it actually hurt.

He was a thief. There could be no other explanation. He'd stolen these jewels—too many to have come from one source, which meant he was a professional thief— and hidden them in this bag. The stranger in his dream? Probably his cohort demanding his share of the bounty. Maybe Grant had tried to swindle him out of it, and that's why he'd been attacked and left for dead.

God, how can this be? I don't feel like a criminal. This is the last thing I wanted.

But the evidence was right there in his hand.

Jessica was right. Her first instincts were spot-on.

Grant felt ill. Head throbbing, he replaced the jewels, all the while considering running. He could travel to another town and drop the travel bag at a bank or jail. Or a church. That would work. A pastor would make sure they were returned to the authorities and from there the rightful owners. He'd keep moving until he was hundreds of miles from here. He could find odd jobs along the way. Of course, he'd have to make up a sympathetic story, adding deception to his list of sins.

Extinguishing the light, he crawled into bed. The thread of optimism he'd been clinging to snapped, and he was left with ugly reality.

Chapter Fifteen

"I wish we didn't have to go," Jessica said. "I wish we could stay for another week."

Juliana's eyes were wet. "The time passed too fast."

The clearing was abuzz with activity. While some families would be staying on, many were packing up and heading home, their wagons jammed full of chestnuts to be sold at market.

Evan came up behind Juliana and, snaking his arms around her middle, nuzzled her cheek. For a brief moment, she closed her eyes and leaned into him, a tiny sigh escaping.

"We'll plan a visit to Gatlinburg soon," he promised.

Twisting in his arms, she encircled his neck. "Can we go for Thanksgiving?"

The smile he bestowed on her spoke of deep affection. "For you, I'll make it happen."

Jessica darted a glance in Grant's direction. Waiting beside their wagon at the clearing's edge, he shifted his stance, his gaze constantly moving about the crowd. With his beard heavier than usual, his good looks had a rough edge to them. He'd been tense and standoffish since breakfast. After their time in the forest and hours of making music together, his attitude stung. She'd replayed those tender moments in his arms a thousand times. It amazed her that an outsider had been the one to dismantle her self-recrimination.

He's not an outsider anymore, is he? He's a treasured friend. And I can't stop wondering what it would be like to be more.

"How about a goodbye hug for your brother-in-law?"

Snapped out of her reverie, she embraced Evan. "We'll see you next month?"

When Evan committed to something, he followed through. Grant was dependable like that. Honorable. A man worthy of her trust and admiration.

Evan smiled. "Lord willing, we'll be there."

Juliana watched her husband lope over to speak to Caleb. Her suddenly troubled expression put Jessica in mind of that odd moment from before. Suspicion surfaced. "What's wrong?"

Her hand pressed against her heart, she frowned. "He's keeping secrets, Jess. I can hardly believe it of him."

"What do you mean?"

"I first noticed something was off about a month ago. He started spending an inordinate amount of time with his cousin, Lucas. They'd talk for hours, and when I asked what they'd discussed, he refused to say." She frowned, twisting her wedding band about her finger. "Since we've been here, he's been glued to Caleb's side. I'm worried, Jess. We've never hidden our problems from each other."

Jessica didn't have sage advice to dispense. Her one serious relationship had been based on lies. "What are you going to do?"

"I've given him plenty of time to confess." Jerking her chin up a notch, she said, "I'm tired of waiting. I'm going to confront him during the trip home. That way, he can't duck into the barn to fix a tool or come up with an excuse to avoid me. There'll be no escape."

Jessica hugged her tight. "I'll be praying. Just remember, he loves you. Whatever he's keeping from you, he has good intentions."

Juliana pressed her lips together. "I'm sure he believes he's doing the right thing, but secrets have a way of destroying a relationship."

"You don't have to tell me that," she said drily.

"I'm sorry. I didn't think."

"It's fine." Her focus gravitated to Grant. "I've made a promise to myself. My next relationship will be based on openness and trust and mutual respect."

Juliana followed her line of sight. "I like him, Jess."

"Oh, no, you misunderstand. I wasn't talking about him. I—"

She touched her wrist. "You're forgetting I'm your older sister. I can see how much you like him. He feels the same, judging from the way he looks at you."

"I'd be crazy to pursue a relationship with him, Jules."

Her assessment turned sly. "That's what I told myself about falling for an outlaw."

"But Evan wasn't an outlaw."

"I didn't know that until *after* I fell in love with him."

Sensing Grant's perusal, she shifted her gaze and, sure enough, he was staring right at her. Blushing as if he'd overheard the entire exchange, she lifted a finger to let him know she'd be a minute more.

"I love you, sis." She gave her hand a squeeze. "Write to me as soon as you get home. I want to know what Evan has to say for himself."

"I will."

Weaving through the throng of people, she made her way to Grant's side. "I'm ready."

His hat shaded his eyes. The lower half of his face was in direct sunlight, his sculpted mouth bracketed by irritated lines. With a terse nod, he took her elbow and assisted her onto the high seat. She set her straw hat on the space beside her and straightened her skirts. Grant climbed up, not sparing her another glance as he put the team in motion. Behind them, the conveyance's bed was tightly packed.

"Where's Will?"

"Riding with Caleb." He waved a gloved hand in the direction of her cousin's wagon not far from theirs. "Would you like to switch places?"

"And leave you with all the treasure?"

His head whipped round. "Treasure?"

"The chestnuts."

His Adam's apple bobbed. Lips forming a flat line, he returned his attention to navigating the team through the crowd to the winding, uneven route down the mountain.

"They do bring a good price, especially with the impending holidays."

He grunted, his profile marble-like as he concentrated. Jessica didn't speak again until they'd left the campsite far behind and the trail wasn't quite so hazardous.

"What's bothering you, Grant?"

His forearms flexed. "Just eager to get back, is all."

He wouldn't even look at her, which sparked her temper. What was his problem? "You're not a very good liar, you know."

His blue eyes were stormy when they finally met hers. "History has proved you're not such a good judge of that."

Jessica gasped. His words dug beneath her skin like stubborn splinters.

Regret splashed across his features, but he didn't retract

his well-aimed barb or apologize. Facing forward, he proceeded to ignore her, a muscle jerking in his unshaven jaw.

Dizzy with hurt, she put her hat on and averted her face, staring unseeing at the passing scenery. Pain blossomed in the area around her heart. How could he do that? After she'd let him in, confessed her darkest moments, made herself vulnerable? The tenderness he'd shown her, the compassion...had it been a mirage?

No. He hadn't faked it. Sometime during the night, he must've thought through all she'd told him and come to the conclusion that she was to blame, after all.

A small voice inside rebelled.

I can't go back there, God. I can't live bearing this guilt, day in and day out.

No matter what Grant Parker thinks of my actions.

Grant deserved to be thrashed for what he'd done.

Consumed by his own misery, he'd lashed out at her in the worst possible way. He'd taken her private shame and used it to wound her. To force her attention elsewhere. If she'd continued to question him, he would've caved and told her about the jewels.

He wouldn't soon forget the hurt shimmering in her eyes. She'd remained quiet and unmoving, her focus turned inward, until they pulled off to the side around six o'clock for a break and quick supper. When it was time to head out, Will had climbed into Grant's wagon, mumbling something about grouchy females. Grant had caught Caleb's perplexed frown as Jessica made herself at home in his wagon.

Directing the team onto Alice's farm hours later, he told himself again it was best this way. They'd been growing too close. When the truth was finally revealed, she'd thank him.

He refused to be like that snake Lee Cavanaugh, refused to willingly inflict further hurt.

Caleb surprisingly didn't question him. No doubt impatient to get home to his wife and sons, he didn't disembark once Jessica had descended.

Will yawned. "Let's unpack tomorrow morning."

"Fine with me. I'll see to the horses," Grant said.

The younger man gave him a hearty nod and ambled toward the cabin. When Jessica passed within inches of where Grant stood, he shot out a hand and grazed her upper arm with his fingertips. She jerked away, glaring at him.

"What do you want?"

Good. He could deal with her anger. What he couldn't handle was her sadness, especially knowing he'd caused it.

"Can I borrow Galahad?"

"What for?"

"I have an errand that can't wait."

Emotion flashed, but she clamped it down, shrugging. "Do what you want." Spinning on her heel, she left him there, aching for a different outcome.

Any illusions of a promising future shattered, he parked the wagon inside the barn and unhitched the team. Once he had the animals brushed down, watered and fed, he saddled Galahad. The travel bag in his possession, he rode for town, praying Shane Timmons was in his office. He couldn't pass another night with this terrible secret hanging over his head.

The streets were empty. Most folks were snug in their homes at this late hour, preparing for bed. He hitched Galahad beside the sheriff's mount. A light burned through the bare window.

Seated at his desk, Shane looked up in surprise at Grant's entrance.

"I've been wanting to speak with you," he said, laying down his pencil.

Grant dropped the bag on his desk and folded his arms. "What about?"

"It can wait." He nodded to the bag. "What's this?"

"I found something hidden in the lining, and you're not going to like it."

A frown line marring his forehead, the other man stood to inspect the contents. As the jewels spilled across the scarred desktop, Grant felt like a man sentenced to be tossed into the ocean, a sack of rocks tied about his neck. He was doomed.

He whistled. "When did you discover these?"

"Last night at the campsite."

"Do you recognize them?" His gaze pinned him in place.

"No."

Shane continued to inspect the various pieces until Grant thought he would crawl out of his skin. "So which cell is to be mine?" He strove for humor and failed. "I'd like a street view, if available."

Hands on his hips, the sheriff quirked a brow. "I have no cause to hold you, Parker."

Grant snorted, waved his hand over the bounty. "This isn't reason enough?"

"We aren't sure if this bag even belongs to you."

"I thought you'd seize the opportunity to keep me away from the O'Malleys."

"A guilty man wouldn't have brought this in. A dishonest man would've kept it for himself."

"That's just it. We don't know what kind of man I am."

Sinking onto his chair, Shane motioned for Grant to take a seat. "I've come up with a theory. Wanna hear it?"

"Do I have a choice?"

"Let's say I'm out rounding up bad guys and get knocked on the head, losing most of my memories in the process. Am I then going to become a wholly different man? Lying, cheating, stealing. Would amnesia alter my basic personality?"

Grant rubbed at a stubborn stain on his pant leg, mulling over his words.

Steepling his hands atop his chest, the sheriff continued, "I'm having a tough time accepting that prior to your accident, you were a base-minded opportunist out for number one, and now you're suddenly a law-abiding citizen. That's why, when I heard you were interested in the livery job, I had a chat with Warring."

His head came up. "How did you know about that?"

"Same way I know Jessica kissed you in the middle of Main Street."

That spontaneous kiss on the cheek? "No secrets in small towns."

"That's right."

"Warring's not inclined to take a chance on me. And with this most recent development, I can understand why."

"He's changed his mind. You can start tomorrow if you're so inclined." Pushing his chair back, he began to replace the jewels. "I'll keep this with me overnight, then place it in the bank's safe first thing tomorrow morning. Looks like I'll be posting more letters."

Removing the folded paper from his pocket, he held it out. "I've remembered someone who I suspect might be linked to my former life. There's a crude sketch, as well as a list of details."

Unfolding it, Shane scanned the information. "I'll check his likeness against my stuff here, then send it out with my other correspondence." When Grant didn't move, he waved to the door. "You're free to go, Parker."

Grant had come here expecting to be locked up. Not only was he going to remain free, but the sheriff had used his influence to get him a job. "Why would you help me?"

"Everyone deserves a chance to prove themselves." He flicked him a glance. "Besides, you can't leave town without money. I figure this is the best way to be rid of you."

Chapter Sixteen

She was waiting for him on the porch.

His mind like a dry wheat field on fire, thoughts churning and melding before he could fully process them, he'd ridden without thought to his surroundings. Fortunately, Galahad knew the way home. After settling him in the barn, Grant trudged across the short grass, his tread heavy on the steps.

She stood off to his right, using the railing for support.

"Will went home."

A sign of good faith. "You waited up to tell me that?"

"Don't flatter yourself," she scoffed.

He climbed another step. Moonlight washed her features in dreamlike radiance, her unbound hair like crimson waves of silk. She was still in her traveling clothes, the scooped-neck blouse with flowing sleeves tucked into a plain navy blue skirt. She looked like a prim schoolteacher in the outfit. Funny. Jessica was anything but prim.

"Couldn't sleep, then?" he said, his arms too empty without her in them.

"Something like that."

He reached the top step. "Well, I'm exhausted." If he

lingered, he wasn't sure he'd make wise decisions. "I'm going to bed."

Jessica was suddenly blocking his way. Face lifted, eyes troubled, she fisted her hands at her sides. "You hurt me. More than I can express."

He bowed his head. "I know, and I'm sorry. I should never have said what I did."

A soft sigh shimmered between them. "That's the thing, Grant. It's not in your nature to lash out. Something happened between the time we said good-night last night and this morning. I want to know what it was."

After everything she'd done for him, he owed her an explanation. The word would eventually get out, anyway.

Meeting her searching gaze, he said, "I discovered valuables in my bag. Deliberately stashed in the lining."

She sucked in a sharp breath. "What sort of valuables?"

He described the pieces. "There's too much for it to have come from one source."

Understanding dawned. "You took them to Shane, didn't you? That's where you've been?"

"He's going to store them at the bank until he finds out more." He kneaded his stiff neck muscles to keep from reaching out to her. The need to hold her was like a fire in his blood. "I'll understand if you want me to find another place to stay."

"No." She shook her head, moonlight glimmering in her locks. "No. I don't want you to leave." Before he could guess what she was about, she wrapped her arms around his neck and leaned into him. "You're innocent, Grant."

Her lips grazed the sensitive skin above his collar. He shivered. Not from the drop in air temperature, but because of her soft curves, her sweet, sweet scent, her overwhelming faith in his goodness. Resting his hands on either side of her waist, his cheek skimmed hers before he buried his face in her hair.

"I hate myself for hurting you."

Her fingers danced along his nape, explored the breadth of his upper back. "It's okay. It's forgotten."

"I was cruel, and that's not okay."

Shifting, forcing him to lift his head, she framed his roughened cheeks. Her palms were cool, soothing. "I forgive you."

He swallowed hard. "Jessica."

His inner voice of reason muted, he mirrored her stance, skimming trembling fingers over her pronounced cheekbones and the smooth curve of her jaw. Her gaze locked on to his. There was an absence of fear in her. No hesitation. Only a shared awe of what was unfurling between them.

Settling his hand beneath her hair, he cupped her nape and dipped his head. He brushed his mouth against hers once. "I don't want to hurt you ever again," he murmured, struggling to rein in emotions threatening to boil over.

She exhaled, her warm breath mingling with his as she tunneled her fingers into his hair. "I trust you, Grant."

Her words were a gift. One he didn't deserve.

When he didn't move, adrift in an impossible internal battle, she tugged his head down. Her kiss was tentative, searching. Any lingering doubts scattered like dandelion seeds on the wind. A rumbling sound of surrender vibrating in his throat, he crushed her to him, holding her fast. Her embrace was purity and joy and hope, and he clung to those ideals with a hint of desperation.

I can never leave her.

They each possessed what the other required. When he was fire, she cooled him. When she was angry, he mellowed her. They balanced each other.

You promised not to hurt her. What will she do if you're already committed to someone else?

It was as if a bucket of ice had pelted him. Jerking away, his breathing ragged, he stared at her kiss-swollen lips and mussed hair.

"We can't do this."

She didn't fight him. Sorrow stole over her and, hugging her middle, she looked lost. "Because of your past? Or because of me? Because of my poor judgment with Lee?"

"No!" Gripping her shoulders, he shook his head. "Don't start questioning yourself again." He gentled his hold. "You and I both know the future isn't mine to do with what I please. Not until I get answers."

Worrying her lower lip, she slowly nodded.

"I might never be free of the past. And I won't ask you to wait for answers that may never come."

"You're right. This can't happen again." Backing away from him, she edged toward the door. "Good night, Grant."

Head held high, she left him alone in the inescapable solitude of night, once again asking God why and getting no answer in return.

Jessica squared her shoulders and entered the Plum Café. It was the first time she'd been in since the new owner so ruthlessly and abruptly canceled her and Jane's agreement. She really wasn't in the mood to see him today. Glancing around the eatery, which was practically devoid of customers midafternoon, she spotted Caroline's elegant form in the far corner, along with two other girls on the committee.

Winding her way through the tables, she greeted them. Caroline's china cup clinked against the saucer. "Thanks for agreeing to join us on short notice."

Pauline and Laura looked up from the ribbons fanned across the linen tablecloth.

Jessica sank into the last empty chair. "Why aren't we doing this at your house?"

"Mother is having the parlor repapered."

"I thought she had it done last year."

"Oh, she did." Her smile was brittle. "She found one she liked better."

Laura sighed. "Must be nice, getting whatever you want."

Pauline nudged her in the ribs and shushed her.

Caroline shrugged. "And yet, she's never satisfied."

The waitress emerged from the kitchen to take Jessica's order. Curious to test their desserts for herself, she ordered a slice of their spice cake and hot tea. When the waitress had gone, the other girls snickered. "Wasted money, if you ask me," Pauline said.

"It can't be that bad."

Laura leaned forward and spoke in hushed tones. "Pa ate their chess pie last week and was sick to his stomach the whole night long."

"Are you sure it was the pie and not something else he ate?" Caroline added more sugar to her tea and stirred with delicate strokes. "Their original cook quit. The food isn't near as good as it used to be. I wish Mrs. Greene would come back."

Winding the string around the ribbon in her hand, Pauline addressed Jessica. "I saw your guest working at the livery yesterday. You didn't mention how handsome he is. The sweat and bits of straw clinging to his clothes didn't detract from his appeal one bit."

Jessica cut her gaze to the huge window overlooking Main Street, scrambling for an appropriate response. Four days later, his kiss still dominated her thoughts.

His position at the livery had proved a blessing. Being around him was suddenly a lesson in restraint, a test of her resolve. She'd liked him before the camping expedition. Her feelings had gone beyond friendship since then, and not simply because of what had transpired on her porch Sunday night. Because of Grant, the guilt and shame she'd been carrying around was dissipating. His insightful, straightforward advice had shaken her out of her skewed thinking.

The day Grant wandered onto her property, she'd questioned God's purpose in bringing another trial into her life. Like Job in the Old Testament, she'd demanded answers of the One who'd created the universe and everything in it. And, while God hadn't owed her a single answer, she'd been granted insight—Grant's arrival had forced her to look beyond her own troubled world and consider someone else's feelings, freeing her from the mire of the past and her own self-absorption.

There was a downside to this freedom.

Where her heart had been locked away in an impenetrable shell, impervious to plunder, it was now exposed and pliable and vulnerable. And it craved a man who was unattainable. A man who could prove to be her ultimate downfall.

Which is why you'll exercise caution, an inner voice reasoned. *You will let common sense rule. You will not ruin the rest of your life by falling for the wrong man.*

"I haven't seen him." Laura pouted. "What's he like?"

Jessica remained quiet as Pauline described him. Tiny sprouts of jealousy poked holes in her composure. She had no right. He wasn't hers to be jealous over.

Her tea and dessert arrived then, saving her from making inane comments about Grant's appeal. The first bite proved the rumors true. The cake was stale, the raisins chewy instead of plump and soft and the icing had a salty twang.

Hurriedly washing away the taste with bracing liquid, she felt three pairs of eyes on her.

Caroline wore a smug expression. "See?"

"That's horrible." Jessica poked the dense cake. "Does the man have no concept of good food?"

"The owner's pretty elusive. Hard to tell what he thinks."

Grant's prediction may prove to be right. She couldn't imagine anyone happy to pay for such poor quality. Scooting aside her plate, she went to work on the ribbons. The conversation turned to the harvest fair and the long list of tasks to accomplish beforehand. Jessica listened with half an ear, preoccupied with a decision she'd delayed long enough.

Once she'd paid for her uneaten dessert, she bade the women good day and headed for the mercantile. The bell announced her arrival. Quinn paused in his sweeping of the aisles.

"Jessica." His smile was warm. "What's brought you in today? If you're looking for Nicole, she's in the back trying to get Violet to sleep."

Violet was their young daughter, who, with her black hair and bright eyes, promised to be a beauty like her mother. A pang of wistfulness gripped her. She was the only one in her family who was still unmarried. No loving spouse or infants to lavish her affection upon.

"I'm actually here to see you."

"Oh?" Leaning the broom against the counter, he folded his arms and waited.

"I've been mulling over your offer—the one where I

use your shelf space to sell my desserts—and I'd like to do it. If you're still open to the idea."

"Come to my office, and you can sign the paperwork."

Surprised, she blurted, "You've got it written up?"

"Jess," he said patiently, "I've been waiting for you to agree for months. Your desserts will sell, guaranteed."

"I don't want to sell by the slice. It's the whole thing, or nothing."

"Sounds reasonable," he tossed over his shoulder.

"And I want to start with cakes only, at first. I can add pies later, depending on the response."

"You're the boss, baker lady." He flashed a grin.

Inside his small office, she scanned the single paper he retrieved from his desk drawer. "This doesn't say anything about your percentage."

"I don't require any."

"You're running a business, Quinn. I can't accept special treatment simply because I'm your sister-in-law."

"It's because you *are* my sister-in-law that you deserve it."

While she appreciated that his intentions came from a good place, she couldn't accept his terms. She replaced the paper on the desk, unsigned. "It wouldn't be fair."

His face screwed up in an adorably boyish fashion. "How about five percent of the profits?"

"Ten percent."

He cocked his head, a lock of inky-black hair sliding forward making him look endearing. "Do you *want* your sister to make my life miserable? Because she has her ways."

This coaxed a laugh out of her. "Fine. Five percent." He slapped a pen in her hand. She signed her name. It was official. She was a businesswoman once again.

I'll be up to my elbows in flour and sugar for the fore-seeable future, too busy baking to think about Grant.

"Get your ledger out," she ordered. "I've got shopping to do."

Chapter Seventeen

Grant pushed his plate away and, nursing the remainder of his coffee, watched Jessica drizzle Tabasco over her eggs and sausage. She'd come to the table later than usual. Another attempt to avoid him, no doubt.

Every night this week, he'd returned from the livery dirty, hungry and exhausted, and yet anticipating spending time with her. But she'd been conspicuously absent, off visiting her sister or working on harvest fair tasks. Evading him.

He drank in her fresh-faced beauty. Her hair shiny and slightly damp around her hairline from morning ablutions, she'd restrained it in her usual simple style, the yellow ribbon perky at this early hour. It would droop and slip as the day progressed, and he wouldn't be here to fix it. Her ruby ring flashed on her hand. Had that been a gift from Lee?

Of its own accord, his gaze found her mouth, and he hated himself for wondering if she'd kissed her former beau the way she'd kissed him.

His gut burned. Getting out of town, if only for a day, would give him a chance to regain the right perspective. To dull the memories of their embrace and extinguish this relentless drive to be near her.

Alice indicated his plate. "Would you like seconds? You've a fair distance to travel today."

"No, thank you." Patting his stomach, he said, "It was delicious, though."

Finally tuning in to their conversation, Jessica's gaze skipped from her mother to him. "Travel? Where are you going?"

"I'm riding along with your cousins Caleb and Nathan. While they're getting the best price for the chestnuts, I'll be visiting Maryville's sheriff. Maybe talk to the local shopkeepers and see if I can get any leads."

Her fork hit the table with a thunk. "And what if someone recognizes you?"

"I can only pray that happens."

Her disquiet deepened. "What if it's someone who doesn't have your best interests at heart?"

Touched by her concern, Grant patted the weapon in his holster. "I'll have this handy."

Alice observed their interaction with motherly patience, as if they were squabbling kids. "Well, I think it's a good idea. And it's kind of Mr. Warring to give you the time off."

"He wasn't thrilled about it."

Grant had given his all to the job. While a tad mundane for his liking, it satisfied him by offering him a chance to earn a wage with honest labor. His initial earnings would go to Alice and Jessica to reimburse them for the many meals they'd fed him and the clothing they'd bought him. The rest he'd use to fund his new life, a fresh start in a city far from here.

He couldn't live in the same town as Jessica and not eventually give in to this unhealthy attachment he felt to her. That wouldn't be fair to her.

"He must be pleased with your work." Ambling out of the chair, Alice gathered her dishes. "Jessica, I'm going to prepare a quick snack for Grant to take with him. Then the kitchen will be all yours."

The floorboards creaked with her departure. Jessica sank against her chair back, her appetite apparently forgotten as she stared at her uneaten meal.

"What did she mean by that?"

Twisting her hair into a long coil, her gaze speared his for long moments before falling away. "I'm going to sell my desserts at the mercantile."

Surprise filtered through him. "When did you decide this?"

"Yesterday. Quinn and I ironed out the agreement. He's confident we'll both make money."

The fact that she hadn't shared her monumental news with him shouldn't hurt. *You can't play an essential role in her life. You made that clear, remember?*

"Congratulations." He drummed up a smile, truly happy for her. "I'm proud of you. It takes courage to pursue your dreams. I share your brother-in-law's opinion. People will vie for your desserts."

"When were you planning to tell me about this trip?"

"I bumped into Caleb in town Monday, and he mentioned they were going. I asked if I could tag along. I would've told you that night, but you haven't been around this week."

Looking chagrined, she said, "I'm always busy right before a community event."

He didn't buy the excuse. No point arguing the point, though. She was dealing with the repercussions of Sunday night's embrace in her own way.

"Right." Downing the last of his drink, he pushed away from the table. "Your cousins will be here shortly. I've got to get my things."

Ten minutes later, he left the cabin as Caleb and Nathan

arrived in separate conveyances. He helped them transfer the women's bushels into Nathan's wagon. He had one
foot on the wheel, about to haul himself up, when Jessica
hurried onto the porch.

"Grant." Jogging up to him, she thrust a cloth-wrapped
parcel into his hands. "I made molasses cookies yesterday
while you were at work. They're still fresh. I thought you
might like some to take with you."

From his perch high on his wagon parked behind theirs,
Caleb watched their exchange with a narrowed gaze. Nathan looked intrigued.

Grant's smile was strained. "Thanks, Jess. I'm sure
I'll enjoy them."

Worry shimmered in her luminous eyes, and the need
to soothe away those worries nearly overpowered him.

"You'll be careful?"

Finding her hand in the folds of her skirt, he gave it
a firm squeeze. "Of course. We'll be home late tomorrow night. Don't want to miss another week of church
services."

"Are you two done? Because I'd like to reach Maryville
before supper." Caleb scowled his displeasure.

Reluctantly, he hoisted himself onto the weathered seat
and tipped his hat. The fact that he hated to leave her,
even for a short trip, indicated serious problems ahead.
Because he wasn't sticking around forever.

Nathan waved to her and set the team in motion. He
didn't ask any questions as they left Gatlinburg behind.
After several side glances at the bundle in Grant's lap,
Grant offered him a cookie. Nathan grinned his thanks.

Grant centered the conversation on the man's wife and
the impending arrival of their twins. The middle O'Malley
brother was more reserved than the others, in possession
of a keen mind and steadfast demeanor. If Nathan was

anxious about becoming a first-time father, he didn't show it. The girl he'd married had grown up on a neighboring farm. They'd been friends since childhood, and he hadn't seen her as anything more until she nearly married someone else. Grant experienced a twinge of envy. Would he ever have a wife and family of his own? Or would he be relegated to a life of solitude, forever wondering, yearning for something he couldn't have?

He repeated the same prayer he'd uttered while waiting for sleep to claim him the night before. *Guide me on the right path, Lord. Lead me to people who can provide clues to my identity.* A verse from Psalms popped into his mind. *I will instruct you and teach you in the way you should go; I will counsel you with my loving eye on you.* God's promise brought comfort and confidence.

The conversation turned to neutral subjects. He could only be thankful he hadn't had to ride with Caleb. He wouldn't have hesitated to interrogate Grant.

The route was a scenic one and well-traveled. The sun was nearly kissing the horizon by the time they reached their destination. Maryville was a large, bustling city tucked amid rolling, green fields, the larger mountains they'd left behind giving way to foothills arrayed in their autumn glory. They would spend the night on the outskirts to save the cost of a hotel bill. When they had readied their camp and eaten the meal the women had sent along, Grant announced his intentions of going to see the sheriff.

Caleb pointed out a horse. "You're welcome to take that one."

"My legs are stiff from the long ride. I'll walk. Thanks anyway."

Nathan offered to tag along. "Jessica wouldn't be too happy with us if we let you get whacked on the head again."

"Or mugged and held at gunpoint." Using a wagon

wheel as a back rest, Caleb sat with one knee drawn up to his chest, his arm resting on it while he twiddled a blade of grass between his fingers. "What's with the hand-holding and the special treatment? You notice she only gave *you* cookies. You were supposed to be keeping your distance."

Nathan tossed another log on the fire. Sparks danced in the air. "How's he supposed to do that when they live under the same roof?"

"Maybe it's time you found other lodgings, seeing as how you have a steady income."

"Believe it or not, I've been giving the matter some thought."

Leaving the O'Malleys' home wasn't what he wanted. But he couldn't be dependent on their hospitality indefinitely.

"We'll be happy to ask around on your behalf."

Caleb's offer and accompanying smirk stayed with him during the short walk into town. While he respected the other men, their continued distrust rankled. He craved a good name and solid reputation. Without it, his intentions would constantly be evaluated, his character called into question, his actions judged.

Asking the first man he encountered for directions to the jail, he found it between a leather shop already closed for the day and a quiet café emitting the mouthwatering aroma of fried chicken.

The desk was vacant, the spacious, high-ceilinged room draped in shadows.

"Hello?"

Snoring came from one of the cells. Walking over, he saw that the sleeping stranger sprawled on the cot wore a sheriff's badge. All the other cells stood unused.

"Excuse me."

When there came no response, Grant entered and

cautiously nudged his shoulder. The sheriff fumbled into an upright position. His considerable paunch quivering, he ran a hand over thready patches of remaining gray hair. "Who are you?"

Grant stepped backward through the cell door, hands raised in a gesture of innocence. "The name's Grant Parker, and I'm in town with some acquaintances of mine from Gatlinburg. I was hoping to ask you some questions."

"Parker, eh?" Brushing past, the sheriff ambled to his desk and opened the top drawer. He slapped a piece of rumpled paper on the desk. "Got this letter from your sheriff a week or so ago. Kept meaning to write a response, but I've had my hands full with town business."

Grant had a feeling it was more a case of laziness. The man's office was as messy as his person. His too-tight shirt boasted stains on the front. And the stench of sweat had nearly overpowered him a moment ago.

"So you're familiar with my situation?"

Hefting up his waistband, the sheriff dropped into his chair and sighed. "I am. Afraid I can't help you. The only Parker I've come across was a young marshal who passed this way about a month ago. And you ain't him." He picked at his teeth with his fingernail. "I never forget a face."

Grant sat without permission into one of two chairs facing the desk, his spirits sagging. "He was a US marshal? Don't their badges look like silver stars?"

"Sure do."

"What was he doing in the area?" When the lawman frowned, Grant added, "If you don't mind my asking. I've had flashes of that badge. Maybe I knew him."

"He didn't have business here. Said he was on his way to Kentucky to set up court proceedings."

Grant's mind raced, frantic for a breakthrough.

A distinctive rumble filled the silence. "My nap ran

long, which means I missed supper." Standing, the sheriff fiddled with the keys dangling from his belt loop. "I've gotta hurry if I wanna make it to Millie's before closing time."

Grant followed the man out onto the street. "I'll be in town until tomorrow evening around this time if you think of anything else that might help."

"Sure, sure." He waved him off, his mind no doubt already on his upcoming meal.

Grant stared after the retreating figure, hands fisting into balls as disappointment collided with frustration. How come the one man with a promising clue turned out to be incompetent?

Grant woke the next morning with a pounding headache.

He'd lain on his pallet staring up at the stars for hours, reviewing the details of his dream and vision, desperate to remember.

The coffee tasted acrid on his tongue, the day-old biscuit nearly choking him. To Caleb's and Nathan's credit, they kept their distance. They'd ridden into town together and dropped him in front of the first hotel they came to. The plan was for him to meet them at the café beside the jail at six o'clock. They'd eat there before heading home.

Grant sized up the modest establishment. The exterior of the brick building was in good condition, the windows clean and shutters sporting fresh paint. Removing his hat, he fluffed his hair and strode inside, where he asked the attendant to direct him to the manager.

The manager's neat appearance and professional manner was a major improvement over the sheriff's. "Lawrence Fisher," he introduced himself as they shook hands. "What can I do for you?"

Grant explained what he was after, and the gentleman graciously agreed to check his ledger.

Grant examined the furnished lobby while he waited.

"Mr. Parker?"

The feminine voice behind him held a note of pleasant surprise. As he spun on his heel, spurts of adrenaline dumped into his system. The young woman wore a uniform of black and white, and her blond curls were partially hidden by a cap.

"Do you know me?" His fingers crushed his hat's crown.

She blinked up at him. "My apologies, sir. I thought you were someone else."

Grant edged closer. "Was this someone a US marshal? Can you give me his description?" The blood rushed through his ears. "Why would you mistake me for him? Do we favor each other?"

Apprehension gripped her rosy features, and she took a step back. "I—I have duties to attend to. Good day—"

"Wait—" He extended a hand.

Mr. Fisher appeared beside them. "Mr. Parker, why don't we go into the dining area. Rose, you will accompany us and answer the gentleman's questions."

Responding to her employer's unruffled manner, she calmed somewhat. "Yes, sir."

His headache blossoming to massive proportions, Grant tried to reclaim calm. His desperation had frightened the poor woman. If he wanted answers, he was going to have to lessen the intensity.

When they'd been seated at a table in the far corner of the spacious room, the manager informed him that a Mr. Aaron Parker had indeed stayed two nights there.

Aaron. The name struck Grant as familiar.

"Rose, what can you tell us about our guest?"

Her hands tightly woven together, she said, "Mr. Parker was very kind and friendly. I believe he was lonely. He said he traveled around the country a lot because of his profession."

Grant found his voice. "What did he look like?"

"Like you, actually. When I saw you from behind, I thought it was him. You have the same fair hair and skin color, but his eyes were green, not blue." She blushed and looked down at her lap. "And he was a few years younger."

"Do you think we look enough alike to be related?"

Her gaze lifted to his. "Yes, I do."

Aaron. The edges of his vision blurred. In his mind, he saw an office. A young man. Talking and gesturing. A silver star pinned to his shirt.

The room tilted. Grant slapped his palms flat on the table. He flashed hot. Then cold.

"Mr. Parker? Are you all right?" The manager's voice barely penetrated the dizziness.

"He's gone pale," Rose exclaimed. "Is he going to pass out?"

"Go and fetch some water," Fisher ordered.

"I'm okay," Grant muttered, embarrassed that he'd had an episode in front of strangers. "I had a memory. I think it was of him. Aaron Parker."

"Would you like a room to rest in, sir?"

"No." Rose brought the glass of water, hovering nearby while he sipped the cool liquid. "I'll be fine in a moment."

"Go ahead and return to your work, Rose."

"Yes, sir."

Obeying the manager at once, she rushed from the dining area. Grant watched her, wondering if she had more information that could aid his search. Fisher stood and, re-buttoning his suit coat, gave him a warm smile.

"You're welcome to sit here as long as you like, Mr.

Parker. Our kitchen staff is still preparing breakfast. Let any of them know if you'd like coffee or something to eat."

"Thank you, sir. I appreciate your help."

"I wish you luck in finding the answers you seek."

Grant stared out the window, his optimism tempered with the knowledge that he had no idea where to find Aaron. Kentucky was a vast state. And who knew if he was still there or had moved on.

He wished with everything in him that Jessica was here, the need to see her, talk to her, find solace in her embrace eclipsing all else.

Chapter Eighteen

"Here, kitty."

Clutching the ladder sides, Jessica beckoned the reclusive cat. The glow from the single lantern she'd brought in didn't extend to the hayloft. She knew Cinders was up here. She'd caught a glimpse of her tail as she navigated the ladder.

"I just want to pet you, silly thing."

And why, exactly, was she seeking out a feline who disdained her?

She told herself again that Grant was fine. Just because it was going on midnight didn't mean they'd encountered problems.

Glaring into the darkness, she spied a pair of glowing eyes. "I see you, you little minx. I don't think it's fair that you ignore the one who feeds you while lavishing all your attention on *him*."

"Who are you talking to?"

The unexpected response startled Jessica. She yelped. As she jerked, the sole of her boot slipped from the rung.

A pair of strong, male hands settled on either side of her waist. Warmth spread outward from his touch, heating her skin through the fabric. "Sorry. Didn't mean to frighten you."

"Grant."

He assisted her to the ground, then sank his hands in his pockets, his lopsided smile making up for every second of worry.

"I didn't hear the team in the yard."

His intent gaze swept the loose waves tumbling about her shoulders. "I had Nathan drop me off at the end of the lane."

She belatedly noticed his borrowed travel bag sitting just inside the open door. His stubble was close to becoming a full beard, his shirt wrinkled from being stuffed in the bag. Dirt clung to his boots. He looked adorably rumpled. To keep from launching herself into his arms, Jessica finger-combed her hair with long, thorough strokes.

"So who were you addressing up there?" He jerked his chin toward the loft.

Craning her neck, she spied a furry face peering at them. "That turncoat right there."

He chuckled as Cinders leaped onto the floor using a series of landings, then trotted over to wind herself around his legs. Her purring sounded like a rusty saw cutting through wood.

"Can I help it if she likes me?" Scooping her up, he scratched her between the ears and promptly sneezed.

Jessica shook her head. Going closer, she ran her hand along the cat's spine. Their hands overlapped. His smile faded. His gaze, fathomless like the ocean deep, searched hers. For what, she didn't know.

Dropping her hand, she cleared her throat. "How did it go? Did my cousins pester you to the edge of reason?"

His smirk was all the answer she required.

"That was a silly question." She sighed. "I know them

well enough to know that Nathan probably remained objective, while Caleb subjected you to the overprotective cousin routine."

"Something like that."

He grew serious then. Lowering Cinders to the floor, he took off his hat and paced to a hay square shoved against the wall, nudging it with the toe of his boot. Something was on his mind. Something big.

Her tummy flip-flopped. "Please tell me you didn't come to blows."

Caleb could be overbearing and irritating at times, but surely he wouldn't have let things go that far.

"No. Nothing like that."

She let out a long breath. "Did you find a clue to your identity?"

She waited, muscles tense as she braced herself for bad news.

"Apparently a US marshal traveled through Maryville not long ago who could pass for my brother."

Shock shimmered through her. "You're serious."

"His name is Aaron Parker."

"You know this how?"

Continuing to pace, he told her about the unhelpful sheriff, the accommodating hotel manager and the young staff member who'd mistaken him for Aaron.

"Grant, this is wonderful news!" She held her arms out at her sides. "Why don't you look happy?"

"I'm cautiously happy. It's the breakthrough I've been praying for." Shoving his fingers in his hair, he said, "But how am I to locate him? All I know is that he was on his way to Kentucky. Shane can't post letters to each and every lawman in the state. It will take considerable time to save enough money to hire a private investigator."

"You could write the Marshals' headquarters. Aren't they in Arlington, Virginia?"

"You're right. I could."

"But?"

His features were stamped with unease. "What if my resemblance to him is simply a fluke? We're going on the opinion of one young woman who I suspect was smitten with the man. What if I was operating on the wrong side of the law? Who's to say I didn't ambush him? He could've fought back and escaped. That could be his travel bag you found. His Bible."

Jessica threaded her fingers through his, intent on making him see reason. "That is a possibility, albeit an unlikely one. The logical route north would be through Knoxville. He wouldn't have traveled this direction."

"Maybe he had friends in this area."

"Aaron was working. According to the sheriff, he was due in Kentucky to set up court proceedings. Do you think a marshal would disregard his duties to the federal government for an out-of-the-way stopover with friends?"

Hanging his head, Grant pinched the bridge of his nose. "I don't know."

"Let's go with the improbable theory that you attacked him." Still holding his hand, she trailed her other fingers up and down his forearm, the fine hairs soft and springy. His muscles twitched. "Why would he disappear? We searched the woods and found no one. He would've gone straight to the local authorities and reported you."

"There's something else."

"What?"

Slowly, deliberately, he described his most recent vision. "I can't shake the feeling that I knew him, Jess."

"You could be his friend. Or a relative."

"Or his prisoner."

Jessica rejected that notion. It was too terrible to consider. "What are you going to do?"

His gaze flooding with tenderness, he smoothed her hair over her shoulder. "Right now, I'm going to escort my beautiful hostess to the house so she can get some rest."

"What about you?"

"I'm going to clean up and then head to bed myself. We've got church in the morning."

"That we do."

At the door, she stopped abruptly.

"Did you forget something?" he asked.

In fact, she had. It was the first time in over a year that she'd been inside the barn and hadn't once thought about Lee.

"Glad to see you're feeling better, young man." The reverend stood on the church's porch, shaking hands with the parishioners as they filed out. He resembled a penguin in his black suit and snowy-white shirt.

"Thank you, sir."

He gave Jessica's hand a fatherly pat. "I heard you're embarking on a new business venture. Carole and I are anxious for one of your apple spice cakes. It's been a long time."

He wasn't the first person to express his excitement. However, unlike the others, he hadn't vented confusion and irritation with the reclusive café owner.

"In that case, I'll be sure to put it at the top of my list."

A stiff breeze whipped through the yard, and she put a hand to her hat's crown to keep it in place. The sun was nowhere in sight. Thick clouds stretched across the sky like a woolen blanket.

Her smile might've fooled the reverend, but not Grant. The strain of the attention they'd received throughout the morning services was wearing on her. Until today, he hadn't given much thought to how her association with him might possibly sully her reputation. She'd weathered a major scandal once already. He didn't plan to be the cause of another.

He didn't want to cause her pain. Jessica deserved to be loved and cherished by an upstanding man in the community. Someone respected and above reproach.

That wasn't him.

If he truly cared for her, he'd distance himself.

His chest spasmed painfully in rejection of that notion. *Don't be selfish, Parker. You may not have control over a lot of things, but you can control your actions.* He remembered the kiss, aware that in that moment, he hadn't been considering what was best for her.

As they descended the steep steps, he steadied her with a hand on her elbow. Any man should be proud to be by her side. Her outward attractiveness aside, she was courageous and spirited, tenderhearted and loving. Life with Jessica would never be boring.

Grant noticed a pair of men glaring daggers at him in the shade of a maple tree. He recognized them from that day outside the mercantile. "Your friends don't look happy to see you with me. I can walk on ahead if you'd like to visit with them."

She noted their presence and frowned. "No, that's all right. I shouldn't linger. Ma's worried about the pot roast drying out."

With a brief wave, she continued past, her rust-colored dress rippling with each long stride. The color put him in mind of a copper penny.

"I've been meaning to tell you something," he said.

Boots thudding on the boardwalk, they passed businesses closed for the day.

"While on our trip, your cousins and I discussed my current living arrangements. I think it's best if I find other temporary lodgings."

Her chin jutted and lightning flashed in her stormy eyes. "Caleb insinuated you're a burden to us, didn't he?"

"He brought up a valid point. My injuries have almost completely healed, and I'm able to work on a consistent basis. Staying on with you and Alice will only serve to stir up gossip. I don't want that for you."

"You can't stop it. Folks will talk no matter what we do."

"I thought you'd be throwing a party," he teased, lightly bumping her shoulder. While unhappy, he wasn't about to show it.

Turning her face away, she studied the river. "I won't miss the extra laundry. Or your derogatory comments about my food preferences."

"And I won't have to watch you eat what any sane person would consider disgusting."

They came to the bridge. "Do you have any prospects?"

"Your cousins are looking into it."

"Cinders will miss you. You should take her with you."

"I'd like that, but it's hardly practical. We don't know if I'll be leaving Gatlinburg a free man or heading off to prison somewhere."

Jessica abruptly rounded on him. "You know, when I first met you, I got the sense you were an optimist."

He stopped. "I'm a realist. There are two possible outcomes. Either I'm on the right side of the law, or I'm not."

"You know, it's a good thing you're moving out. Some space will do us good."

Whirling away, she marched away from him. He quickly caught up to her. Snagging her arm, he forced her to slow down. "Not so long ago, *you* were the one with the wild theories about my true identity."

"I didn't know you then," she retorted, wriggling free.

"Jess, why are you upset?"

"Why? Maybe because I can't stand the thought of you turning out to be just another criminal like Lee. Maybe because I know how devastated you'll be if you do." Tears glistened in her eyes but didn't fall. "I once told you that you didn't matter. That was a lie. You're important to me, and that scares me."

Grant closed his eyes and, sucking in a fortifying breath, asked God for wisdom.

"Jessica, you and I...we can't be together."

"You think I don't know that?" she demanded. "After Lee, I promised myself that I wouldn't take foolish risks with my heart. You, Grant Parker, are the biggest risk of all. I said you're important to me. It wasn't a confession of love."

He felt ridiculous and annoyed. Ridiculous, because he'd made the wrong assumption. Annoyed, because she'd so cavalierly declared she wasn't in love with him. He was tempted to howl in frustration.

What was wrong with him? *Of course* she shouldn't have romantic feelings for him. He was all wrong for her.

It bothers you that she loved Lee, though, doesn't it?

And the memory of their kiss would always stick with him. Even now, he could imagine hauling her into his arms and repeating what they'd done on her porch, despite the fact it was broad daylight and anyone could pass by at any moment.

"I apologize," he said stiffly. "I shouldn't have leaped to such an unlikely conclusion. I appreciate your concern. And I agree with you on one point. A little distance would do us good."

Chapter Nineteen

❦

"Can you believe the nerve of that man?" Jessica marched along the creek's edge. "To presume that I'm in love with him... What arrogance!"

Jane relaxed on the quilt they'd spread out across the grass, the smooth tree trunk providing support for her back. Tom's fishing pole bobbed in the slow-moving water. Normally Jessica was disposed to adore her brother-in-law, but today his grin infuriated her.

"Surely he didn't arrive at that conclusion for no reason." Jane rubbed a spot low on her stomach. Having freed her hair from its sophisticated twist after arriving home from church, she'd draped a crocheted shawl around her shoulders, the pastel pinks, yellows and greens a riot of color atop her plain white dress.

Jessica stopped her constant motion to study her twin. While radiant with her increasing pregnancy, she bore obvious signs of fatigue. The delicate skin beneath her eyes appeared bruised. Strain bracketed her drooping mouth.

Sitting cross-legged on the quilt's corner edge, Clara ceased playing with her dolls and gazed up at Jessica. "Are you getting married, Auntie?"

"No. Probably not ever," she muttered.

"You don't mean that," Jane said.

Setting aside her ire—and underlying hurt caused by Grant's casual, firm dismissal of any possibility of a relationship with her—she knelt before Jane, balancing herself with her fingers splayed in the short grass.

"How are you feeling?"

Out of her peripheral vision, she saw Tom lay his pole on the rocks and get to his feet.

Jane gave her a wan smile. "Tired. Achy. Ready to meet this baby."

When Tom stood over them, concern wreathing his features, she laughed softly. "You're both hovering like I'm about to go into labor any minute. We have three weeks to go."

"Sometimes babies come early." Kneeling on her other side, Tom gingerly smoothed the hair from her forehead, his gold wedding band vivid in the overcast gray day. Then he bent to drop a kiss on her stomach. "Be a good girl," he murmured, smoothing the white fabric, "and let your ma get some rest."

Her throat suddenly thick with confusing emotion, Jessica stood and transferred her attention to the clearing where Tom and Jane's small cabin stood surrounded by towering trees. They didn't have much in the way of material possessions, but they were rich in ways that couldn't be measured.

"It could be a boy, you know." Jane's voice deepened with playful affection.

"Clara has made her wishes plain. She would like a sister to play with," he pointed out. "Isn't that right, my little bird?"

"Right!"

Jessica tuned out their conversation. Her sister had been blessed with a loving, attentive husband, a man she'd secretly loved for years before he'd finally noticed her. They were building a fine life together. *A life you'd like to mirror. With Grant.*

Her heart stuttered in her chest.

Don't torture yourself.

"Clara—" Jessica forced herself back to the present "—why don't you and I clean up this mess and afterward I'll read you a book?"

"Do I have to take a nap?"

"I'm afraid so." Stacking the food containers in the basket, she said, "But if we get this cleaned up quickly, I can read you two books."

Popping up, Clara eagerly pitched in to help.

"You don't have to do that," Jane inserted.

"You could use the rest."

"Jess."

"What?" She paused to stare at Jane.

"Someday God will bring the man He's chosen for you into your life. You'll know when it's right."

She bent her head to evade her twin's perceptive gaze. Caring about Grant felt right, but the circumstances were all wrong.

After cleaning up the lunch dishes, reading not two but three books and singing a handful of silly songs before Clara drifted off to sleep, Jessica headed home. She was ready for a nap herself. How Jane was able to manage the needs and wants of a small child, in addition to the farm's everyday demands, she had no idea.

The sight of her aunt and uncle's wagon in the yard was not an unwelcome one. However, she'd been planning to escape to her room for the remainder of the afternoon. No chance of that now.

The assembled group turned to regard her as she untied

her hat ribbons and set it on the hutch. "Ah, there you are," Alice greeted her with a smile. "How is Jane today? I didn't have a chance to speak with her after services."

"As well as can be expected."

Jessica came to stand beside the chair her uncle Sam occupied. Aunt Mary sat alone on the couch. Grant leaned against the mantel, a coffee mug in his hand.

He looked strange. Not angry, exactly. Or upset.

Resigned. That's the word.

"What's going on?"

"Jessica," her mother admonished, teacup rattling in its saucer as she shifted on the cushion.

Mary patted the empty space beside her. "Come sit. We have good news."

Holding in a sigh, she complied, willing her gaze not to stray to Grant. She pinned a bright smile to her face. "Tell me."

"Caleb and Nathan came to us with Grant's dilemma. As you know, we have several rooms that aren't being used. We offered Grant one of them, and he's accepted." Mary beamed.

A born nurturer, Mary had already taken in Caleb's adolescent sister-in-law, Amy. Adding a stranger with a murky past wouldn't faze her.

"I see." Jessica quieted the protest brewing inside. "And Caleb's okay with the arrangement?"

"He's the one who suggested it," Sam said between bites.

Not for Grant's benefit, she was certain. Her cousin would've moved him into his own cabin if it meant getting him away from her.

Deliberately searching out Grant's gaze, which was un-readable, she said, "You'll be in good hands. My mother and aunt learned to cook from my grandmother. Their skills in the kitchen are evenly matched."

His mood somber, he looked from Sam, who was quietly eating his cobbler, to Mary. "I appreciate your willingness to take me in. I'll be paying for room and board, as well as pitching in with daily chores."

"You don't have to pay us."

His jaw set in stubborn lines. "I insist. I don't know for how long I'll be staying. Could be weeks. Maybe months. If at any time you decide our arrangement isn't working, let me know and I'll move on."

Mary scoffed at that suggestion. "You're welcome to stay for as long as you'd like."

"If we must lose you, at least you'll be with family." Alice's tone held a hint of sadness, and Jessica realized her mother had grown attached to Grant, too.

"I'll never forget your kindness." Frowning, he drained his cup of its contents. To Mary, he said, "If it's all right with you, I'll stay this last night here. It'll give me time to get my things together and clean up the room."

"Certainly. You can come tomorrow after work. I'll have supper on the table."

Sam finished off his dessert and stood. "It's settled, then. You'll move in tomorrow."

Hands woven tightly in her lap, Jessica fixed her attention on the floor. Her insides churned. Amid the goodbyes, she escaped to her room and shut everyone out, reminding herself that this was what she'd wanted all along.

At the livery the following morning, Grant's attempts to banish Jessica from his thoughts failed. He'd anticipated spending his last evening in Jessica's home conversing with her, playing their instruments or relaxing on the porch and stargazing. She'd made it clear, however, that she wished to be left alone. So he'd filled the hours with chores. After assembling his meager belongings, he'd stripped the bed and replaced the soiled quilt with a fresh one. He'd swept and mopped the floor. Then he'd gone to the barn and mucked out the stables until his muscles burned and his back ached. Unlike Jessica, his feline friend had craved his company, curling up on a hay square to watch him work. The hopeful part of him had thought Jessica might join him at some point. Around eleven, he'd heard a footstep, but it was Alice bidding him good-night.

"Parker, we got a customer." His boss's statement brought him back to the present.

Looping a bridle over a peg in the tack room, he went to greet the gentleman and handle the transaction. Warring continued to oversee the money exchanges. He didn't trust Grant not to pocket some of the coin. He did trust Grant's capability with the horses. Being around the magnificent animals felt as natural as breathing. They didn't intimidate him. He'd calmed more than one ornery beast with soothing words and a firm hand. And while he enjoyed the work and being outdoors, he yearned for something more challenging. Less repetitive.

Once he had their newest boarder brushed down, watered and fed, he scrubbed the soap sliver over his hands at the wash barrel and bid his boss good evening.

He strolled along Main Street, nodding at those who acknowledged him in passing. Folks were starting to tolerate his presence. Acceptance from an established, respected family like the O'Malleys went a long way in convincing others of his decency. His work at the livery brought him into regular contact with the townsfolk. He wasn't so much of a mystery anymore.

Nearing the mercantile, he slowed to study a handwritten sign taped to the window glass. He smiled as he read the words advertising Jessica's desserts. He was proud of her for pursuing her dreams. She possessed the talent and work ethic necessary for success.

The bell jingled. A woman emerged onto the boardwalk, her profile hidden by her hat. A bouncy red ponytail trailed between her shoulder blades.

Head bent, she was tucking something into her reticule and didn't notice him.

He gave her hair a playful tug. "Raking in the profits already?"

"Grant." Sidling away from him, she looked at him, her widened gaze raking his dusty clothing. "I thought you finished at five."

"We had a late customer." He gestured in the direction of the barbershop, the last business on this side of the street. "You going home? I can accompany you. I have to pick up my things before heading to your aunt's."

She hesitated. "I've concluded my errands."

Grant got the distinct feeling she didn't want him around. After last night, how could he doubt it? Had she deliberately come to town at this time in the hope of avoiding him?

"You know what? I forgot something at the livery." Jerking his thumb over his shoulder, he made to leave. "I'll see you around."

"Grant—"

Whatever she'd been about to say was lost amid the thundering of horse hooves rounding the corner. They recognized Tom simultaneously. Moving into the street, Jessica waved her hand in the air.

He pulled up sharply on the reins, flecks of dirt spraying her skirts as the horse pranced sideways. "Jane's water broke. She's having regular pains." Worry stamped his features. "I've come to fetch Doc."

Grant joined them. Jessica's freckles stood out in stark contrast to her milk-white complexion. "Where's Clara?"

"I dropped her at your ma's. Could you stay with her so Alice can be with Jane?"

"Of course."

With a jerky nod of thanks, Tom prodded his mount's flank and continued on to the doctor's home.

Grant resisted the urge to hug her. Lower lip caught in her teeth, she looked torn.

"I can watch Clara if you'd like to go with your ma."

Her green eyes flicked to his. "That's kind of you to offer, but she doesn't know you. She may be frightened or upset. A familiar face will help keep her mind off things."

She started in the opposite direction Tom had taken, her skirts rippling with each long stride, the flowers on her hat quivering. He kept pace with her, determined to help whether she wanted it or not. He couldn't leave her alone. Not when she was consumed with worry.

"I didn't realize Jane's baby was due already."

"It's not. Not for another three weeks."

They crossed the bridge and entered the shaded lane. "She's healthy and strong," Jessica broke the silence. "Until now, her pregnancy has proceeded normally. She was so tired yesterday. I wonder if she has overdone it."

Hearing the tremor in her voice, he sought to dispel her apprehension. "Would her husband have allowed that? Is he the oblivious type or one to notice details?"

"Tom's attentive to my sister's needs. With this being their first, he's been vigilant to make sure she's been eating enough and getting the proper rest."

"What about Clara? Does he help with her?"

"Oh, yes." A small smile eased her features. "Clara's mother died when she was only two. Her father, Tom's brother, sought solace in the bottle, leaving Tom to care for her. He's been her primary caretaker for years. He oversees bedtime and pitches in with the meals when he's not out in the fields. He's a good father."

"Sounds like your sister made a good match."

"She did." Her countenance darkened again as she became lost in thought.

Searching for a distraction, he asked her to tell him the story of how Jane and Tom got together. She launched into the surprising tale. The lengthy account served to pass the minutes until they reached the cabin.

They found Alice and the little girl at the kitchen table. The smell of chicken and dumplings warmed the cozy space, and his mouth watered. Cathead biscuits, green beans sprinkled with bacon crumbles and corn on the cob rounded out the meal.

Jessica bent to give Clara a hug. "Clara, this is my friend Grant Parker. You met him at church. Can you say hello?"

With springy brown curls, big green eyes and a rosebud mouth, she looked like a doll he'd seen in the mercantile.

She eyed him with curiosity, but her manner was subdued. "Hello."

Removing his hat, he hooked it on the chair back. "Pleased to meet you, Clara."

Turning her attention to her plate, she picked at her food. Jessica tugged her own hat off and smoothed her hair. "We ran into Tom in town. He told us everything. I'm going to stay here while you go to Jane, Ma."

"Are you sure?"

"I'm going to stay with them." Grant helped himself to the coffee on the stove. "Want some?" he asked Jessica.

She shook her head. "You don't have to stay."

"I want to."

"My aunt's expecting you."

Alice abandoned her half-eaten meal. "I can swing by Mary's and tell them what's happening. That way they won't worry. Besides, Jane and the baby need all the prayers they can get."

"They have ours," Grant said.

Gratitude shone on Jessica's face.

She may not like to admit it, but she needed support. And he was the only one around right now to give it to her. After all she'd done for him, keeping her and the child company was the least he could do.

Chapter Twenty

A tear trickled down Clara's cheek. "Is Mama going to be all right?"

Jessica knelt beside her chair. "God's watching over her and the baby. Did you know He loves your mama more than we do?"

Her wispy brows crinkling, she shook her head.

"He does. And He has a plan for each and every one of us."

Grant sat opposite Clara, and his expression turned thoughtful. Jessica somehow knew he was reflecting on his own life and wondering what God's plan was for him. If God hadn't led him to her door, how would that have affected her? Would she still be mired in her old mistakes?

"I'm glad my plan is here. Papa—I mean Uncle Tom, not my other pa—was sad in Kansas. Now he's happy. He smiles and laughs every day. Sometimes he sings, but he sounds like a sick cow." She scrunched up her nose.

Jessica smiled. Tom and Jane had let Clara choose what she'd like to call them. In the beginning, she'd stuck with Jane and Uncle Tom. And now more and more she referred to them as her parents.

"I don't believe I've heard him sing," Jessica said.

"You don't want to."

His head bent over his plate, Grant choked out a laugh.

"I wonder if the baby will like his singing." Clara's tiny mouth puckered.

Jessica exchanged a wary look with Grant. He put his fork down. "I have an idea. How would you like to search for treasure?"

"Treasure?"

"Sure. With all the creeks and streams running through these mountains, you never know what you might find. There could be gold."

"Truly?"

"Or silver."

Clara's eyes grew round.

Gaining his feet, he started opening cabinet doors and peeking in the pie safe.

"What are you doing?" Legs cramping, Jessica straightened to her full height.

"Looking for this." With a triumphant grin, he waved a metal colander in the air. He then snagged a shallow pie pan. "Here, hold these." He thrust them at her. Retrieving a stack of clean towels, he covered the leftover food. "We can deal with this mess later. Let's go."

As the three of them marched across the yard and into the forest, Jessica marveled at his gift of distraction. He'd done it with her on the trip from town. His charm in full-on mode, he was chatting up her niece as if they were long-term friends. For certain Clara was no longer dwelling on Jane and her ordeal.

His knowledge of the plants and insects they encountered astounded her. How did he know these things? Livery work wouldn't satisfy him for long. Not with his keen intelligence and appreciation for nature. In the great outdoors, he was in his element. She fancied him as some sort of government explorer, like Meriwether Lewis or William Clark. Or a journalist set with the task of reporting on the West.

Jessica perched on a rock and observed the pair. Hunkered side by side in the water, unheeding of the water seeping into their shoes, they scooped handfuls of pebbles and silt and dumped them in the colander.

"Oh! Look at this one," Clara exclaimed, lifting a tiny rock for Grant to see. "It has gold flecks."

He smiled warmly at her. "I'm not sure that's real gold, but it's very pretty."

"Can I keep it?"

"I don't see why not."

Jessica's heart melted like warm chocolate. He would make a wonderful father someday. Caleb's earlier accusation spoiled her contentment. She stared at Grant's profile. What if he already had a child?

A stiff breeze barreled through the understory, rattling fallen leaves, the treetops gently swaying. She shuddered. Grant shrugged out of his new lightweight jacket and, splashing through the shallow water, approached her and draped it about her shoulders. His residual body heat chased away the chill. She inhaled his distinctive scent clinging to the material.

As he tugged the lapels close, she looked into his face. "Won't you be cold?"

"Nah." He grinned, spun on his heel and returned to Clara's side.

The sweet gesture made her heart sing.

Unbidden, a memory of Lee resurfaced. They'd been on one of their many picnics. A fly had landed on her pie and, revolted, she'd pushed it away. Lee continued to eat his portion without offering her a single bite, then proceeded to eat hers, commenting on her weak constitution. *It won't kill you*, he'd said.

Grant was the type of man who'd share his pie. He was the type of man who'd give her his coat without thought to his own discomfort. He was the type of man who'd treat her with respect and not do anything to tarnish her reputation.

In Grant's embrace, Jessica had felt utterly safe. She'd known, deep in her soul, that he would never press her to do anything inappropriate. There was a line he wouldn't cross. Grant Parker was a gentleman who lived by a code of honor.

Lee hadn't been as careful. Around him, she'd had to keep up her guard, not entirely certain that her virtue was his top priority. And while she'd enjoyed his displays of affection, they hadn't moved her to an emotional place like Grant's.

Touching her cool fingers to her lips, she recalled Grant's tenderness, the slight tremor in his hands as he'd cupped her face. And shocked herself by wishing his was the only kiss she'd ever experienced.

This isn't love, she reassured herself. *It's friendship and affection. Yes, looking at him is like looking at a spectacular autumn sunset. Being near him brings the same satisfaction as a perfectly crafted confection. And despite all the unknowns, I'd trust him with my life. But that's not love, necessarily.*

She'd loved Lee, and her feelings for him were different than what she was experiencing now.

"I have to talk to Jane," she whispered. She'd know what Jessica's feelings meant.

"Did you say something?" Grant tipped the brim of his hat up.

"Nothing important." Cheeks burning, she was grateful he couldn't read her thoughts.

Her peace of mind would have to wait. Jane had a baby to bring into this world. A brand-new life to nurture and care for.

Hunkering into his jacket, Jessica prayed for Jane, Tom and the baby. She prayed for Grant, as well. *God, for so long, I've demanded answers from You. I needed to know why You allowed certain things to happen. But I made a choice to place my future in Lee's hands without seeking Your will first. Because he attended Sunday services faithfully, I assumed he followed Christ's teachings in his daily life. I ignored my family's warnings. I didn't seek Your guidance, stubbornly pursuing my wants and desires. And yet, in all my stubbornness, You protected me. You kept me safe. I don't need answers anymore. But Grant does. He won't ever experience true peace until he finds out who and what he used to be. He can't move forward without the truth. Please help him.*

Clara yawned widely. Grant noticed and tilted his head back to study the sky. "We're going to have to continue our treasure hunt another time."

Her lower lip protruded. "But I haven't found any gold."

He locked gazes with Jessica. "This stream isn't going anywhere, and your aunt and I have dishes to wash. Not only that, but I bet Sadie is impatient to be milked." Cocking his head, he studied Clara. "Are you a good drawer?"

She nodded.

"Why don't you draw a picture for your ma and pa while we tend chores?"

Rolling a pebble between her first finger and thumb, she considered his suggestion. "I could draw a picture of the woods and the stream."

"That's a fine idea."

With that settled, they gathered their things and began the trek home. Jessica tried to return his jacket, but he wouldn't hear of it. He hurried to do the milking while she took Clara inside and located paper and pencils for her. She'd gotten the leftovers into the icebox and was grating soap into the water basin when Grant brought in the milk and, after complimenting Clara's progress, joined Jessica at the counter to dry and put up the dishes.

At half past nine, it was clear her niece was ready for bed. Jessica located an old chemise for her to wear. Washing away the grime from the child's face and gingerly combing the tangles from her curls, she put her in Jane's bed.

"Are you going to read me a story?" Her lids drooped as another yawn overtook her.

Jessica tucked the blankets around her small form and sat on the edge of the bed. "Not tonight. You're tuckered out, as am I."

Clara's gaze shifted beyond Jessica's shoulder. "Do you like my picture?"

Angling slightly, Jessica saw Grant propped against the door frame. Having him here tonight had been a blessing. He'd kept them both too busy to dwell on what was happening just across town.

"I do," he said. "I'm sure your ma will like it."

"Can we pray for the baby?" she asked Jessica.

"Of course, sweetheart."

Clara held out a hand to Grant. "Are you going to pray, too?"

Entering the room, he stopped directly behind Jessica. Clara's pudgy hand looked tiny in his large, tanned one. His heat radiated outward, warming her back like the gentle sweep of sunlight on a brisk day.

"You and Auntie have to hold hands, too."

A chuckle rumbled in his chest. Prickles of awareness fanned across her exposed nape.

"I don't think that's possible from where I'm standing."

Clara considered this. "You can put your hand on her shoulder." She patted her own to show him. "That's what my pa does to Mama."

He was quiet a minute. Then Jessica felt his fingers settle on the curve between her neck and shoulder. She held her breath. His touch was firm and familiar. Beneath her ponytail, his thumb scraped over the top of her spine. Fireworks went off in her midsection, a not unpleasant feeling.

As they took turns asking God to protect and watch over their loved ones, Jessica experienced a strange longing. *So this is what it feels like to have a family of one's own. Working together toward a mutual goal, supporting each other, loving each other.*

What you feel for Grant isn't love, remember?

Afterward, Grant led the way to the living room. Too aware of him in the quiet house, she kept the sofa between them. "Please give my aunt my regards."

Shooting her a knowing look, he lifted his hat from its peg. "I'm not leaving, Jess."

"We'll be fine."

"I don't feel right leaving you. I will be sleeping in the hayloft, though. Do you have old bedding you can spare?"

She waved a hand over the furniture. "If you're determined to stay, you're welcome to the sofa. It's not like we're alone here."

"I don't want to give anyone an opportunity to cast doubt on your reputation."

His response was so different than what Lee's would've been. He would've jumped at the chance. Not only had Lee sought his own comfort, he would've grasped the excuse to be close to her without other adults around.

"Thank you."

"For?"

"For keeping us company tonight." For being you.

"I'd do just about anything for you, Jessica."

Unable to endure the emotions shimmering in his blue eyes, she looked away. This wasn't supposed to happen. She wasn't supposed to care this much.

He wasn't sticking around. She was afraid to consider how much it would hurt when he left.

Jessica balanced the miniature bundle along her forearm. "She's perfect in every way." Testing the downy silkiness of her new niece's thin cap of dark hair, she smiled. "I'm smitten."

From his spot on the sofa, Tom placed a finger on the storybook's page to hold his place. "We would never have guessed. You've only visited every day this week."

"Can you blame me?"

Tom and Jane shared an amused glance. Clara tapped his chin and asked for him to continue the story. Seated in the rocking chair Tom had surprised her with a day or so ago, Jane appeared content to relax and watch her family. She'd had a normal delivery and was basking in the happiness of motherhood. Family and friends had inundated the couple with meals, baked goods and homemade gifts for the baby.

"You've been here more often than Ma," Jane remarked good-naturedly.

Jessica had been walking the baby around the cabin. She stopped beside Jane's chair. Joy's lids fluttered. Her tiny body squirmed. Gently swaying, Jessica patted her back through the blankets, and she settled into sleep once more.

"Fine. I won't come tomorrow." She studied the dainty mouth, the fine outline of eyebrows. "Maybe."

Jane's gaze turned serious. Pitching her voice low, she said, "Is there another reason you're wanting to get out of the house?"

Her stomach dipped. "No."

"You're lying."

Jessica rolled her eyes.

"You forget I know the signs. Your voice does this funny dip when you're not being truthful." She waggled her finger. "Why hasn't Grant come to visit? I wanted to thank him for helping with Clara."

"He's been working during the day. Not sure what he does with his evenings."

"She's talked almost nonstop about their treasure hunt I think she fancies him. I think she's not the only one."

"Maybe more than fancy," she confessed on a whim.

Worry clouded Jane's eyes. Folding her arms across her chest, she audibly exhaled. "Do you trust him?"

She stopped swaying at the unexpected question. "Yes."

"And you believe him to be worthy of your feelings?"

"I do."

"Does he have feelings for you?"

"If he does, he hasn't voiced them."

One kiss didn't amount to love. But he liked her. She knew he did. Whether or not it was more, she couldn't be certain.

A frown hovered about Jane's mouth. "Then I pray nothing from his past causes you pain or regret."

Bending slightly, Jessica placed Joy in her mother's arms. Suddenly cold, she chafed her arms in an effort to warm herself. The meager flames in the fireplace did little to chase away her chill. Every time she recalled their kiss, every time she allowed herself to wonder what a lifetime with Grant might be like, she pictured a faceless woman somewhere in their vast country who'd be crushed by his connection with her. The thought of Grant belonging to someone else filled Jessica with a sick sort of dread. It made her want to curl up in a lonely meadow somewhere and cry until there were no more tears left.

Pressing her hand to her forehead, she shut her eyes tight.

I love him.

"Do you have a headache?" Jane's soft query pierced her misery.

"No. I'm, uh, just tired."

"Your voice is doing that dipping thing again."

Straightening her shoulders, she bussed her twin's cheek and strode for the coat stand. She wrapped her shawl about her shoulders and wished for Grant's jacket suffused with his heat and scent.

"It's getting late. I'm going to head home and work on the baby blanket I didn't get to finish, since Joy decided to make an early appearance."

"Good night, Jess." Tom studied her thoughtfully. "See you tomorrow."

"Maybe."

She bid Clara good-night before slipping out the door into the chilly October evening. Far above, a fingernail moon floated in the blackness. Pinpricks of light winked like faraway candles.

Jane had been right. Doting on Joy hadn't been her only reason for spending so much time away. She hadn't seen Grant in four days, and she found she couldn't handle the sad emptiness cloaking the cabin. Funny, in the beginning, she couldn't have imagined feeling this way. She'd been desperate to be rid of him then.

In spite of all her hard-won lessons, contrary to her

best intentions, she'd lost her heart to a stranger. The best and worst man she could've chosen. Grant Parker wasn't hers to love.

Chapter Twenty-One

Sitting in another borrowed room, on another bed that wasn't his own, Grant ran his fingers over the Bible's thin parchment. What was the illegible first name? Gregory? George? Gustave? Nothing sounded right. He'd gotten used to being called Grant.

Of course, this might not even be his. It could belong to the real Parker. The US marshal he couldn't stop thinking about. He'd recalled something from his childhood, a memory of himself playing with another boy, one with blond hair like his own. They'd been climbing trees. Laughing. Lobbing acorns at squirrels. Grant wondered if this boy was the same man in his other memory. The man wearing the silver star badge.

He'd been tempted to ride over to Jessica's right away and share this new revelation with her. He'd resisted. As much as he ached to see her, severing the unexpected bond between them was the wisest course of action. He was trouble. A hidden bomb that could explode at any time, scattering destruction in his wake.

Closing the heavy book, he left it on the bedside stand and crossed to the window. Situated on the upper level, this room had an unobstructed view of the O'Malleys' farm and the lane that led to town. A sizable garden stretched in long, even rows in the clearing. Bright orange pumpkins and assorted squash were nestled in the dirt. To his right, a massive barn was flanked by toolsheds and other outbuildings. One of those buildings housed Josh's furniture workshop. The pieces he built here were transported into town for display in his store. Josh and his wife, Kate, along with their children, lived behind this main house in a home of their own.

His gaze searched the tree line where the forest took over, snagging on the one-story cabin tucked beneath the branches of an ancient oak. Caleb's cabin. He lived there with his wife, Rebecca, and their young sons.

Surrounded by all these couples and their offspring, he couldn't help but think of Jessica. Alone. Unwed. Did she feel left out? Awkward about her single state? He hadn't heard anyone tease her about it, and he hoped he never did.

He'd stayed away from Jane and Tom's, even though he'd love to see the new baby girl. He was curious what she looked like. If she favored Jane, she also favored Jessica. And he'd get to see what a daughter of hers might look like.

Whenever Mary had spoken of baby Joy, Grant's mind had wandered down dangerous paths...like what a child of his and Jessica's might look like. Green eyes or blue? Blond hair or red? Strawberry blond? Creamy skin with freckles or tanned?

Would a little girl turn out to be feisty and independent like her mother?

His fist closed around the filmy white-and-blue curtain, crumpling the starched fabric.

Stop torturing yourself, Parker. Nothing good will come of such thoughts.

A knock reverberated on the open door. He turned

to see Nathan in the hall. He and his wife, Sophie, had arrived shortly after lunch. Will had told Grant that he missed spending nights at Alice and Jessica's. Grant didn't mention he missed it, too.

"We're setting up for the husking bee. Feel up to joining us?"

"Explain to me what a husking bee is again?"

Nathan's silver gaze twinkled with mirth. "Neighbors and friends come together to shuck the mounds and mounds of corn. In addition to the work, there are games and food."

"Not sure if I've ever attended one, but it sounds interesting."

He trailed the other man to the stairs, thankful his wounds had healed and he wasn't relegated to spending his days in the sickbed. He'd go mad if that was the case.

The females were gathered in the kitchen. Delightful aromas filled every nook and cranny of the homey cabin. Just as they reached the bottom of the stairs, Alice stepped through the main door, an unwieldy crate in her arms.

Nathan relieved her of her burden and headed for the kitchen. "I'll be in the barn," he said over his shoulder.

"Be there in a minute," Grant said before being wrapped in a motherly hug.

Alice pulled away, her gaze searching. "How are you? I've missed having you underfoot."

"Everyone has made me feel welcome." Even Caleb. A surprising development.

When she caught him looking behind her, she said, "Jessica won't be here until later. She's working on her orders for the mercantile."

Nodding, he massaged his stiff neck muscles. "How does it feel to have another grandbaby?"

"Too wonderful to describe. You should go and see her."

"Maybe I will."

Her brow creased. "Have you had any news from Shane?"

"None, I'm afraid."

The sheriff had come to see him at the livery yesterday. Somehow, he and the bank owner had managed to keep the existence of stolen jewels a secret. Shane had sent letters to authorities as far away as New York. No one could tell him anything about missing gems. Nor was anyone searching for a man of Grant's description. Together they'd penned a letter to the US Marshals' headquarters and were awaiting a response. Grant suspected the competent sheriff was growing frustrated with the lack of answers. This whole mystery identity case had him baffled.

Grant couldn't fully relax. He worked and lived with one eye on the horizon, constantly on alert, half expecting the authorities to swoop in and cuff him for some unknown crime. It was a difficult way to live. Peace wasn't achievable.

Alice patted his cheek. "It may not seem like it, but God's working behind the scenes on your behalf. He brought you here for a reason. You just don't know what it is yet."

What reason? To learn some elusive lesson? To pay for a past sin?

To realize what it was to want something with every fiber of his being, only to be denied?

"He's not a cruel father," he murmured, somehow convinced of that truth.

"No, He's not."

A passage from the New Testament scrolled through his mind. *Are not two sparrows sold for a penny? Yet not one of them will fall to the ground outside your Father's care. And even the very hairs of your head are all numbered. So don't be afraid; you are worth more than many sparrows.*

"So my only choice is to trust Him and His plan."

"No one said it would be easy. When the girls' pa died, I couldn't see how I would manage alone. Not only raising five daughters, but keeping the farm afloat. God gave me the strength and courage I needed to make it through each day. My family and friends helped. They prayed for me, listened to me whine, pitched in around the farm. It was a dark time. Eventually, though, I began to smile again."

"I'm glad I had people like you and your daughter to support me."

"What you don't know is what a blessing you've been to us." Her smile fond, she bustled off to join the others. The conversation made him long to know his own mother. Was she kind and wise like Alice? Did she have a sense of humor? Was she a good cook? And what was his father like?

From his vantage point, he could see the long dining room table was already littered with serving dishes and bowls of assorted meats and vegetables. Will emerged from the kitchen, snagging a roll as he passed the table.

Grinning, he opened the door and spoke with a full mouth. "You coming?"

"Yeah, I'm coming."

Following the young man out into the yard, he told himself to enjoy the present moment. No telling how much time he had left to spend with his new friends.

Jessica didn't arrive until the gathering was in full swing. Folks milled about her aunt and uncle's yard, balancing their plates and mason jars of tea or lemonade. A few had chosen to eat their supper on the porch steps. The watery yellow haze of dusk had descended, and her uncle and Josh were lighting the lamps sitting on makeshift tables. The cabin windows blazed with light.

Laughter competed with the hum of conversations.

Fiddling with the ends of her shawl, she searched out men with fair hair, hoping to see Grant and dreading it at the same time. She was the teeniest bit hurt that he hadn't bothered to stop by and say hello or ask after Jane and the baby. He would've gotten updates from her aunt or cousins. Still, would it have inconvenienced him that much to pay them a short visit?

A blond-haired woman broke from her group to pick her way across the yard. Jessica recognized her older sister at once. In their mountain town, only Megan had ringlets the color of moonlight combined with a peaches-and-cream complexion.

As she approached, her pretty, robin-egg-blue dress skimming the grass, she assessed Jessica's hair with a humorous glint in her eyes. "If I didn't know Jane had stayed home, I would've mistaken you for her. What made you arrange your hair that way?"

Self-conscious, Jessica touched a finger to the crown of her head. "I wanted a change. Does it look horrid?"

Megan made a circling motion with her finger. Jessica complied, hoping everyone else was too engrossed in their socializing to notice.

"Well?"

"It looks wonderful. You did a bang-up job."

"Thanks," she mumbled, wishing she'd gone with her usual no-frills style. But no. She'd sought to impress Grant. In doing so, she'd courted questions.

She pressed her hand flat against her dress's bodice. Crafted of gossamery fabric that whispered across her skin, the deep green hue mimicked the forest canopy. The overskirt was made of two panels that draped from the waist in thick ruffles, revealing a black lace under-panel.

"I'm overdressed." Most of the women wore dark skirts with blouses. "I should change."

Megan grasped her wrist. "No, you aren't. And no, you shouldn't. You look stunning."

"You're sure?"

"It's not like you to care. What's going on?"

When Jessica pressed her lips together and refused to answer, Megan surveyed the crowd. Stilling, she tipped her head close. "Is our local mystery man the one you intended to impress? If so, you succeeded."

Jessica's heart hammering in her chest, she followed Megan's gaze to the crowd's periphery. The barn's massive doors had been thrown wide to reveal the mounds of corn waiting to be shucked. Grant stood slightly apart from her cousins Caleb and Nathan. He made no effort to hide the fact he was staring straight at her.

She waved. He raised his glass in response, but he didn't smile. That was unlike him.

Was he unhappy in her aunt and uncle's home?

Turning away, he said something to Caleb and stalked off toward the outbuildings. Caleb watched his retreat before continuing his conversation with Nathan.

Her spirits flagged. She could've been wearing a flour sack for all he'd noticed.

"Well." Megan looked as confused as Jessica felt. "Have you and he had a tiff?"

"Not that I'm aware of."

"Caleb's coming over."

Indeed, he was weaving through the clusters of people with single-minded determination. When he reached them, he arched a brow at her.

"What have you done to Grant?"

"Excuse me?"

"He was in a fine mood until you showed up." He paused to rake her with his gaze. "You look pretty, by the way."

"Um, thanks?"

Caleb folded his arms across his chest. "And another thing, the man isn't going to have enough funds to leave if he keeps buying your cakes."

Megan looked intrigued. "She's only been stocking the mercantile since Monday. How many has he purchased?"

"After working a half day today, he stopped on the way home for his fifth."

Jessica's jaw sagged. That was one a day since Tuesday.

"Ma's starting to worry about the quality of her cooking," he tacked on. "Not to mention it's stirred up talk. I overheard Gerard and Wilton laughing about it moments ago. They're certain he's besotted with you."

Her cheeks burned. "I didn't tell him to do that. I wouldn't."

"So do us all a favor and give him one for free."

Megan touched her arm. "Maybe you should go and talk to him."

Jerking a nod, she gathered her skirts and swept around the nearest side of the cabin, eager to hide from prying eyes. Was everyone laughing at her? Did they think she put him up to it? Or worse, that Grant felt sorry for her?

The apple orchard stretching across gently undulating fields was washed in the final rosy hues of daylight. In the distance, the roof of Josh and Kate's home was visible through a break in the forest. Movement to her left alerted her to Grant's presence on her aunt's back porch.

Rising from his seat when he spotted her, he waited with his hands at his sides, his expression unreadable. As she neared, his eyes lingered on her upswept hair and exposed throat, darkening to blue black. Admiration shone there.

She drank in his appearance, the casual farmer's clothes not quite appropriate for his proud, military-like stance. She hadn't noticed that before. Maybe because he'd had a bum ankle and tender side. He'd favored those injuries. Now that he was healed, he stood with his shoulders back, spine straight, boots planted wide on the smooth planks.

If a mountain lion were to come charging through the fields behind her, he'd be prepared to fight it off.

In the low light, his hair didn't shine as usual. Washed and combed, it lay against his head, longer than when he'd arrived. A stray lock fell over his forehead, and she would've forfeited a week's earnings to experience its silky texture between her fingers once more. To be in his arms again.

Curling her arms about her middle, she expelled those thoughts with difficulty. She stopped on the opposite side of the porch railing. There was no step up, so they were on eye level.

"Contrary to what you might think, I don't want your pity," she bit out.

He gripped the railing's top edge and leaned over it, his face close, his expression defiant. "Why would I pity you?"

"Everyone's talking about how you've gone to the mercantile every day this week and bought one of my cakes."

"Everyone?" One brow quirked. "No one's said anything to me about it. Why would that upset you? Word of mouth is good for business."

Upset without knowing why, Jessica dropped her arms and, not paying attention, placed her hands on the railing on either side of his. "You think I'm going to fail."

His head reared back. "That's the exact opposite of what I'm thinking."

"I don't believe you."

"Are you calling me a liar?" His voice was steel cloaked in silk. His hands shifted, imprisoning hers against the weatherworn wood. His face was close enough that his coffee-scented breath puffed across her lips. His beautiful, glittering eyes delved deep into hers. Was he angry for the same reason as her?

This wasn't about cake. This wasn't about rumors. Inside, the truth burned. She loved him…and she craved his love in return.

"I happen to be of the opinion that you can succeed at anything you set your mind to, Jessica O'Malley."

His sure hands slowly skimmed her bare arms, creating chilled bumps in their wake, curving around her shoulders until finding her nape. He gave a gentle tug. Anchoring her against his chest, the railing an inconvenient barrier between them, Grant brought his mouth down on hers. Branding her as his.

She slid her hands up the muscles of his back, reveling in his strength, the broadness of his chest cradling her, the taut security of his arms enfolding her.

I love you.

The words coursed through her, begging to be uttered. His lips were firm and searching. Warmth against the coolness of the night.

It was of dire importance that she memorize every detail of this experience. On the lonely days and nights to come, she'd wrap this memory around her like a toasty blanket warding off the chill of his absence.

His lifted his head a fraction, eyes ablaze. *"Jessica."*

The way her name rolled off his lips made her shiver. His fingertips skimmed her hairline at her temple. "When I saw you tonight, I thought I was dreaming. Your beauty has no equal."

While his words brought her pleasure, they weren't the ones she yearned for him to say.

She stroked his shaven cheek. "There's something I need to tell you."

His brows drew together even as he brushed another kiss across her sensitive mouth. "I'm listening."

Her pulse out of control, she gathered her courage. She opened her mouth to speak.

"Grant?" Caleb's distinctive growl split through the night. "The competition's about to start."

Gasping softly, Jessica jerked away.

A muscle ticked in Grant's jaw. Coming around to her side, he hesitated.

Caleb prowled closer. Grant moved so that his body blocked hers. "Don't take your anger out on her. Say whatever it is you have to say to me."

She braced herself for her cousin's blast of temper, but it never came.

"I've made my feelings plain—getting involved is a dumb idea at this point. You're both mature adults, however. I can't stop you from pursuing this course."

Grant's sigh seemed to be jerked from the depths of his being. Jessica squeezed his upper arm and stepped out of his shadow. "Go on to your competition. I'll speak to Caleb alone."

His gaze delved into hers, seeking reassurance. Appearing satisfied, he murmured, "We'll talk later."

"Okay."

With a parting glance at Caleb, Grant strode away, disappearing into the darkness.

"I'm worried about you, Jess."

She wished she could make out Caleb's exact expression. "I'm not that little girl who trailed you around anymore. I'm not your responsibility."

"No matter how old you get, I'll never stop trying to protect you."

Without a father or older brothers to look out for them, her uncle and cousins had stepped in to do the job. She understood his actions were born of love.

She touched his shirtsleeve. "I appreciate your concern, Caleb."

"But you're not going to heed my warnings."

"You've warmed to Grant. I know you have."

"He's not a bad person," he agreed. "It's his history, his situation I'm concerned about."

"I'm aware of the risks. Let me do this my way."

He was silent awhile. "Just be careful, okay?"

She hugged him and, craving a few moments to regain her composure before facing the guests, slipped inside the silent house. Upstairs in her aunt and uncle's bedroom, she checked her appearance. Not a hair was out of place. Only her heightened color and feverishly bright eyes bore testament to her high emotions. Returning to the living room, she lingered as sounds of merriment filtered through the windows.

When she finally went outside, the first round of competition was over. People were cheering and clapping. From her vantage point on the porch, she saw Nathan and Josh clapping Grant on the back.

"Did he win?" she asked the elderly woman beside her.

"No, but he found a red ear of corn."

Flutters erupted in her middle. Tradition held that the gentleman who found a rare red ear of corn got to kiss the woman of his choosing.

She watched as her cousins explained. Grant's lips parted in surprise. He searched the crowd, stilling when his gaze landed on hers. He started forward.

Anticipation pulsed inside her, along with a heavy dose

of caution. The young men whistled. Everyone in attendance tracked his progress, which seemed to her painfully slow. Was he really planning on kissing her right here in front of her neighbors and family?

He neared the porch, and his attention broke from her. Stopping before a group of older women, he extended the corncob and, with a wink and a playful grin, kissed her ma's wrinkled cheek. Clapping filled her ears. Good-natured laughter, too.

Jessica joined in, able to see her ma's fiery blush from her position. Grant spared Jessica a long glance, communicating with his eyes whom he truly would've liked to kiss. Happiness suffused her. He was ever mindful of her reputation. He put her needs above his own.

Surely he felt something deeper than friendship for her.

The sound of a fast-approaching rider thundered along the lane. The gaiety dissipated as the sheriff's form became distinguishable. He didn't dismount. Instead, he located Grant and beckoned him over.

"I need for you to come with me."

Chapter Twenty-Two

Numb to the activity around him, Grant approached the sheriff on wooden legs. Jessica rushed to join him.

"What's happened?" The question was directed toward Shane.

Not one emotion flickered in his somber features. "Not here, Jessica."

Apprehension slithered along Grant's spine, wrapping around his ribs and squeezing the life out of him. That old familiar panic beast pounced. Sweat popped out on his forehead. This was it. He'd been found out. He was guilty. Doomed to a life behind bars.

No. I can't accept that. Dear Lord, please. I can't...

Jessica's hand found his. It wasn't easy meeting her gaze. The tremulous smile she gave him lessened the turmoil roiling inside him. She had faith in him. In his goodness.

Grant couldn't bear to see that faith blasted to pieces. Squeezing her hand, he said, "Maybe you should stay here."

"I'm coming with you." Her tone brooked no argument.

He looked to Shane, who nodded his acquiescence. Nathan brought a horse for him to borrow. "Take this one."

"Thanks."

The O'Malleys gathered around, forming a human barrier in an effort to afford him a modicum of privacy. With his arm slung about his wife's shoulders, Caleb looked serious. Mary wore a frown.

Alice patted his shoulder. "Everything will be fine. You'll see."

Nodding, he turned to Jessica. "You're sure about this?"

"I'm sure."

With everyone watching, Grant climbed into the saddle and, holding out a hand, assisted Jessica onto the horse's back. She settled in behind him, one arm going about his waist. Shane turned his horse around, and Grant's trotted after him.

Mingled with the worry about his own future were worries about Jessica's. Would scandal and gossip follow her long after he was gone?

That kiss—on another isolated porch, no less—never should've happened. But he couldn't bring himself to regret it.

The ride into town passed in a blur. Tension radiated from Jessica's body.

Maybe he should've insisted on coming alone. He had no clue what or who was awaiting him at the jail.

A lone horse stood hitched to the post, one that had traveled a great distance if the amount of gear attached to its saddle was anything to go by. As Shane slid to the ground, Grant contemplated bolting for parts unknown. Instead, he guided his mount beside the sheriff's.

"Who's inside, Shane?" Grant stopped the man outside the door.

"Someone who claims to know you."

"Male or female?"

"A man." Sighing, Shane glanced between them. "Let's go in and let him explain."

Grant took one final look at Jessica, searing her face into his memory. After tonight, she may never look at him the same again.

His throat tight and dry, he nodded. "All right."

Shane led the way into his office. Grant and Jessica followed. Out of the corner of his eye, he noticed a figure turning from the window. Looking to be in his fifties, the man was tall, reed-thin, and sported thick auburn hair and a mustache.

His narrowed gaze raked Grant from head to toe. His mustache wobbled as his mouth broke into a grin. "Parker! It truly is you." Striding over, he grasped Grant's shoulders and pulled him in for a quick hug and hearty slap on the back. Grant was stunned into silence.

Jessica edged closer. "You know Grant?"

Belatedly, he noticed the silver star. This man was a US marshal.

Stepping back, the other man spared Jessica a quick glance. "Know him? We've only served our country together for the last six years. I was friends with his father." He twirled his mustache ends, a gesture that struck Grant as familiar. "His legal name is Garrett Sebastian Parker."

The name ricocheted through his skull.

"I think I need to sit." Using his foot, he scooted over a chair and sank into it before his knees gave way.

Shane tossed his hat on his desk and, using the corner as a seat, motioned for Jessica and the marshal to follow suit. "Grant, I've apprised Marshal Taylor of your situation. He knows everything."

"You don't remember me, do you?" Taylor's sunburned face looked sad. "I can see the lack of recognition in your eyes."

"I'm afraid not."

"I'm Winston Taylor. You call me Taylor." His mouth quirked. "Or Skinny."

"How did you find me?"

"We've been searching for weeks. The prisoner you were transporting to Arlington, Wayne Thacker, was captured just over the mountains near Asheville. His cohorts ambushed you and left you for dead. In fact, we were beginning to fear that was the case. Aaron's been going out of his mind with worry."

"Aaron?"

Jessica's eyes were huge in her pale face. "Isn't that the name of the marshal those people in Maryville mistook you for?"

"Aaron. Your younger brother." Taylor's frown turned thoughtful. "It's no wonder someone thought you were him. The two of you bear a strong resemblance to your father."

"Can you describe this prisoner? Wayne Thacker?" Grant said.

Taylor's description matched the first man Grant had remembered in a dream. The angry one. All this time, he'd believed he was on the wrong side of the law. When in reality, he'd been the one enforcing it. "I'm a marshal."

"That's right. A good one, too."

Grant turned his attention to Shane, who'd been listening intently to their exchange. "Did you tell him about the jewels?"

"Yes. It's likely you hid them in your bag on the off chance Thacker's gang attempted a rescue. Your instincts proved useful."

Taylor snorted. "There's a jewelry store in Chicago that will attest to it being far more than merely useful."

Grant was silent, trying to absorb the details of a life

he didn't remember. He had a brother. And a father. He flexed his left hand. What else didn't he know?

Jessica caught the movement. Sitting rigidly in the chair, she looked fragile. "Are there any more family members Grant—I mean, Garrett—should know about?"

"Apart from aunts and uncles scattered about, he has no other immediate family members."

Grant shifted on the hard seat. This was weird, asking a stranger about personal details. "So I'm not married?"

Understanding lit Taylor's gaze. Stroking his mustache, his voice dipped in sympathy. "You were married once. About five years ago."

Jessica's soft gasp punctuated his own shock.

"Were?" he grated.

"Susannah died before your first anniversary."

Pushing to his feet, Grant wandered to the window overlooking Main Street, his mind and heart numb, as if pumped full of laudanum. How? How could he have had a wife and not known it? Questions pelted his brain from all sides. What was she like? Had he loved her?

Pivoting, he avoided looking at Jessica. Did she suspect him of lying? Or toying with her emotions?

"How did she die?" he demanded.

Taylor didn't answer at first. "Perhaps we should discuss this in private."

Jessica started to rise. Grant threw out a hand. "No. Please stay." Still looking at the marshal, he said, "Whatever you have to say can be said in front of them."

He licked his lips. "Susannah was expecting. She died of complications related to her pregnancy."

Jessica felt as if a part of her had died. The shock and disbelief etched on Grant's face rent her heart into pieces. She longed to go to him, to try to ease his suffering. She didn't feel free to do so. Hearing about this whole other life, a noble, exciting life as a marshal, with friends and family who cared about him, opened her eyes to how foolish she'd been.

She'd known he could never be hers. The knowledge that he'd courted, loved and married another woman crushed her. Made her feel crazy jealous and ashamed at the same time. The poor woman was dead. And his lost baby... Tears welled up and spilled over onto her cheeks.

Wiping at them surreptitiously, she wished she could disappear. A handkerchief was dropped on her lap. Lifting her head, she met Shane's sympathetic regard. There was no condemnation in his eyes. Thinking back, there hadn't been any all those months ago when she'd given him her account of events surrounding Lee's death. Oh, there'd been frustration. But that had stemmed from his concern, hadn't it?

"If it's any consolation, you weren't there when it happened."

Grant stared at the older marshal. "Where was I?"

"You were protecting a judge whose life had been threatened."

He looked haggard. "Let me get this straight. I left my pregnant wife alone so I could go gallivanting about the country protecting a judge who likely had been taking bribes in exchange for leniency? She suffered and died with no one around to help her?"

Taylor stood, hands out in a placating gesture. "You were doing your duty, Parker. Serving your country as you've done faithfully since you pinned on the badge."

Shoulders sagging, Grant's head bent low.

The auburn-haired man went and grasped his shoulder. "I'm sorry you're having to relive this all over again, my friend."

Jessica gained her feet. "Shane, would you mind taking me home? They have much to catch up on."

Nodding, he snatched his hat. "Before we go, I have one more question."

"What's that?"

"If Grant found Thacker in Kentucky, what was he doing here? Gatlinburg wouldn't have been on his route to Arlington."

"You're right." Hefting a huge leather satchel onto the desk, Taylor rifled through the contents and brought out a sheaf of papers. "He was making a stop here to inquire about another case." Licking his fingertips, he flipped through the papers until he found what he was looking for. "Ah. Here it is. The case is about two years old. Involves a bank robbery. Five men dead, including the banker and one female clerk. Our information led us to believe the perpetrator traveled here."

Shane took the proffered paper. Through the thin parchment, Jessica could see the bold letters describing the criminal and bounty. She couldn't make out the photograph.

Shane suddenly stiffened, nostrils flaring. His gaze shot to hers.

"You know him?" Taylor asked.

A sense of foreboding filling her, she moved to stand beside the sheriff. There, staring up at her, was a photograph of Lee. A small cry of protest escaped her lips. She covered them with shaking hands. Her stomach roiled.

Grant came and snatched the wanted sign, his mouth going slack when he read the name. "Jessica, I'm sorry. I didn't know."

Shane said something to the marshal. Jessica couldn't make sense of it through the roaring in her ears.

Grant had come to Gatlinburg in search of a murderer. In search of Lee, the man she'd trusted and loved and lost.

Whatever respect he'd had for her must surely be gone. Grant was a man whose job it was to uphold the law and punish those who broke it. She had aided a federal criminal. How would he ever look at her as anything other than a fool?

"I—I have to go."

"Don't," he intoned as she bolted onto the boardwalk. "Jess!"

Behind her, she heard the scuffle of boots on wood. Heated words between the sheriff and Grant.

She didn't stop. Didn't slow down.

She couldn't face US Marshal Grant—Garrett—Parker again.

Chapter Twenty-Three

"You weren't at the church service this morning, so I came to check on you."

Grant turned the hat in his hands in a complete circle. He remained at the foot of her porch steps, oddly uneasy in this place he'd considered home for weeks. He would've thought learning he was an honest citizen in service to the government would make him feel as if he belonged, as if he had a right to be here. But the truth hadn't brought healing. The truth had acted like a disease, eating away at his and Jessica's relationship until he wasn't sure if there was anything left to salvage.

Jessica's attention was on the pile of pink fabric in her lap. The sun's light blocked by thick, low hanging clouds rendered her unbound hair a darker hue in contrast to her slate-gray dress.

"Go away, Parker."

"Not until we talk."

"There's nothing to talk about."

Of course she'd be stubborn. He balanced one boot on the bottom stair and rested his forearm across his thigh. "I disagree. I can be just as obstinate as you, so unless you'd like for me to stick around all day, you'll hear me out."

Pink mouth compressing, she lifted her gaze. The turmoil in her eyes punched him in the gut. If Gatlinburg hadn't been his destination, if he hadn't been searching for Cavanaugh, he wouldn't have had the opportunity to inflict pain. The prospect of missing the chance to know her, to *love* her, made his chest ache and his heart kick in protest.

What good is loving her going to do either of you? an insidious voice demanded. *Your life is dedicated to bringing criminals to justice. A treacherous existence not suited to marriage.*

After she'd fled, he and Taylor had spoken long into the night. He'd answered Grant's myriad questions as best he could. Those pertaining to his marriage to Susannah Baker hadn't been as clear-cut. According to the older marshal, Grant hadn't been one to share private details with just anyone. Aaron would be better suited to supply the information he needed. What Grant was able to glean, however, was that after her death, he'd planned to remain single.

One thing was certain—Jessica would've been better off never meeting Garrett Parker.

"I thought you'd be packing," she charged, the needle and thread held aloft.

"That's what Taylor wants."

Something flickered in her expression. She pressed her lips more tightly together.

"I'm not leaving town until I talk to my brother. Taylor's sending word for Aaron to come here at his first convenience. In the meantime, I'll continue working and going about life as usual."

The thought of meeting his brother filled him with anticipation. Apprehension, too, if he was honest. He didn't know what to expect, what sort of relationship they shared. Without knowing their history, he was a blind man fumbling about in the dark.

"And will Taylor stay, as well?"

"Shane found a family willing to take him in for the time being."

"He seems like a decent man." She tilted her head. "You don't remember him?"

"That mustache of his is hard to forget. And the cheroot scent clinging to his clothes. Do I recall working with him? No."

"Maybe, when you return to Arlington, to your home, and you're surrounded by your possessions, you'll remember more."

She dipped her head, but not before he glimpsed her deep sorrow. The specter of his marriage loomed between them. And the fact he'd been pursuing the man she'd loved.

The distance between them seemed insurmountable. Grant hated it. He wasn't about to leave Gatlinburg with things unsettled and broken. He couldn't leave her with hurt feelings. If it weren't for Jessica, he might've died. He certainly wouldn't have adjusted to his altered existence without her.

"Let's go for a walk."

He thought for a minute that she'd refuse him. Clearly unhappy, she put her sewing project inside the cabin and halted before descending the steps. She didn't come near. Waving her hand, she said, "After you."

Grant yearned to hold her close, to promise her everything would turn out fine. He couldn't lie to her, however. Things wouldn't be fine. How could they when his future didn't include her? Staying in Tennessee wasn't an option. He had a responsibility to his fellow marshals. To the US Government. Even if Jessica agreed to a future visit from him, who knew how long it would be before he could travel this way again?

By that time, she could be in a courtship with someone else.

His heart heavy, he focused on keeping his stride matched to hers. They entered the forest. Without the sunlight peeking through the canopy above, the understory assumed a mysterious quality. The humidity moistened his skin and made the ends of his hair cling to his nape.

Jessica maintained a healthy distance, looked everywhere but at him. "How are you coping with...everything?"

His chest heaved with a sigh. "It's a lot to take in at once. I don't doubt Taylor's sincerity, but it feels as if the life he's described belongs to someone else."

He stepped over a moss-encrusted fallen log. Jessica avoided his outstretched hand and climbed over it without his assistance. He thought of their most recent embrace, clung to the memory of her sweet kiss and soft expression.

Memories fade. They won't be enough to sustain me.

"US marshal wasn't one of the jobs we thought of, was it?" She finally deigned to look at him, attempting a half smile that didn't reach her eyes.

He silently willed her to hold his gaze, to read everything he couldn't articulate into words. "No. It wasn't."

She stumbled over an exposed root and, pulling away from his fleeting touch, put even more space between them. "It's a noble profession."

He tamped down his frustration. "According to Taylor, my father was a respected constable for many years. That's the reason Aaron and I went into law enforcement."

Walking into church that morning, he'd recognized the not-so-subtle change in folks' regard. Admiration and respect had replaced suspicion. He wouldn't lie. It felt good to be rid of the troubling imaginings, to slay the panic beast that had hovered below the surface since awakening in these woods. To know he'd lived his life righting wrongs. Upholding justice. Ensuring criminals got what was coming to them.

He wished he could remember. The job. His father. Aaron. Susannah. His unborn child.

Sadness overtook him. How could he have forgotten something that monumental? That tragic? He didn't know how he'd met Susannah, how they'd come to be married, whether or not he'd truly loved her. The old questions had been replaced with a whole new set.

"I probably shouldn't mention it." They'd reached the stream. Bracing a hand against a gnarled tree bent sideways, she observed the rippling water. "I didn't have a chance to express my condolences last night. I—I'm sorry about your w-wife and child."

Boots making impressions in the soft earth, he clenched his fists. Minnows darted through the water. "I want to remember everything. There's a part of me, though, that thinks maybe not knowing the details is best."

"I can't imagine what you're going through." Tenderness wove through her voice.

Grant fought the impulse to confess his feelings. More than anything, he wanted to take her in his arms and not let go until she believed in his love for her. No matter what the past contained, Jessica was the only woman who'd possess his heart. His dreams of a future resided solely with her.

Rubbing his temples, he called on all his strength of will. She wasn't ready to hear it. And he wasn't in the position to tell her such things.

"Guess this explains your affinity for the outdoors," she mused, glancing about at their lush surroundings. "You traveled a lot for your work."

"Spent my nights stargazing." He hadn't memorized the constellations from a book, as they'd supposed, but from lonely nights sitting by a campfire.

"You must've seen so many places." Crouching at the water's edge, she plucked a yellowed leaf from the surface and twirled it in her fingers, unmindful of the moisture dripping on her skirts. Her glorious hair spilled down her back, shiny and luminous like a new copper penny. "Your interest in your surroundings must stem from that."

"Possibly."

"You knew the year Tennessee went dry without having to think about it." As her statement registered, her gaze shot to his, and he saw the shame come flooding back.

Striding over before she could retreat, he bent and clasped her shoulder. "We've been through this already. Don't reclaim guilt that doesn't belong to you."

Jessica averted her face. Long ropes of hair cascaded over his hand. Gently, he smoothed the silky strands into place. "Jess, look at me."

When she wouldn't, he curved his hand about her cheek and nudged her face in his direction. Her expression was awash in misery. "You don't know how humiliating it is," she burst out. "That you were only here to search for him. I was so blind!"

His thumb stroked her cheekbone. "No," he intoned. "You trusted someone who failed to see what a treasure he had in you. He willingly deceived you. I don't need my memories to know there are some people who take advantage of others' generosity and trust. They use others to get what they want without thought to the consequences." He shook his head. "You aren't the only one who has regrets."

"What do you mean?"

Unable to be this close any longer, he reluctantly shoved

to standing. "I can't stop thinking about what Taylor said about my—" He swallowed hard. "About Susannah."

Her eyes dimmed. "What about her?"

"Instead of staying home, I left her alone to track outlaws. What does that say about my character? My priorities?" Slapping his hat against his thigh, he tunneled his fingers through his hair. "Taylor said she didn't have relatives nearby. I don't know how long she suffered before… She must've been frightened out of her mind. Do you know what the worst part is? I don't even remember what she looked like. She may as well have never existed."

Jessica approached, her hands together in a gesture of pleading. "Don't do this to yourself, Grant."

"I feel like a monster."

Lying in bed last night, he'd tried to force the memories to break free of the black void, to recall Susannah's face. Her laugh. Her voice. Anything. He'd wound up with a headache the size of Mount Le Conte.

Mimicking his earlier entreaty, she laid a hand on his chest, directly over his heart. Her eyes burned with conviction. "You are the most compassionate, caring man I've ever met. You wouldn't have left her if you'd had a choice."

He would like to think that was the case, but he couldn't know for sure. Maybe Aaron could give him insight into his marriage.

Covering her hand with his own, he rested his forehead against hers. They stood there for long moments, the trees rustling softly and the trickling water echoing through the forest.

Jessica pulled away first. "I don't think we should see each other again," she said in a thick voice.

While he could see the wisdom of her words, his entire being rebelled. He wanted to fill every minute remaining with her. Pack moments and memories into these last days before he returned to Virginia.

In the end, he accepted what was best for her.

"I'd like to say goodbye before I leave town," he managed at last.

Nodding, she worried her lower lip as she gazed beyond his shoulder. "Okay."

Jessica walked away then, and he let her.

Three days had passed since she'd told Grant to leave her alone. Three interminable, horrible, miserable days. Knowing he was working and sleeping a couple of miles away made the separation tougher to bear. Several times she'd been tempted to go to him. To toss aside her pride and common sense and beg him to stay.

Thankfully, she'd risen above the momentary weakness and logic had prevailed.

He was a marshal with responsibilities elsewhere. He had friends in government positions. Why, he could very well be acquainted with the nation's president, Grover Cleveland! What made her think he'd give up such an honorable, glamorous life to be with her, a mountain girl with poor judgment and who associated with criminals?

Tuning out the hustle and bustle of the mercantile's patrons, she slid the last cake into the glass case and closed the lid. Five cakes of different heights and flavors occupied the case. She'd tucked handwritten description cards in front of each one. Business had been steady. Nothing had gone to waste, which was an aggravation of hers and something she'd fretted over when trying to decide whether or not to launch this venture. God had blessed her efforts. Once again, she had a steady income to help with expenses.

Satisfied everything was in order, she straightened, her

gaze settling on a gentleman in the corner. Only his jet-black hair was visible from this angle, but he looked too much like her brother-in-law for it to be a coincidence. But what was Evan doing in Gatlinburg?

Her last conversation with Juliana filtering through her mind, she rounded the counter, dodging customers to reach him."

"Evan?"

Replacing the handsaw on the shelf, he turned and acknowledged her with a smile at odds with the caution in his larkspur-blue eyes. "Jessica. How are you?"

She accepted his hug. "I didn't realize you were planning a visit. Are Juliana and the kids with you?"

Tugging on his collar, he shook his head. "No. They're at home. This was a spur-of-the-moment visit, actually."

Crossing her arms, she leveled a meaningful stare at him. To her knowledge, he'd never made the trip alone. "What are you here for?"

"Business."

He didn't hesitate. Nor did he look guilty. She knew, however, that Evan Harrison was adept at subterfuge. After all, he'd infiltrated a gang of outlaws in search of his brother's murderer and even convinced Juliana that he was one.

Aiming for his weak spot, she said, "When we were camping together, Juliana confided in me. Whatever secrets you're harboring have her worried. As her sister, I don't approve."

His lids flared. Anxiety pinched his rugged features. Casting his gaze about, he moved closer. "What did she say exactly?"

"That you're acting strangely and avoiding her." A

horrible thought struck her. "You haven't taken up with another woman, have you?"

The color drained from his face. His gaze turned deadly, and Jessica wished to recall the words. He gripped her upper arm none too lightly and, steering her outside and onto the boardwalk, marched her to the alley beside the building.

"How could you suggest such a thing?" he demanded, throwing his arms wide. "Your sister is the only woman I've ever loved. I wouldn't do anything to risk losing her. Surely you know me better than that."

"You're right. I spoke before I thought." Evan was a loving, devoted husband and father. "But why all the secrecy? What's going on, Evan?"

He kicked at the dirt beneath his boots. "I'm working on something. A surprise for Juliana."

"What is it?"

"I'm not telling my sister-in-law before I've told my wife."

Jessica studied his face, instinct telling her to trust him. "Fine. You'd better tell her soon, though. Who knows what scenarios she's cooked up to explain your behavior."

His smirk vanished. "I know. She's tried to pry it out of me every way she knows how. I've managed to keep her questions at bay. I don't like worrying her."

"How long before your surprise is ready?" Curiosity made her temporarily forget her own sorrows for a moment. Would a man ever go to this much trouble for her?

"Not much longer, I hope. Keeping secrets from your loved one, even innocent ones, takes its toll on a relationship."

Jessica stared at the livery building, desperate to see Grant but aware it wasn't a good idea. She didn't need the reminder. She'd gotten burned by Lee's secrets, and now she was harboring one of her own. One she'd take with her to the grave.

Why tell Grant she loved him when it wouldn't change a thing?

Chapter Twenty-Four

Grant left the stuffy confines of the livery and, stalking to the copse of trees yards from the rear entrance, discarded a bucketful of dirty water. He squinted into the sun and swiped his shirtsleeve across his brow. They were having an unseasonably sweltering day. His boss assured him the cooler weather would return by next week. Grant didn't bother reminding him he might not be around next week.

Like the attitudes of the rest, Warring's, too, had undergone a drastic change since his true profession had become common knowledge. The older man didn't hover anymore when Grant cared for the horses and mules, nor did he bother overseeing the customers' transactions. It appeared the title of US Marshal evoked instant respect, whether it was deserved or not.

Billowing the front of his shirt to unstick it from his skin, he didn't hear anyone approach.

"Garrett?"

Grant stilled. He didn't have to turn around to know who stood behind him. No one called him that.

Lord, give me strength. Lowering the bucket to the ground, he turned, coming face-to-face with his brother.

Heart thudding, he looked into a face remarkably like

his own. "It's Grant, actually. That's the name I go by. Folks are used to calling me that, and I'm used to hearing it."

"I don't care what name you use, big brother," the shorter man grunted before enveloping him in an enthusiastic hug. Pulling back, Aaron gripped his arms. "We've had some close calls before, but this time around I was beginning to think I'd lost you for good. Praise God you're all right!"

Grant subtly disengaged from his hold. He didn't want to ruin this reunion, but he wasn't up for more displays of affection, either. He'd half hoped—irrationally that one glance at his brother was all that it would take to unlock the past. His damaged brain was stubbornly refusing to cooperate, however. As he stared into his younger brother's face, he sensed a deep connection. He just didn't have facts or events to attach to it.

Dressed in neat blue trousers and a white button-down shirt beneath a gray-and-blue vest, Aaron was cleanshaven, with blond hair that was cut military short. Despite his travels, his boots were immaculate. The shiny silver star nestled proudly over his heart. A small scar was visible on his chin, where a bullet or knife blade had nicked the skin, perhaps? Theirs was a risky occupation fraught with danger.

"Did Taylor tell you about my problem?"

Aaron's smile vanished. Stroking his jaw in a weary gesture, he said, "Yeah. I got into town about an hour ago and went straight to the sheriff's office. Timmons and Taylor were both there. They told me everything."

"So you understand that I don't remember you."

Pain flashed in Aaron's eyes. Grant's lack of recognition and cautious reception was hurtful, that much was clear. He tried to put himself in Aaron's place. The most significant person in his life was Jessica. The idea that she would wake one day and not remember a single thing about him was devastating.

"I know that's difficult for you to comprehend," Grant tacked on.

"I understand you have questions. And I realize it will take time for you to trust me. You're the cautious type."

The bit of insight thrilled Grant. Here was the one person in the world who'd known him since childhood, who knew his likes and dislikes. His strengths and faults. Aaron had the keys to unlocking his history.

"I am? Why?"

"It's something you develop over time in this line of work. Dealing with criminals on a regular basis makes you cynical." He scowled. "Susannah's behavior didn't help matters."

"What's that supposed to mean?"

Aaron exhaled. Twisting slightly, he scanned the lane behind the row of businesses. "We've a lot to talk about. But I've been riding like the wind these past days to get to you. I'm saddle-sore, in need of a bath in a real copper tub, not a river, and I'm famished. Is there somewhere we can get something to eat? I'll answer your questions over a cup of coffee and a hot meal."

Grant belatedly noticed Aaron's eyes were bloodshot and fatigue tightened the skin across his cheekbones.

"Sorry. I didn't think." Gesturing toward the main thoroughfare, which was hidden by the livery, he said, "Let me tell my boss I'm leaving. We can get something to eat at the Plum Café."

Aaron gave him a strange side-glance. "Your boss is Governor William Cameron."

"For now, it's also Milton Warring."

"Whatever you say."

Warring waved him off without a word of complaint. Apparently the presence of three marshals in their mountain town was a rare and unique occurrence. The livery owner wasn't about to go against their wishes.

He met Aaron out front after divesting himself of his apron and washing the grime from his face and hands. Their walk to the café did not go unnoticed. Aaron didn't seem to mind. He was probably used to people staring when he arrived in a new town.

Questions about his brother's life bubbled to the surface. Was Aaron happy doing this job? Was there a girl somewhere out there who pined for him?

As usual when he strolled through the heart of town, Grant found himself scanning the boardwalk for a glimpse of flame-red hair. He hadn't seen Jessica in almost a week, and he was miserable without her. Living with her relatives made the situation nearly untenable. Once this week, he'd returned from work to find Jane ensconced in the living room, her newborn tucked in her arms. For a split second, he'd seen Jessica in place of her twin. He'd envisioned coming home to her and their children. Clara's chattering and spinning about in circles had wrenched him back to reality before he could make a fool of himself.

When Jane had asked if he'd like to hold the baby, he'd muttered an inane excuse and escaped upstairs. He'd been so upset that he'd remained in his room rather than risk seeing her again at supper.

He kept telling himself it was bound to get worse before it got better. That the throbbing, bleeding hole in his heart would eventually scab over and heal once he'd put miles between them. Like the wound in his side, he'd be left with ugly scars. But he'd survive. He had to.

There were no good choices available to him. He had a life in Virginia to resume. Responsibilities. As much as he yearned to stay, he couldn't. *It's not just the job or the duty, though, is it?* an inner voice needled. *It's the possibility you were a miserable excuse for a husband that's holding you silent.*

"Who are you searching for?" Aaron paused outside the café, his hand on the knob.

Grant tore his gaze from the passersby. "No one."

One blond brow quirked in disbelief. "Right."

Grant remembered something. "I've been on the receiving end of that particular look plenty of times, haven't I?"

Laughing, he pulled the door open. "As your little brother, it's my job to pester the truth out of you."

Settling in a semiprivate corner table, they placed their orders. Aaron aimed a wide smile at the hostess and asked for a whole pot of coffee to be brought to their table. She blushed and stammered before rushing to do his bidding.

Grant shook his head at how naturally Aaron switched on the charm.

Discarding his hat on the seat next to him, Aaron leaned back in his chair and toyed with the napkin atop the table. "I suppose you'd like to hear about your marriage first."

"Actually no. I'd like to start with you."

His brows shot up. "Me?"

"Have you ever been married or engaged?"

Laughter burst out of him, causing several patrons to turn and stare. "No, thank you. I enjoy teasing the ladies, but that's as far as it goes. I'm too young for all that serious stuff."

"How old are you?"

His humor faded. "This is strange. You not knowing anything about me or yourself. Our history."

"I can imagine."

"I'm twenty-three. Three years younger than you. My

birthday is October twentieth. Yours is January twenty-sixth."

"Where did we grow up? What was our home like? Our father?"

He'd learned from Taylor that their mother had died shortly after giving birth to Aaron. Their father had raised them with the help of their paternal grandparents. It hurt to know they'd all passed on. Grant would've liked to meet them, speak with them, gain insight into the past.

The waitress arrived with their coffee. Aaron chatted with her while she poured the fragrant brew. By the time she returned to the kitchen, Grant was positive she was besotted.

"Are you angling for free dessert?"

He spread his hands and adopted an innocent look. "I'm simply being friendly."

He felt himself smiling. "I have a feeling you've left a string of brokenhearted young women across this great country of ours."

They shared a laugh. He noticed Aaron didn't deny it. As they waited for their order, he launched into an abbreviated account of their childhood. Their father had been a stern, serious man who'd worked long, odd hours trying to keep the peace in their city. Fortunately, their grandparents had been happy to help raise them. Fredrick Parker had taken them fishing, taught them how to build things in his work shed, let them help care for the horses. Kind, nurturing Marjorie Parker had read them stories, taken them with her to the mercantile, doctored their minor cuts and scrapes and always greeted them after school with a plate of cookies. They'd also made sure the boys memorized Scripture and attended church regularly.

Hearing about his grandparents made him wistful for

lost memories. He didn't want to merely imagine what they'd been like. He wanted to remember for himself.

"So that's why I remember so many verses. For a while there, I kind of thought I might be a preacher."

Aaron laughed again. "A preacher? You?"

"That was Jessica's response, too," he said drily.

Interest roared to life. "Who's Jessica?"

He bit into his corn bread, wishing he hadn't mentioned her. His brother was going to give him a hard time about her. "Jessica O'Malley and her mother, Alice, are the ones who found me. They took me in."

"Is she married?"

"Eat your meat loaf." He jabbed a finger at his plate, slipping into the role of big brother without a thought.

Aaron's expression warned he wasn't done fishing for information. Dropping the matter, he scooped up a large forkful of his meal. The food wasn't anything to rave over. The corn bread was dry, the potatoes tasteless. Grant had yet to meet the new owner who'd spurned the twins' desserts. Half the tables were empty, and it was a quarter past noon. Did the man even care that his business was in trouble?

When they'd finished, Grant tossed his napkin over his plate. "How did I meet Susannah?"

"It was at one of the governor's fancy soirees. A Christmas party. She was a friend of the governor's daughters and was clearly intrigued by the marshals' presence."

"What was she like?"

"Beautiful. Sophisticated. An accomplished flirt." He described her sleek black hair, flawless skin and blue eyes. Grant tried to picture her and failed. "You weren't interested in pursuing a relationship and wouldn't even agree to dance. Then one of our fellow marshals introduced her to a group of us. She asked you to dance. You couldn't refuse without embarrassing her. She didn't leave your side for the rest of the night."

"Why wasn't I interested?"

"Our lifestyle. On the trail more months out of the year than we are at home. The danger. Loneliness."

"Something about Susannah changed my mind. I must've loved her."

The absence of emotion besides regret troubled him. The woman was his *wife*. She'd carried his child in her womb before death tragically claimed them both.

"Susannah Baker was the type of woman who dazzled a man. Made him forget, temporarily, his priorities."

"You didn't approve."

"There was something calculating about the way she looked at you. When I confronted you, you dismissed my doubts. You insisted she was worth the sacrifice. You had a whirlwind courtship and were engaged within three weeks' time."

"Wait. What sacrifice?"

"Your independence. Your career."

Grant sagged against the wooden slats. "I was going to quit the marshals?"

"She'd convinced you to give up your life's dream. But shortly after the wedding, we got word the Nelson gang had struck again, this time wiping out a group of women and children. Taylor needed us both to help track them down. Susannah was livid. I waited outside, but I could hear the crashing plates, her shouting. She accused you of breaking your promise, of loving the job more than her."

A dull ache blossomed behind his forehead. "Apparently I'm not a man of my word."

Aaron's expression turned bullish. "That's rubbish. Taylor needed you. Those innocent victims' families needed you. She refused to look at the situation from your perspective. You didn't lie. You promised the mission would be your last." Frowning deeply, he ran a finger along the handle of his butter knife. "Only problem was, it took us a lot longer to locate the gang than we thought."

"Did I know she was pregnant when I left?"

"No." His blue eyes took on a sad quality. "Through Taylor, she was able to get a message to you. You were ecstatic about being a father, but I could sense there was tension between you. You were torn up about not being there, anxious to return. But it was too late…"

"No need to say any more." Grant scooted his chair back and, tossing down enough coins to cover the bill, gestured to the door. "I can fill in the rest."

Outside, Aaron turned to him. "I know this is difficult, but things will get better once we reach Arlington."

"That's what I keep telling myself."

"Believe it." Aaron slapped his back, a grin once again curving his mouth. "But before we leave, I'd like to meet the women who nursed you back to health. Jessica, in particular."

Chapter Twenty-Five

Of course she chose an uncommonly hot November day to roast chestnuts.

Her scalp tingled from the persistent rays. The large fire added to her misery. Jessica peered into the kettle suspended above the flames. "Water's boiling."

Sitting in the shade of their back porch's overhang, Alice carefully slit openings in the chestnuts' shells. She pointed her knife to the pan at her feet. "I've got a batch ready for you."

Jessica retrieved it and shook the contents into the roiling water. A bead of sweat trickled beneath her collar. Sighing, she returned the pan to the porch.

"Have you seen Grant lately?" Alice didn't look up from her task.

"No." Lifting her heavy ponytail off her neck, Jessica fanned the sticky skin. She moved to stir the nuts.

How could she have known missing him would hurt worse than anything she'd ever experienced? Even worse than grieving Lee? Grant was alive. He was close by. And he was *choosing* to stay away. To live without her.

You're the one who told him not to come around, remember? an accusatory voice prodded.

Whether or not they spent these last days together, he was still leaving Tennessee. Leaving her.

"I thought you might've stopped by the livery after delivering your cakes earlier."

"Why would I do that?"

She sensed rather than saw her mother's perusal. "Because he's your friend?"

"He's going home soon." She struggled to keep her voice casual. "Once he leaves, we'll probably never see him again."

The sooner he left, the sooner she could get on with the business of mourning his absence and healing her battered heart. Something told her it would be an excruciating process.

"Jessica, look at me."

Turning, she obeyed, striving to keep the sadness locked away. Her mother was too perceptive, however.

"You care for him." Her knife in one hand, a chestnut in the other, Alice studied her. "More than that. You love him, don't you?"

"Yes."

Imagining her life without Grant was like imagining a world without sunshine or bright autumn flowers or soothing rain on a hot day. He made her laugh. Teased her out of her bad moods. Challenged her to face the problems she'd rather hide from. When he held her, kissed her, everything else fell away until it was the two of them alone on the earth.

Compassion was reflected in her eyes. "Are you planning on telling him?"

Blinking away unwanted tears, she set her jaw. "That's not something I'm willing to do. He doesn't belong here. I won't burden him with unwanted sentiment. Nor will I mar his memories of this place with regret."

"What if you tell him, and he asks you to go with him?"

Jessica hadn't even considered the possibility. "This is my home. Besides, I'm not sure that's what he'd want."

"Here's your chance to find out."

Brows drawing together, she followed Alice's line of sight to the patch of lane visible from their spot behind the cabin. "Is that…" She trailed off, nervousness skittering through her.

"Looks like his brother has arrived."

Alice laid aside her things and, leaving Jessica by the fire, went around to greet them. Jessica glanced down at her plain green blouse and skirt and her dirt-streaked apron, put her fingers to her moist hairline. Perfect.

Their voices preceded them as they rounded the corner. Jessica steeled herself, lifting her chin and willing all emotion away.

But the moment Grant came into view, his celestial blue eyes homing in on her, the love she harbored in her heart expanded, flowing into every fiber, every particle, almost too powerful to hold inside. Surely he could see it. Feel it seeping into the air and surging toward him like an invisible tidal wave.

She forced her feet to remain motionless as he came around the fire. His deep blue shirt lent his irises a more distinct hue. He was in need of a shave; the bristles along his jaw and chin had a reddish tint she'd never noticed before. He looked tired. But there was a sense of belonging in his eyes, the thrill of discovery and connectedness, put there by Aaron Parker.

Grant introduced the man whose resemblance was undeniable.

"Aaron, these are the women I told you about, Alice and Jessica O'Malley." His gaze was intent on hers. "Ladies, meet my younger brother."

Aaron greeted her mother first. Then he turned to Jessica. Her hand was enveloped by a roughened, trail-worn one. Instead of the customary shake, Aaron lifted her hand and kissed her knuckles. "A pleasure to meet you, Jessica."

Mischief and curiosity danced in the eyes so like Grant's.

Grant rolled his eyes. However, indulgence played about his mouth. To an objective observer, it was clear their relationship had a strong foundation. Amnesia or not, they'd be on sure footing within a couple of days.

Jessica was happy for Grant. He'd need support and understanding as he adjusted to his new reality. "Likewise. Welcome to Gatlinburg. When did you arrive?"

"A couple of hours ago."

When her mother started to fetch chairs from the kitchen, Grant waved her off. "Stay here. I'll get them."

Aaron removed his hat and placed it over his heart. "I'd like to thank you both for taking Garrett in and helping him get back on his feet. Not many would've done that in light of his situation."

Alice smiled. "We were glad to help. Grant's a special young man. We're blessed to know him." Looking flustered, she snapped her fingers. "I can't seem to remember to call him Garrett."

He emerged from the cabin then and bestowed a smile on her. "It's all right. I've decided Grant will be my nickname from now on. Most of my colleagues will call me Parker, anyway."

Aaron accepted the chair with a nod. Lowering his wiry frame onto the seat, he swept an arm about him. "Looks like we've interrupted your work. Garrett was reluctant to stop by. He said you'd be busy. Can we help in some way?"

Jessica's heart sank. Grant hadn't wanted to see her.

He was here because of his brother's need to express gratitude.

Turning to the fire, she stirred the pot again, leaving her mother to reply. Alice declined his offer and asked how he'd fared during his journey. Jessica listened as he explained the long days of travel and short hours of sleep he'd snatched.

"Where are my manners?" Alice exclaimed. "There's a tray of fresh cinnamon rolls on the stove. Would either of you like one? I can prepare coffee, too."

"I'd love one." Aaron popped up. With a side-glance at Grant, he strode forward to hold the door open for Alice. "How about I give you a hand?"

"I can give you a tour," she said. "I'll show you the room where Grant stayed."

The door closed behind them. The resulting silence was broken by the bubbling water, the hiss and pop of the firewood, a hawk's cry as it flew over. Keenly aware of Grant's presence, Jessica snatched up an empty pot and started to transfer the chestnuts into it.

"Here, let me help."

Suddenly, he was beside her, his arm brushing hers. He held the pot while she scooped.

"What will you do with them now?" His husky voice wrapped around her like whispering satin.

"Put them in the stove to roast." She kept her face averted. "Then put towels over them to let them steam. Makes them easier to shell."

He glanced over his shoulder at the bushels on the porch. "That's a lot of work. Aaron and I can stay and help."

"No, thanks," she said quickly. Having him around was exquisite torture. Pausing in her work, she allowed herself to look into his face. "He's nice, Grant. I'm really glad you have someone like him in your life."

His gaze seemed to drink her in. "I haven't remembered any specific memories about him, but it's like I recognize him anyway. Does that make sense?"

"Yeah. It does." Her mouth dry, she retrieved the last of the kettle's contents. "He seems to be handling your memory loss well."

"He's been patient. He told me things about our childhood. Our grandparents practically raised us. He also told me how I met Susannah—"

Jessica threw up her hand. "Stop. You don't have to divulge the details."

Hurt flashed in his eyes. "I merely thought you'd want to know. After everything we've been through."

"You're wrong. I don't."

He digested her words. His scrutiny nearly broke her determination to remain silent. Throwing a glance at the kitchen door, he set the pot in the grass and pulled out a folded piece of paper. He held it out to her.

She hesitated. "What is it?"

"My address. In case you decide to write."

Jessica took the soft paper. She wasn't going to write. Judging by the melancholy stamped across his features, he knew.

She slipped it into her pocket. "When are you leaving town?"

"Early tomorrow."

"So this is goodbye."

"Jessica... I don't know if I'll ever travel this way again." Reaching out, he proceeded to straighten the ribbon nestled close to her nape. She held very still as longing surged. His arms dropped to his sides. A sad smile curved his lips. "I hope you'll write. I hope you don't mind if I write to you."

She was very close to tears. "Wait here. I have something for you."

Inside the dimmer interior, she hurried to the living room, thankful her mother and Aaron were upstairs. She retrieved her desired object and rushed outside.

Grant took one look at the guitar case and put up his hands. "I can't take that. It belonged to your father."

"Why let it go unused when you make such beautiful music with it?"

His fingers brushed hers as he reverently accepted the gift. His eyes were bright. "I'll think of you and these mountains every time I play."

A tear escaped. Bowing her head, she dashed it away with the back of her hand. She felt his fingers come under her chin.

"Jess, don't. Please." A world of emotion accompanied his groan.

Voices floated through the kitchen. Footsteps thrummed against the floorboards. Then the door was opening.

Their time was coming to an end.

"Be safe, Grant," she whispered.

Unable to corral her emotions, she murmured an excuse and, brushing past a surprised Aaron and her startled mother, sought refuge in her room.

Grant huddled into his jacket and, using the wagon wheel as a prop for his back, tossed another twig onto the fire. Tiny sparks spun out in the darkness. Above him, stars twinkled in the endless black sky.

Aaron returned from the woods and plopped down beside him. "What's eating you?"

On the other side of the fire, Taylor shifted on his

pallet, his snores cutting through the stillness. While the older marshal possessed certain habits that grated on Grant's nerves, he'd developed a soft spot for him. He supposed it was a result of their friendship and close work relationship.

Grant plucked a blade of grass to fiddle with. His hands were as restless as his mind.

Aaron propped an arm on his bent knee. "Ever since we left Gatlinburg, you've walked around with your own personal thundercloud hanging above your head. I thought you'd be anxious to get home. Stir up memories."

"There's no guarantee seeing my old place will spark anything."

"It's not your *old* place. It's your home. You haven't been gone that long."

"Gatlinburg feels like home."

Aaron was silent, contemplative. "I can see why you'd feel that way. Give Arlington a chance, all right? Give your friends and me a chance."

Somewhere in the distance, a cow lowed, followed by dogs barking. Just over the rise from their campsite, a large farm occupied the rolling fields. They'd been on the trail for three days. With each passing mile, Grant's heart and mind rebelled, insisted he was making a huge mistake.

"I didn't intend to upset you," Grant said at last, sorry for making his only living relative feel unnecessary.

"You didn't. We both have adjusting to do. I guess I've been waiting for you to remember me, and it's frustrating that it hasn't happened yet." Holding off Grant's response with an uplifted hand, he said, "I'm trying to be patient. And focus on the fact God spared you. You're all I have left in this world."

Grant's respect and admiration grew. "You've got a

good head on your shoulders, little brother. I'd like to see you in action as a marshal."

Aaron's chest puffed with pride. "I learned from the best. You were a marshal a full two years before I followed suit."

He proceeded to regale Grant with tales of their exploits. Grand tales that were both awe-inspiring and sobering. For the marshals, duty to their country was paramount. Loyalty. Honor. Brotherhood. Grant admired those sentiments. And yet, he couldn't help thinking it was a lonely life.

When the flames had died down and they'd settled on their pallets for the night, Aaron's voice reached him.

"You miss her, don't you?"

Grant's chest tightened. No use denying it. "Yeah."

Memories of her flooded in. Would he ever see her again? He was pretty sure she wasn't planning on contacting him. She could be resolute about some things. *Stubborn would be a more fitting description.*

He couldn't blame her. So many things about his life were unsettled.

"Did you consider asking her to come with you?"

Grant sat up and stared at his brother. His features were indistinct. "Why would you ask that?"

"I've got eyes, brother." The sarcasm wasn't lost on him. "The pair of you looked miserable. She didn't want you to leave."

He slumped onto the hard ground and blinked up at the sky. Her tears had nearly broken him. "I didn't have a choice."

His only recourse was to make the best of his situation. And while he was thrilled to have Aaron back in his life and relieved to know he was an upstanding citizen, a tiny part of him wished his identity had remained a mystery for a bit longer. Because then he'd still be in Tennessee. And he'd still be close to the woman he loved.

Chapter Twenty-Six

I have a lot to be thankful for, Lord.

Her gaze roaming about her aunt and uncle's living room, crowded with relatives on this Thanksgiving Day, Jessica prayerfully listed her blessings. The brightest one lay nestled in her arms. Joy slept deeply, despite the loud conversations and occasional outburst of laughter. Her perfect, dainty mouth made sucking motions. Her tiny fingers held on to Jessica's with surprising strength. What she wouldn't give for a baby of her own.

Funny, she'd contemplated marriage to Lee, but it had been an abstract notion. She certainly hadn't given much thought to children. Grant was different. She had no trouble envisioning being his wife, living with him day in and day out, raising a family. He'd be a tender, giving husband, a wise and patient father.

She held in a sigh, lest she earn another worried look. Her loved ones had been walking on eggshells these past weeks. Afraid to make a reference to Grant. Afraid to say anything remotely upsetting.

Had her feelings for him been that obvious? Had her mother let the truth slip to Aunt Mary, and it spread from there? Or, more worrying, had they simply put two and two together—his absence and her lingering despondency?

Evan entered the cabin and called for the room's attention. "Juliana? Will you come here, please?"

A slight frown on her face, Juliana rose from her chair and hoisted their sleepy two-year-old son onto her hip. Jessica tensed. The couple had written ahead about their plans to spend the holiday in Gatlinburg. Whatever he'd been busy arranging these past months, Jessica prayed it would please her sister.

When Juliana reached him, Evan curved an arm around her waist. Love shone in his gaze. There was tension in him, though.

"Juliana, as you know, I've been working on a surprise for you. Something I hope you approve of very much."

She gave him a tremulous smile. "You know I trust your judgment. I won't lie and say I haven't been anxious these past weeks, however."

"I appreciate your patience, Irish. The wait is over." Turning to the expectant gathering, he said, "Everyone, we're going on a short trip. The wagons are waiting outside."

They filed out into the yard. Four wagons had been readied, the beds lined with hay squares for seating. The kids bounced up and down. Nicole cradled her sleeping daughter to her chest. She leaned close to Jessica. "I wonder what this is about."

"I can't imagine."

"Quinn knows something. I'm sure of it." Her violet eyes snapped. "But no amount of pestering would budge him. I didn't glean even a bit of information."

The baby in her arms squirmed. Cooing softly, Jessica rocked Joy until she settled.

"You're a natural with her," Nicole said with a smile.

"Any chance your marshal will trade in the badge for mountain living?"

"You're the first to mention him to me."

"No use avoiding the obvious. You're miserable without him."

"Why would he want this when he can reside in a bustling city, hobnob with government elite and get paid to live out adventures?"

"What if that no longer appeals to him? What if he's miserable without you, too?"

If Jessica allowed herself to hope for such a thing, she'd live with constant disappointment. No. Better to focus on getting through each day the best she could.

Ahead of them, Nathan assisted a heavily pregnant Sophie into the wagon bed. Because of her petite frame, her belly looked large and uncomfortable. Surely the twins would be born soon. With her situated, he turned and helped Nicole and then Jessica. The wagons finally started off down the lane. Instead of heading toward town, their procession turned toward Jessica and Alice's. They passed their property and, about a mile down the lane, parked alongside a newly cleared field.

Evan led the way into the middle of the field, leading Juliana by the hand. Alice held Sammy, and young James huddled close to her side.

When everyone had gathered around, Evan took his wife's other hand so that they were facing each other. "My darling Juliana, for years it's been your dream to return to your home. I know how much you've missed your family. The land you're standing on is ours. If you agree, we'll start work on our new home right away. We can be moved in by Christmas."

There were gasps and clapping. Tears streamed down Juliana's cheeks. "*This* is what you've been planning?

Truly?" she exclaimed, glancing about her at the fields, the trees and the mountains in the distance.

"Are you happy?"

For an answer, she squealed and threw her arms around his neck. Evan's smile bore testament to his relief, as well as his adoration for his wife. Jessica found herself blinking away tears. She could hardly fathom that her entire family would be together again.

As everyone gathered around the couple, she hung back, apart from the celebration. While she was thrilled for Juliana, sadness permeated her soul. All around her, her sisters and cousins stood with their spouses. Some, like Megan and Lucian, had large families. Others, like Nathan and Sophie, Jane and Tom, were just starting theirs.

In that moment, she experienced Grant's absence, his *permanent* absence, as if a part of her heart had been ripped from her chest. Solitude was a bitter friend. Jessica ached to see his lopsided smile. His bright eyes full of mirth. To hear him humming along to a tune he was playing on his guitar.

She longed to have him beside her, a ring on his hand proclaiming to the world that he belonged with her.

It was nothing but a pointless, silly dream. He was in Virginia now. And he wasn't coming back.

Grant answered the succinct rap on his door. His brother waited on the stoop. Behind him, single riders, conveyances and pedestrians traversed the busy thoroughfare. After the peacefulness of the mountains, the constant activity was jarring.

"Taylor said you were looking for me." His cheeks were chapped from the blistering wind.

"Come in."

Grant moved to admit him into his quarters, a spacious but utilitarian room in the marshals' barracks, located in the heart of Arlington. It was large enough to hold a bed, wardrobe, desk and chair. He'd had a clapboard house once upon a time, he'd been told. One he'd sold shortly after Susannah's death.

Aaron eyed the open trunks and the wardrobe's doors thrown wide. Before he could comment, Grant said, "I've remembered something."

"Seriously? When did this happen? Why didn't you tell me right away?"

Striding to the bed, he rifled through a box of their grandparents' things, mementos Aaron had given him, and lifted out a necklace with a heart-shaped locket.

"I was looking through this box late last night when I came upon this." He closed his fingers around the locket, the thrill of the memory still fresh. "I saw her, Aaron. I remembered Grandmother."

His brother's elation was plain. "What did you remember, exactly?"

"She and I were sitting at her kitchen table. The table-cloth was made of lace. And faded. She wore her silver hair in a bun." Closing his eyes, he recalled the details, warmth infusing him as if he were back there in that kitchen with her, the smell of cinnamon cookies in the air. "Her apron was pink and white and frilly."

"That was her favorite apron," he said. "Did you remember Grandfather? Or anyone else? Pa?"

"No. Just her. She gave me this locket and explained that it had belonged to our mother. Grandmother was a sweet lady, wasn't she?"

"She was the best." He clapped him on the back. "This is just the start, Garrett. Before long, you'll get all your memories back. Life can finally return to how it used to be…you and me, making the world a safer place."

Grant carefully returned the necklace and turned to face his brother. This was the hard part. "I'm leaving, Aaron. Memories or no, I can't resume my former life as if nothing happened. I can't pretend I haven't changed." As he watched Aaron struggle to accept his decision, he added, "This wasn't a decision I made lightly."

In the six weeks he'd been here, he'd struggled to re-adjust to his former life. He'd done everything he could think of to jog his memory. He'd visited his grandparents' old homesite. Taken flowers to their graves and his father's. He'd stood on a busy street and stared at the home he and Susannah had briefly inhabited. Taylor had gifted him with a new silver star and, while he'd felt proud to wear it, he didn't deserve it. Without his memory, he didn't have the knowledge or skills to step into his former role. And deep down inside, he didn't want to.

His colleagues had been patient with him. They'd plied him with story after story about how he'd tracked down notorious outlaws, protected federal judges and witnesses, arranged for court proceedings. Just that morning, when he'd handed in his letter of resignation, Taylor had advised him to give it more time.

He didn't need more time. What he needed was to see Jessica again. Thoughts of her crowded his mind at all hours of the day. Sleep didn't bring relief. He worried that she was sad. He worried that she wasn't, that she'd completely put him out of her mind, that she didn't ache for him as he did for her.

"I had a feeling this was coming. I kept thinking that regaining your memory would solve everything." Aaron spun the desk chair around and straddled it, his bulky wool coat bunching at the sleeves. "It wouldn't, though, would it? You'd still choose to leave."

Grant folded another shirt and placed it in the trunk. Then he came and sat on the corner of the bed. "This isn't the life I want anymore."

"Words I never thought I'd hear you say." Unhappiness wreathing his features, Aaron waved a hand to encompass the room. "Being a marshal was your lifelong dream."

"Dreams change. God allowed this to happen to me for a reason. Has it been easy? Of course not. I'd give anything to be able to remember working alongside you. As much as it would hurt, I want to remember what happened with Susannah. But if I hadn't been ambushed, I never would've met Jessica…" He trailed off as fierce emotion gripped him. Fisting his hands, he stared at the swept floor, willing himself to regain control.

Aaron didn't speak at first. "Have you worked out what you're going to say to her?"

He lifted his head, grateful for Aaron's effort to understand. He cleared his throat. "Not yet. Thought I'd practice my speech on the way. Maybe I should purchase a ring first."

"I didn't get a chance to really speak to her, but from what I saw, she'd accept you with or without a ring."

He didn't share his confidence. "I shouldn't have left her."

Not once had she ever said she loved him. There were no guarantees, no way to know if she desired a future with him.

"But then you would've always wondered if you'd made the right choice. You gave this life a try. Discovered it's not for you." Aaron chuckled softly. "If our father knew you'd given up the marshal's life for that of a farmer…"

"He wouldn't understand."

"Not at all." Pushing to his feet, he shoved the chair beneath the desk. "Plan on frequent visits from me, big brother."

Grant stood as well and pulled him in for a hug. "Whether I wind up a happily married man or a miserable hermit, you'll always be welcome."

"Trust me. She'll say yes."

Clapping him on the back, Aaron broke the embrace and walked over to the wardrobe. "Let's get you packed."

Grant joined him, praying with everything in him that Aaron was right.

With only twelve days until Christmas, it was far too cold to be outside on the porch. Jessica sat bundled into a layer of quilts. Her cheeks and nose tingled and the tips of her ears burned. Everything else was relatively warm. The creak of the rocker was the only sound in the tranquil December night. If she stopped the motion and strained her ears, she could just make out the patter of snowflakes landing on the brittle earth.

She would've been toasty inside by the fire but hadn't been able to resist observing their first snowfall of the winter. And this spot, more than any other, held special memories of Grant.

Closing her eyes, she relived their many conversations on this porch. The music they'd made together. Even after all this time, she could clearly picture his teasing smile, the way his eyes danced with mischief. Countless times she'd been tempted to pick up pen and paper and write to him. Countless times she'd discarded the idea.

Why prolong her agony?

The air was heavy with the scent of pine, reminding her of those fleeting moments she'd spent in his arms. Feeling the rush of sorrow stemming from broken dreams, she reluctantly squirmed to standing. Stringing popcorn for the tree they'd cut that day would divert her thoughts. She just had to be quiet and not disturb her mother.

Jessica had her hand on the door latch when the indistinct tinkling of bells reached her.

Treading to the top step, she held on to the railing and waited as the musical sounds drew closer. Was this a late-night visit from one of her sisters? They'd all done their very best to cheer her. Not that their efforts had paid off, at least not for any length of time. But she appreciated what they were trying to do. It proved how much they loved her.

Lanterns swinging from a conveyance scattered shards of light onto the lane. Snowflakes whirled and dipped as a pair of horses clopped through the wet accumulation, their breaths creating white clouds of steam.

Jessica considered going for the gun inside her room. She didn't recognize the team or the lone figure leading them. Something held her there, something about the way his Stetson was pulled low on his head and the set of his shoulders.

Hope exploded deep inside, and her knees threatened to buckle.

The team jerked to a stop near the barn. After setting the brake, the man leaped to the ground and strode across the yard, his attention on the layer of snow beneath his boots. Her grip tightened on the rail.

"Grant?"

He stopped short, startled, his head snapping up. His gloved hands fisted and opened, then fisted again. The glow behind her living room windows was enough to illuminate his beloved features. She'd recognize that mouth anywhere. The stubble along his jaw. And his eyes. They burned into her like twin blue flames.

"Is it really you?" The words tripping from her mouth

were a few seconds behind her thoughts. "I thought it was but couldn't be sure. Until now. What are you doing here? It's almost Christmas. Aren't you spending the holidays in Arlington with your brother?"

Grant ascended the steps one at a time, his gaze never leaving hers. He stopped once they were on eye level.

One trembling hand gingerly cupped her cheek. The leather glove was soft and warm. "You're beautiful, you know that?" he murmured. "Far more than I remembered."

Jessica didn't register the blankets slipping to the planks at her feet. She didn't register the cold. Inside, joy heated the blood fizzing through her veins. Anticipation chased the chill from her skin.

"Did you come back just to tell me that?" she whispered, her heart beating a drum tattoo against her rib cage.

One side of his mouth curved. "Not just that, no."

Quickly divesting his hands of his gloves, he let them drop to the step and reclaimed her face. She shivered at how amazing his skin felt against hers. Needing to reassure herself this wasn't a dream, she curved her fingers about his wrists. The fine hairs tickled her skin. *He was real. He was here.*

"What else did you come to tell me?"

"I'm sorry I left without telling you how I felt. I can't pinpoint exactly when I fell in love with you. All I know is that I do love you, and I'm desperate to know if you love me, too."

Happiness filled her until she thought she might burst. "I've missed you so much I could hardly function." With her fingertips, she traced the outline of his jaw. "Nothing cheered me." Removing his hat, she tossed it aside, uncaring where it landed. She smoothed the lines creasing his forehead. "I lost count how many cakes I had to scrap because I forgot to put in an egg or substituted salt for sugar."

"Jessica." His voice was a mix between a plea and a growl.

Smiling, she dipped into his hair, sighing at the soft strands threading through her fingers. He curved his arms about her and, pulling her against him, nuzzled the corner of her mouth.

"Keep talking," he softly ordered.

"I thought my chance at happiness was gone forever. I thought I'd live the rest of my life alone." Looking deep into his eyes, she stroked his cheek. "I shouldn't have let you leave without telling you how I felt."

"And how, exactly, do you feel?" His fingers flexed on her waist. "I need to hear you say it."

"I love you, Grant Parker. I have for a long time."

His eyes blazed. He lowered his head and kissed her with such tenderness it brought tears to her eyes. Easing away, he gathered the forgotten blankets and patted the top step.

"Sit with me."

When they were sitting side by side, he tucked the blankets around them, forming a cocoon of sorts. His arm was around her shoulders, mooring her to him. She snuggled into his chest.

"If I never moved from this spot, I'd be happy."

"Me, too." He kissed the top of her head. "I doubt the horses would be, though."

"Tell me about your home. Did being there spark any memories?"

She reveled in his closeness, the rumbling of his voice in his chest as he described the city, the quarters where he lived, the offices where he worked.

"Just before I left, I remembered being with my grandmother. And during the trip here, I was drifting off to sleep one night when I was hit with an image of my father. He was in his office. Aaron and I had gone to see him after school."

"Oh, Grant, that's wonderful!" she exclaimed. "I'm so happy for you."

"I can't describe how it feels to finally be getting pieces of my past back. It's like I'm discovering more of my old self."

"I pray you'll discover it all."

He rubbed her shoulder, his expression peaceful.

"Arlington sounds like an exciting place."

"I suppose."

Her fingers fisted in his coat lapel. "Grant, when are you going back?"

He stilled. "I'm not." Shifting, he gazed down at her. "I thought you understood. Jessica, I want to marry you. I want you to be my wife. I thought that's what you wanted, too."

"I do." Her brows pulled together even as his words thrilled her. "But what about your career? Aaron and Taylor? Your friends? I'm willing to move to Virginia. I don't know the first thing about being a marshal's wife—"

"Hold on. You'd uproot your life, leave your family, your business, for me?"

"I love you. I want to be where you are, whether that's in Arlington, some remote outpost or a deserted island."

"What about in Gatlinburg? Would you be content as a farmer's wife?"

"Building a life with you here would be a dream come true." Slipping her hand beneath his coat, she splayed her fingers over his heart. The steady beat was comforting. "But is that what you truly want?"

A thin layer of snow covered the steps, the flakes hitting their boots melting quickly away. The horses stamped and snorted. He'd have to leave her in a few minutes to care for them.

"Aaron and I spent a lot of time together these past weeks. He told me that I'd wanted to be a marshal ever since I was a kid. I was good at my job. I loved it. Couldn't imagine doing anything else until I got married. Apparently I couldn't reconcile the lifestyle with being a devoted husband and father. That's why I determined to remain single after her death. I knew I couldn't be successful at both." He stroked her arm, a lazy smile brightening his features. "Then I got ambushed in these mountains, and a beautiful, feisty redhead rescued me. She made me see how meaningful and satisfying family life can be when you're with the right person."

"What if your memory returns completely and you have a change of heart? I wouldn't want to be the reason for your regret."

"I will never regret being with you. We can't know what the future holds. Whatever happens, we'll work through it together, all right?"

Caressing her cheek, he captured her lips in a kiss full of promise. His heat enveloped her, making her oblivious to the falling snow just beyond the overhang. This was her beloved. The man who'd crashed into her life when love was the last thing on her horizon. The one who'd restored her faith in love and trust and commitment.

"So what do you say, Jess?" he breathed, his arms going even tighter about her. "Marry me?"

"Jessica Parker… I'm not sure if I like the sound of that." She grinned, teasing.

His smile turned impish. "Let me set about convincing you, then."

Grant pulled her close, and she lost herself in his kiss.

Epilogue

Valentine's Day, 1886

Grant rapped on Jessica's front door and hid his hands behind his back. The curtain at the nearest window wavered and suddenly she was there before him, hurriedly shutting the door behind her.

Bewilderment formed a pleat between her brows. "Grant, what are you doing here?" she admonished. "You're not supposed to see the bride before the ceremony. Ma would have a conniption if she knew."

"I know. But I had to see you."

Trepidation flared in her lovely green eyes. "Is something wrong? Are you having second thoughts?"

"No, of course not!" Going closer, he bent at the waist to kiss her lightly on the mouth. "I had to see you to give you these. I missed you yesterday." They'd been deliberately kept apart by her romantic-minded sisters. Apparently there had been last-minute wedding preparations to tend to. Presenting her with his gifts, he said, "Happy Valentine's, my love."

Her eyes lit up when she saw the box of chocolate creams and beribboned card. "How thoughtful, Grant. Did you make this?"

As usual, her smile made his heart sing. He enjoyed seeing her happy. "Nicole helped me gather the supplies."

"You're very creative. My first Valentine. I'll put it in a frame to keep for always."

"As long as I'm able, I'll present you with one every Valentine's Day for the next seventy-plus years."

Laughing softly, she encircled his neck and hugged him, landing a quick kiss above his collar that made his skin tingle and his pulse speed up.

While they'd wanted to get married in December, they'd decided to postpone the wedding until they could figure out living arrangements and make proper plans for the future. His future mother-in-law came up with the perfect solution. He and Jessica would live in the cabin—plenty of rooms for any children that came along, she'd pointed out—while she would reside in a smaller cabin on the property. The community had come together during a mild week in January to construct her new home. She'd slowly transferred her belongings and would spend her first night there tonight.

He'd enjoyed courting his bride-to-be, but he was eager for their relationship to be official. Permanent. He wanted to proclaim his love for her in front of the entire town.

"Just think," he said, "this time tomorrow, you'll be mine."

A pretty blush climbed into her cheeks. Her eyes sparkled like jewels.

"One last kiss as an engaged couple," he cajoled.

Her sisters would soon be arriving to help her prepare. And any minute now, her mother would notice she wasn't in the house. They'd all be outraged at his flaunting of tradition.

"Just one," she agreed and, depositing her gifts on the rocking chair, turned to envelop him in her embrace.

Minutes later, he forced himself to retreat to the yard. "See you at the altar, Jessica O'Malley."

"You'd better not be late, Grant Parker."

With a wink and a wave, she disappeared into the house. And he went away whistling.

"You're not supposed to be crying, Jane," Jessica gently chided. "The ceremony is over."

"I know." She sniffed. "It's just that I've never seen you look so at peace. So content."

Jessica smiled and hugged her twin. "God has truly blessed me."

After a poignant, tear-inducing ceremony at the church, their wedding guests had assembled in Lucian and Megan's spacious Victorian home for refreshments and the opening of gifts. The garden-themed parlor was Jessica's favorite room in the house, the floral prints and bright furnishings keeping at bay the cold February weather beyond the large windows.

"I'm glad you agreed to wear your hair up," Jane said. "For a moment there, I thought Grant was going to faint when he first saw you."

Nothing could describe the way his awe-filled expression had made her feel. Nicole had fashioned her wedding dress out of the finest fabrics. Constructed of creamy satin, the bodice hugged her upper body. The hems of her three-quarter-inch sleeves were ringed in silk tulle to mimic her full skirts of the same material. The tulle gave the dress a floaty, romantic appearance. Juliana and Jane had arranged her long locks into a formal chignon and stuck sparkly pins in her hair. Megan had lent her a pearl necklace and pearl-and-emerald ear bobs. Clara had taken one look at her and pronounced her a queen.

Indeed, Jessica felt as if she were royalty. She'd married a prince of a man.

Juliana joined them. "The cake is gorgeous," she told Jane. "Tasty, too. You outdid yourself."

"It was my gift to Jessica and Grant. I knew she'd be preoccupied with other details. Anyway, a bride shouldn't have to bake her own cake."

Megan descended on them and, linking arms with Juliana, bounced on her tiptoes. "Have I told you lately I'm over-the-moon excited that you're living here now?"

Juliana laughed. "Only about a hundred times. I still can hardly believe it myself."

"Believe what?" Nicole sipped her ginger water and grimaced.

Jessica noticed how her lavender dress, normally a perfect foil for her inky-black hair and violet eyes, highlighted her wan complexion. "Nicole, darling, are you expecting again?"

All the sisters gaped, their gazes shooting to her middle. Nicole managed to look simultaneously sheepish and elated. "Quinn and I hadn't planned on sharing the news this early."

Their squeals drawing attention, they took turns hugging and congratulating her. For someone who'd disdained the idea of motherhood, Nicole had surprised them all with her strong maternal instincts. It was nice to see her nurturing side. Having Quinn for a husband had changed her life for the better.

Taking in the room's occupants, comprising mostly family members, Jessica silently thanked God for providing loving, faithful spouses for each of her cousins and sisters. And now, at long last, for herself.

Josh and Kate, hands clasped, approached to congratulate Jessica. Kate pointed to the long sofa. "Looks like your new husband has been bitten by the baby bug."

Grant sat at one end, his tailored navy suit the perfect complement to his golden-blond hair, tanned skin and intense blue eyes, his attention on the twin babies tucked in his arms. Swaddled in matching blue blankets, Nathan and Sophie's one-month-old sons were oblivious to their surroundings.

Jessica's heart melted. "He looks perfectly natural, doesn't he?"

In the months since his return, Grant had recalled more segments of his past, not all of it pleasant. His memories of Susannah, their courtship and brief, tumultuous marriage had filled him with sorrow and regret. Jessica had comforted him as he relived the loss of a child he'd never known.

Unaware of her thoughts, Josh teased, "Who knows, cuz? You may be next."

"That's my prayer," she replied truthfully.

"Don't rush her." A smiling Kate kissed Josh's cheek. "Let them enjoy each other for a little while first."

On the cushions beside Grant, Nathan cuddled Sophie close. Whatever he was whispering in her ear brought a charming blush to her cheeks. Caring for twins was a demanding job for any young mother, but Nathan had pitched in and made sure Sophie was getting the proper rest. Her brother, Will, was enchanted by his new nephews and volunteered to rock them to sleep and even change their diapers.

Close by, Tom propped his baby girl against his shoulder, patting her lovingly as he chatted with Caleb and Rebecca. Quinn and Lucian, whose similar upbringings and business interests had led to a firm friendship, spoke together near the arched entryway. Jessica noticed that both men periodically searched the room to locate their wives, relaxing into the conversation again once they'd done so.

Jessica's gaze returned to Grant, who was now focused on her, his expression saying a multitude of things…pride in her as his wife, relief that the wedding was behind them, impatience to be alone with her.

He said something to Nathan, who passed one of his sons to Sophie and took the other for himself. Grant rose and crossed to her. To her sisters, he said, "If you'll excuse me, ladies, I'd like a word with my wife."

They exchanged significant glances and, with knowing smiles, waved them away. His hand pressed low against her spine, he guided her to the nearest exit. Aaron met them in the hallway.

With a mischievous glint in his eyes, he said, "Whoa. Where are you off to? I haven't had a chance to chat with my new sister-in-law."

"You'll have plenty of time to do that before you return to Virginia next week," Grant said smoothly. "But right now, she's all mine, brother."

With an exaggerated smile, Aaron bowed and waved them on. "Fine. I guess you're allowed to be selfish just this once."

Shaking his head, Grant smiled and led her to the deserted library. He closed the door. Sighing, he turned to her. "Remind me why we decided to invite so many people."

"Because we wanted to celebrate our union with our dearest loved ones."

"Right. And why are we required to stay?"

"Because…" She lost her train of thought as he planted his hands on either side of her waist and urged her closer. He kissed her jaw. "Um, I can't recall right this minute."

"Mrs. Grant Parker," he murmured, taking her left hand and examining the way his ring sparkled on her finger. "I'll never tire of saying that."

Jessica curled her arms around his neck. "I'll never tire of hearing it."

"You know what's been going through my mind the last couple of days? The verse from Genesis. 'But as for you, you meant evil against me; but God meant it for good.' Like Joseph's brothers, Thacker's gang meant me harm. God turned the situation around and allowed good to come from it."

"He brought you here, to me, even though I didn't deserve such a gift."

"None of us deserves His goodness. He chooses to bless us because of His love and grace."

"How did you get to be so wise?"

"Marrying you is the smartest thing I've ever done."

"Happy Valentine's Day, Grant. Out of all the gifts you've given me today—the chocolates, the card and the ring—my most prized gift is you."

* * * * *

Dear Reader,

It's hard to believe I began this journey five years ago. This book marks the final one in the O'Malley saga, and it's sad to say goodbye to the characters I've lived with for so long. Thank you for sharing in this journey. I hope these stories have made you laugh, cry, shake your fist at the characters, and kept you up reading until late in the night.

During research for this book, I read about the chestnut trees that used to inhabit the Smoky Mountains. Settlers gathered and preserved these nutritious nuts. What they didn't keep for themselves, they sold to local markets and shipped to larger cities, where they were in high demand. Wildlife such as turkeys, deer and bears depended on the chestnuts. But in the early 1900s, a fungus entered the country, wiping out millions of acres of chestnut trees. The loss was a blow to humans and animals alike. I enjoyed adding this aspect of mountain living to Grant and Jessica's story.

My hope is to write a few more books in this Smoky Mountains setting revolving around some of the townspeople. I'm sure the O'Malleys would make appearances in those books from time to time. You can find further information on my website, karenkirst.com, and on my Facebook page. You can also follow me on Twitter, @KarenKirst.

Until next time,
Karen Kirst

COMING NEXT MONTH FROM
Love Inspired® Historical

Available March 1, 2016

THE COWBOY'S READY-MADE FAMILY
Montana Cowboys
by Linda Ford

Susanne Collins has her hands full raising her brother's four orphaned children and running the farm. When cowboy Tanner Harding offers his help in exchange for use of her corrals, will he prove to be the strong, solid man she's been hoping for?

PONY EXPRESS COURTSHIP
Saddles and Spurs
by Rhonda Gibson

When Seth Armstrong arrived at recently widowed Rebecca Young's farm to teach her seven adopted sons how to become pony express riders, neither expected they'd soon wish for more than a business arrangement.

THE MARRIAGE BARGAIN
by Angel Moore

Town blacksmith Edward Stone needs a mother figure for his orphaned niece, so when hat shop owner Lily Warren's reputation is compromised, he proposes the perfect solution to both of their problems—a marriage of convenience.

A HOME OF HER OWN
by Keli Gwyn

Falsely accused of arson, Becky Martin flees to the West and takes a job caring for James O'Brien's ailing mother. With her past hanging over her head, can she open her heart and learn to love this intriguing man?

REQUEST YOUR FREE BOOKS!

2 FREE INSPIRATIONAL NOVELS
PLUS 2 *FREE* MYSTERY GIFTS

Love Inspired HISTORICAL

YES! Please send me 2 FREE Love Inspired® Historical novels and my 2 FREE mystery gifts (gifts are worth about $10). After receiving them, if I don't wish to receive any more books, I can return the shipping statement marked "cancel." If I don't cancel, I will receive 4 brand-new novels every month and be billed just $4.99 per book in the U.S. or $5.49 per book in Canada. That's a saving of at least 17% off the cover price. It's quite a bargain! Shipping and handling is just 50¢ per book in the U.S. and 75¢ per book in Canada.* I understand that accepting the 2 free books and gifts places me under no obligation to buy anything. I can always return a shipment and cancel at any time. Even if I never buy another book, the two free books and gifts are mine to keep forever.

102/302 IDN GH6Z

Name	(PLEASE PRINT)

Address	Apt. #

City	State/Prov.	Zip/Postal Code

Signature (if under 18, a parent or guardian must sign)

Mail to the **Reader Service:**
IN U.S.A.: P.O. Box 1867, Buffalo, NY 14240-1867
IN CANADA: P.O. Box 609, Fort Erie, Ontario L2A 5X3

Want to try two free books from another series?
Call 1-800-873-8635 or visit www.ReaderService.com.

* Terms and prices subject to change without notice. Prices do not include applicable taxes. Sales tax applicable in N.Y. Canadian residents will be charged applicable taxes. Offer not valid in Quebec. This offer is limited to one order per household. Not valid for current subscribers to Love Inspired Historical books. All orders subject to credit approval. Credit or debit balances in a customer's account(s) may be offset by any other outstanding balance owed by or to the customer. Please allow 4 to 6 weeks for delivery. Offer available while quantities last.

Your Privacy—The Reader Service is committed to protecting your privacy. Our Privacy Policy is available online at www.ReaderService.com or upon request from the Reader Service.

We make a portion of our mailing list available to reputable third parties that offer products we believe may interest you. If you prefer that we not exchange your name with third parties, or if you wish to clarify or modify your communication preferences, please visit us at www.ReaderService.com/consumerschoice or write to us at Reader Service Preference Service, P.O. Box 9062, Buffalo, NY 14240-9062. Include your complete name and address.

LIH15

SPECIAL EXCERPT FROM

Love Inspired HISTORICAL

*Susanne Collins has her hands full raising her brother's
four orphaned children and running the farm.
When cowboy Tanner Harding offers his help in
exchange for use of her corrals, will he prove to be the
strong, solid man she's been hoping for?*

Read on for a sneak peek of
THE COWBOY'S READY-MADE FAMILY
by **Linda Ford**,
available March 2016 from Love Inspired Historical.

Tanner rode past the farm, then stopped to look again at
the corrals behind him. They were sturdy enough to hold
wild horses…and he desperately needed such a corral.

He shifted his gaze past the corrals to the overgrown
garden and beyond to the field, where a crop had been
harvested last fall and stood waiting to be reseeded. He
thought of the disorderly tack room. His gaze rested on
the idle plow.

This family needed help. He needed corrals. Was it
really that simple?

Only one way to find out. He rode back to the farm and
dismounted to face a startled Miss Susanne. "Ma'am, I
know you don't want to accept help…"

Her lips pursed.

"But you have something I need so maybe we can help
each other."

Her eyes narrowed. She crossed her arms across her chest. "I don't see how."

He half smiled at the challenging tone of her voice. "Let me explain. I have wild horses to train and no place to train them. But you have a set of corrals that are ideal."

"I fail to see how that would help me."

"Let me suggest a deal. If you let me bring my horses here to work with them, in return I will plow your field and plant your crop."

"I have no desire to have a bunch of wild horses here. Someone is likely to get hurt."

"You got another way of getting that crop in?" He gave her a second to contemplate that, then added softly, "How will you feed the livestock and provide for the children if you don't?"

She turned away so he couldn't see her face, but he didn't need to in order to understand that she fought a war between her stubborn pride and her necessity.

Her shoulders sagged and she bowed her head. Slowly she came about to face him. "I agree to your plan." Her eyes flashed a warning. "With a few conditions."

Pick up
THE COWBOY'S READY-MADE FAMILY
by Linda Ford,
available March 2016 wherever
Love Inspired® Historical books and ebooks are sold.

www.LoveInspired.com

Turn your love of reading into rewards you'll love with
Harlequin My Rewards

**Join for FREE today at
www.HarlequinMyRewards.com**

Earn **FREE BOOKS** of your choice.

Experience **EXCLUSIVE OFFERS** and contests.

Enjoy **BOOK RECOMMENDATIONS**
selected just for you.

PLUS! Sign up now
and get **500** points
right away!

Earn **FREE** REWARDS
HarlequinMyRewards.com
Join Today!

MYR16R